Book Description

He broke her heart once. Can she take a chance on him again?

Carly Milner is doing all she can to make ends meet. Left pregnant and alone by her high school sweetheart, Carly has struggled to provide for her daughter while getting her career off the ground. Just when she is getting her life back on track, Ryan Melrose walks back into her life. Can she trust him again?

Realizing too late that he should never have listened to his parents, golden boy Ryan Melrose is ready to admit he was wrong. He never should have deserted Carly or their daughter. Now, he wants to live the life God intended for him and work for a second chance at love. But Carly struggles to trust him. Can he prove his faith and his love for her by showing Carly and their daughter his true devotion?

Chapter One

Carly Milner steered her tired old Honda Civic into the staff parking lot of Ocean View Community College. She pushed it into Park and gave the accelerator a few "*vroom-vrooms*" with her foot. The engine roared to life ... for a few seconds. Then, it conked out.

Carly sighed. She looked around, wondering if any of her new co-workers were watching. Then she remembered that it was her first day, and she had no idea who her co-workers were. A young man in a shirt and tie peered in her direction from about ten feet away, and she waved, giving him a friendly grin. She murmured to the Civic, "Thank you for getting me here. Now, get a rest, and make sure you get me back home, too, you hear?"

She opened the door and stepped out, giving the blue exterior a pat. She and the vehicle had an understanding: it would continue to deliver her safely to where she and Grace needed to go, and when she finally had a little money socked away, she'd dole some out for engine repairs. Now that she had a decent job, maybe that would come sooner rather than later.

But first things first. She followed a small line of people into the side door of the college, located the Admissions Department, and walked in. Seeing no familiar faces, she went to a chest-high counter. The young woman standing behind it tapped away at a keyboard.

"Good morning. I'm Carly Milner. Today's my first day of work."

The young woman looked up. "Oh yes! Dave told us to expect you. He's in a meeting till nine, but I'm supposed to show you to your desk and get you logged into your email. You can go see him in his office when he's free."

A rush of pure adrenaline circulated through Carly's body. A real office job. A desk. A computer! Gone were the days of wearing a polyester uniform to work, apron and orthopedic shoes. No carrying trays burdened with food and trying to remember who ordered what. And ... no hairnets in sight!

She smiled at her co-worker and held her hand out. "Well, I'm thrilled to be here, and thrilled to meet you ... um?"

"Haley! Sorry."

"No problem, Haley. You show me what to do and where to go and I'll get out of your hair."

Haley led her into the depths of the big room, past several rows of desks until she reached an empty one. A plastic tag hung, Velcro'd to the fabric wall of the cubicle: Carly Milner. Carly ran her fingers over it and had to remind herself to release her breath. She sat in the desk chair and twirled it excitedly, stopping abruptly when she noticed Haley's amused expression.

"First job?"

Carly considered, restraining a grin. "You could say that, I guess. Not first job ever, but certainly my most professional job, the one that's going to lead me to a bright and successful future."

Haley nodded, impressed.

Fifteen minutes later, Carly was exploring the Admissions guidelines manual on the college's intranet. She was so absorbed that she didn't notice Haley standing in front of her desk until she heard, "Earth to Carly."

Carly looked up, eyes wide. "Sorry. Were you speaking to me?"

"Yes, I was. Only to tell you that a super cute hunk is here asking for you."

"For me? You must be mistaken," Carly said, eyebrows crunched in confusion.

"You're the only Carly Milner who works here." Haley subtly gestured across the room with her index finger, in the direction of the Admissions Office door. Carly let her gaze follow.

She gasped.

"Do you know him?"

Did she know him! Did she ever. Although what on earth he was doing here, she had no idea.

He happened to glance in their direction and raised a hand, a gorgeous smile suddenly covering his face. "Oh hey, Carly!"

Carly groaned discernibly. Those longish chestnut locks, cocoa-brown eyes and white smile. That voice with the cute Low Country accent. It was why she'd fallen for him so deeply when she was just sixteen.

And as much as she didn't want to admit it, it was why they now shared a two-year-old daughter.

"You can bring him to your desk if he wants to talk about taking classes."

"Oh, no, that's all right. Can I take a quick five-minute break to go talk to him?"

"Fine with me. Dave isn't ready for you yet anyway."

Carly tucked her chin into her chest and marched to the front of the office. When she reached Ryan, and he looked like he was about to give her an enthusiastic greeting, she grabbed his arm and dragged him to the front door, opened it and manhandled him through. On the other side of the closed door, she hissed, "What are you doing here?"

"I wanted to see you about something."

She sputtered, not even sure where to start with that one. How about the most obvious question? "How did you know I was here?"

He had the decency to blush, which always meant that he'd done something sneaky and was embarrassed by it. "Ahh, well, I followed you."

"You did what?"

"I mean ... I was coming to your apartment this morning to visit you and Grace, and you were just pulling out. I decided to see where you were going, and you ended up here."

Her mouth dropped as she stared at him, thinking about his words.

"You're working here now?"

"Ryan, I'm giving you two minutes to tell me what it is you're here for and then get out. Yes, I'm working here now. It's my first day and I need to make a good impression. I don't need you to get me in trouble, you hear?"

"Oh. In that case, I guess I need to hurry up and tell you what I came here to say. Even though this isn't how I planned it. No, not at all." He cleared his throat, looked closely into her eyes and lowered his voice to a murmur. "I miss you, Carly. I miss what we could've had all along. I messed up when I put my own needs ahead of yours and our daughter's. Messed up big time. But I'm ready for it now. I want to be a family with you and Grace."

Her eyes popped open wide, and then the rushed morning, the skipped breakfast, the super-caffeinated coffee and Ryan's surprise confession all rushed to her head simultaneously. Bees buzzed in her ears, dark swirls filled her eyes, and she fell ... right into his arms.

SHE WAS SO TINY, HER weight barely strained his biceps. He'd caught her when she'd fainted, and now held her in his arms, gazing down into her freckled face, her complexion almost translucent in its fairness. Her lashes brushed against her cheeks and the crease that had been etched into her forehead a moment ago was now gone. Without thinking, he lifted her closer to his face and inhaled a deep breath of her scent.

He smiled. Still the same: Juicy Couture. It was her trademark scent back in their high school days. It was reassuring to know that some things hadn't changed.

So much between the two of them had changed between then and now. He'd never been so head over heels for a girl before Carly. He used to love spending time with her, making her laugh, surprising her with little gifts or outings.

His decision to go away to college seemed like a good thing to do at the time. His parents, graciously, picked up his slack with his unplanned daughter, seeing her regularly, establishing their side of the family in her life, even paying the court-appointed child support for him. He'd tried to immerse himself into college life, partying on the weekend and studying all week as if he were any other young guy.

A few years in, and it all felt ... wrong. A lie. A ruse.

And everything centered around this beautiful young lady who now lay in his arms. And the other beautiful young lady they'd created together.

Carly opened her eyes, blinking quickly. "Ryan. What ...?"

"Hey baby, you're okay. You fainted and I caught you. How are you feeling?"

Carly shook her head, orienting herself to her surroundings. She looked straight at him. "Put me down, this instant."

Regretfully, because he liked holding her, he tilted her, so her feet landed gently on the ground, then carefully released her.

And then she punched him.

"Oooof!" he grunted. "What the heck?"

She straightened her skirt, then skittered her hands over her hair. "What part of me wanting to make a professional impression on my first day of work, did you not understand, Ryan?"

He recovered from her fist to his shoulder and retorted, "Would you rather that I let you hit the ground? Get a black eye or a bloody cheek? How professional would that be?"

She stared for a second, then took a slight step away from him. "What happened anyway?"

"No clue. We were talking one minute, and the next, you passed out."

"I skipped breakfast this morning."

So typical of Carly. So conscientious, so ambitious. Never put her own needs first. "Can I go get you an Egg McMuffin?"

"No. I need to get back to work."

"You need your protein, Carly. I'll go get it and bring it back for you to eat at your desk."

"I don't know …"

"I do. You can't stop me. You can throw it in the trash if you want, but you can't stop me from getting you some McDonalds goodness."

He was gratified to see the start of a chuckle, which she scaled back to a grin. Her eyes connected with his and his heart increased its rate just a little. "Okay, thank you, Ryan. I do need to take better care of myself, but I was in a rush this morning."

He dared to raise a thumb and drag it over her cheek. Surprisingly, she didn't flinch. "I'm sure it's not easy taking care of Grace all alone, especially when you're on a tight schedule."

"You're right, it's not. She's a handful sometimes. And these are brand new work hours for me compared to my steak house shift. But this is for our future … hers and mine. She'll get used to it. She's a good girl."

She looked up at him, their 12-inch difference in height obvious. "Don't think I forgot what you told me before I fainted, Ryan."

"Oh, yeah! We need to talk about that."

"No, we don't. There's nothing to talk about."

"What …?"

"Absolutely nothing."

And with that declaration, she turned, flung open the door and disappeared. He watched her and couldn't stop the fond smile that crossed his lips. His Carly. Independent, smart, courageous. She'd come around. She'd realize that they'd be good together as a couple and raise Grace together.

She didn't know it now, but she'd get there. He'd make sure of it.

CARLY MADE A BEELINE to her desk, determined not to address any curious inquiries from Haley. The last thing she wanted to broadcast to her new colleagues was the status of her relationship with Ryan. Or, lack thereof. He'd made his priorities very clear when he'd left her with an infant to raise all alone while he'd gone off and lived his collegiate dream. He'd had plans to go away to college before the baby, and nothing was going to stop him from fulfilling them ... even after the baby was born.

Not that Carly would've wanted to stomp on his dreams. If he'd shown any indication of being committed to her and Grace when he'd first graduated from high school, she would've held off on her own plans for a college education until after he was done. People did that when they were in love. But obviously, their love was one-sided. He'd never considered tweaking his plans. Of going to college locally while being a part of Grace's life. While being a part of Carly's life. What had happened to all those professions of love he'd delivered when they were dating? Did all those feelings disappear in his rearview mirror on his way to Chapel Hill?

A tear stung her eye and she brusquely pushed it away. Two years. Two years now, she'd been Grace's mother, handling all the responsibility of raising a baby, with help from Grace's grandparents when she needed to work. Where was Ryan through all of that? He was living the good life at college, studying with no interruptions and earning a perfect grade point average. Partying on the weekends and making friends at the fraternity. He was living the life every college student wanted.

But not every college student had a baby back home.

The phone on her desk rang, bringing her head up and her mind back to business. She hesitated a moment and then answered it, "Ocean View Community College. Admissions Department. This is Carly."

"Carly. It's Haley." Haley's voice not only came to her through the phone, but it also projected from across the open room. Stereo.

"Oh hi, Haley."

"Special delivery coming your way."

Carly stood up and saw that Ryan had returned. He caught her eyes from across the room, a happy smile gracing his face, and held up a bag of fast food. "Haley, just take the bag from him and tell him I'm too busy to see him again. In fact, tell him I have a meeting with the boss."

"Oh, uh ..."

"Please Haley, just do it." She hung up, grabbed a notepad and walked away toward the back of the room. Although she had no idea where the boss's office was, she made sure to walk with enough purpose to fool Ryan.

When she reached the far corner, she turned and looked over the seated heads of her co-workers and saw that sure enough, Ryan had left. Relief flooded her heart. And then a trace of regret.

Ryan had come to see her and tell her he wanted to reunite as a family. He had never ever done that before. Isn't that what she wanted? Isn't that what she'd dreamed of for months on end? Wouldn't that be the best for Grace, to have her daddy and her mommy together, for her sake?

Was there room in her heart to give him a second chance?

And then, a steel door in her brain closed with a firm clank. No. Ryan had absolutely destroyed her with his abandonment. She wasn't about to open herself up to the possibility that he'd do it again.

The coast clear, she returned to her desk and plopped down in her chair. Haley arrived with Ryan's peace offering a moment later. She placed it lightly on her desk, her eyebrows up in an unspoken question. "Soooo, here's your breakfast that the cute hunk went out and bought for you and delivered back to you."

Carly grimaced. "Thanks, Haley."

"I'm sure you have a good reason why you're not happy to see him. But I sure wouldn't kick that one out of bed for eating crackers."

A laugh escaped. "Can it just suffice to say for now that it's a long story and leave it at that?"

"Okay, okay. But I will say that on top of being a total hottie, he really seems devoted to you."

Carly snorted. "Oh, if you only knew …"

Haley continued, "He asked me to make sure you ate this meal because you needed your energy and he made me promise to watch you to make sure you didn't throw it away."

Carly smirked. Devotion in the form of greasy, high-calorie fast food. She reached for the bag, pulled out the sandwich, unwrapped it and stuffed it in her mouth. While chewing, she shrugged and said, "Okay?"

"Okay. Make sure you eat it all. Oh, and …" she reached in her pocket and pulled out a folded-up sheet of paper, "he wanted me to give you this, too."

Carly eyed it suspiciously, eyebrows scrunched. Then she met eyes with Haley. "Thank you." Carly took the paper and laid it on her desk.

Haley watched her expectantly. An awkward moment stretched between them. "All right. I'm going."

Carly waved two fingers at her in farewell. She forced herself to finish the breakfast, and then she pulled the paper closer. She hesitated a second before she opened the paper.

"I'll be over to see you and Grace tonight at seven."

RYAN MELROSE PULLED into a parking space outside of Carly's apartment. He sat, willing his racing pulse to calm. His stomach complained with a slight case of nausea. It had never been easy for him to admit when he was wrong. Of course, he had never been so totally, colossally wrong before in his life.

Growing up as the only child of a ER physician dad and nurse mom, he had everything a kid could ask for. His room was filled with every toy that covered the shelves of Toys R Us. If he wanted it, he asked for it and he got it. What he didn't have was family time. His parents didn't work normal hours, come home for dinner and tuck him in at night. They worked whenever they were needed. Ryan was secondary. Most of his childhood, he'd sit at home, a babysitter in the living room while he was squirreled away in his room playing with his warehouse of toys.

For him, college wasn't a choice; it was an expectation. His parents had inserted that knowledge deep into his consciousness from the time he was in kindergarten. You weren't done with school until you were fully educated and prepared to work productively in your field. He'd chosen Accounting. So that meant a Bachelors, then his CPA and most likely, an MBA or a Masters in Accountancy. His mind raced, counting up the number of years he'd be committed to full-time education, just to meet his parents' expectations. And he was only two years in.

He loved college, just as he knew he would. He'd always been a good student. It's what he did. Life could be a lot worse than attending one of the best universities in the country, focusing on the subject he loved most.

But.

The baby was the surprise factor. No one expected him to knock up his high school girlfriend. No, that was definitely not part of anyone's plan.

He shook his head, closed his eyes and let his head fall back to the headrest. If he had to narrow down the most difficult things he'd ever had to do in his life, admitting to his parents what he'd done was at the top of the list.

His future would be put on hold, he told his mom and dad. He'd get a job, help support Grace, and go to college in a couple of years when things had become a bit more stable. That was the responsible thing to do. The honorable thing.

But his parents didn't see it that way. They put their heads together and decided he wouldn't change any of his plans. Instead, *they* would help Carly when she needed it. *They* would see their granddaughter regularly. *He* would go away to college.

The sense of relief that flooded through his body when they'd delivered their judgement was undeniable. His parents had his back. Their disappointment in him stung. So did their anger at him for jeopardizing his future. But they didn't disown him. They didn't walk away. They loved him and supported him, despite his mistakes.

See? He could still be a success, even with this setback. When they presented their idea to him, his first instinct was to object. But he was so grateful for their forgiveness that he didn't want to rock the boat. If they thought it was the right thing for him, then it must be. He went along with it. Regardless of what that decision did to Grace. And Carly.

Two years later, he could no longer deny the error of his ways. He had no business being away at college, focusing on preparing for his future, while Carly was stuck here, dealing with her present. The reality that he helped create. Where was his commitment? Where were his priorities?

Unlike his parents, his priority would now be his daughter. Not his career. He wanted to know Grace. He wanted Grace to know him. Time was slipping away, and he had to change his circumstances right now.

And he needed Carly's agreement to do it.

He cleared his throat. He drew a hand through his hair and took a quick look in the rearview mirror. *I could use your help, God,* he prayed silently. He got out of the car, straightened his legs and walked toward the building.

THE DOORBELL RANG AT 7 pm sharp.

It didn't surprise Carly. Ryan had always been on time, disciplined in every aspect of his life. It wouldn't surprise her if he'd been sitting outside in his car for fifteen minutes, waiting for the clock to tick to 7 pm. Being early was just as disruptive as being late.

She'd struggled with what to wear. Getting out of her work clothes this afternoon, she took a moment to wonder what would be appropriate attire for this meeting. Then she got angry. This wasn't a date or anything that required a careful wardrobe. She'd wear what she always wore for an evening in the apartment: shorts and a t-shirt. Nothing more.

She pulled the door open and worked to keep her face neutral. The smile that wanted to jump onto her face at the sight of him threatened. Because as much as she didn't want it to be true, she was still attracted to him, and yes, she supposed in a small corner of her heart that was unguarded, she still loved him.

And now a frown also wanted to jump on her face because of what he'd done to her. To them. All of them. Sure, getting pregnant at 17 had a way of changing the way you thought you'd live your life. But wouldn't it have been better if they'd been doing this together all this time? Not her, stuck in their reality while he selfishly lived what was going to be his life's path anyway?

So, neutral it was. "Hello, Ryan. Can I help you?"

He let a chuckle escape, then controlled his smile. He must've realized she wasn't joking. "Yes, hi Carly. Could I come in?"

She didn't respond right away, just stood there holding the open door with one hand, staring him down. Trying to make him sweat a little bit. Despite what he thought, she wasn't a doormat. This was her home, and she'd make the decisions.

"Please?" His voice softened, and a crease marred the smoothness of his forehead. "It's about time we talked, don't you think?"

Her breath shuddered on the way in. The firm façade she'd wanted to present was chipping away, brick by brick. Geez, that didn't take long. When Ryan put on his gentle face, spoke in his soft voice just for her, she never could resist. She loved him, and she had for years.

The problem was, he didn't love her.

She stepped aside and let him pass. He did so, happy as a puppy wagging his tail. "Not for long," she said firmly. She had to retain some kind of control, even though she'd already given in.

"Right. Is it close to Grace's bedtime?" he asked, glancing around the apartment.

Carly shook her head. It was a pity that Grace's father didn't have the first clue about her bedtime routine, but such was life. "Grace isn't home."

Ryan's face fell, just for a second, before he pulled it back to a normal expression. "I'm sorry to hear that. I was looking forward to seeing her."

Carly bit back the mean retort at the tip of her tongue. Of course, he'd expected Grace to be here at his beck and call when he'd finally decided to come by. Why wouldn't he? Life always went his way. "My mom took her shopping for a few fall outfits."

"Oh, I see. That's nice." He turned his head, looking around tentatively, probably wondering if he should sit or wait for an invitation.

"So, what's this about, Ryan?" She didn't want to invite him to sit. She didn't want him to think this was a social call, that he could just come in and sit down and chat and laugh like he was a welcome visitor. There was way too much water under the bridge between them for that.

As if he could read her mind, he stepped over to the higher countertop in her kitchen, and leaned against it, one elbow up. She stayed where she was, arms crossed pointedly over her chest.

He cleared his throat which turned into a cough. "I've been doing a lot of thinking, Carly. And I've been doing some growing up, too. I've been looking back over my decisions of the last few years and I realize, I don't like what I see."

He'd been growing up? Try being almost solely responsible for the 24-hour care of an infant, who'd grown into a toddler. Talk about a crash course in growing up. At the age of nineteen, she was more grown up than anyone else she knew. She clamped her mouth to keep the words from coming out.

"I don't like where I put my priorities," he continued, massaging his forehead, probably unconsciously. "I put myself first, my own needs and education. But what about you? You were left here to raise our daughter."

He stopped and slid onto a bar stool and locked eyes with Carly's. Those brown eyes that reminded her of a delicious bite of milk chocolate. They'd always gotten to her, made her do things, made her *want* to do things to gain his favor. She had to arm herself to resist their power. This was not only her life, this was Grace's too. She couldn't allow Ryan to crash unfettered into their daughter's life if all that would happen was he would lose interest and leave her again. Leave *them* again.

Because as hard as the first time was to deal with, the second time might just kill her.

"And I'm doing a darn good job of it, Ryan. With little help from you."

"Yes!" His hands darted out, a gesture that implied agreement. "You're amazing, and you're raising an amazing little girl. My parents tell me all the time how sweet she is, how loving, how polite. You've done a terrific job with her."

Carly loosened her arm cross, and her legs suddenly tired, she slid onto the bar stool next to him. He turned his whole body to face her. His signature scent smacked her in the face, and she insisted to herself she not breathe it in.

"This isn't about thinking I could improve on what you're doing or thinking I could do anything better. Not at all. This is about me becoming an adult. This is about me recognizing my responsibilities and not being a selfish SOB."

He tentatively reached for her hands, and finding that she didn't pull back, he grasped them both gently. "This is about me being the man God intends for me to be and fulfilling the role of father. I want to make some changes. I need to make some changes."

His voice took on a tone she'd never heard from him before. Determined, convinced, insistent. She had no doubt in that moment that he was speaking from his heart.

What she didn't know was how long it would last.

She sat there, looking into Ryan, this man she had loved for three years of her short life, holding her hands in his, telling her exactly what she wanted to hear. This should be easy. This should make her happy. And yet, she doubted.

She was the guardian of her own heart. She held the key to the lock on the wall she'd carefully built around it, ensuring that never again would she be unprepared to fight off people who could destroy her emotionally.

And Enemy Number One sat right in front of her.

So, before she could argue with herself, talk herself out of it, start to empathize with him and his revelations, she stood, released his grip, walked to the door and opened it.

"You need to leave, Ryan."

HE BLINKED, HIS BODY twisted uncomfortably so he could watch her move across the apartment. He sighed and stood, straightening his long form with slow precision. Full height now, he stilled, his mind whirring with words he could say to get through to her. Of course, Carly wouldn't just listen to his change of heart and welcome him with open arms. He'd need to work to regain her trust.

He moved to the door, thinking while he walked. He'd been going at this all wrong. He'd broken Carly's heart when he'd abandoned her for college. She had every right to be suspicious of him, guarded around him. He'd have to approach this in two separate strategies. First, he'd work to get back into Grace's life. Then, and only then, could he work on getting back into Carly's.

Which meant, no hand holding, no meaningful gazes into her beautiful green eyes. She was the mother of his child, but beyond immeasurable respect for her for doing what she did every day, he couldn't reveal romantic feelings for her. That's what had her putting up the shield.

He reached the door and stood beside her, placing his hands firmly into his jeans pockets. Keep them captured so he couldn't reach out and unthinkingly tuck a strand of strawberry blonde hair behind her petite ear. So he couldn't inadvertently brush a knuckle across her cheek while in the vicinity of her beautiful face.

"I messed up. Again."

She frowned, a crease forming in her forehead. Her lips formed to ask a question, then she must've thought better of it.

"I know you don't trust me, Carly. I've given you absolutely no reason why you should. I want to change that. But I know it will take time. It will take effort. I don't expect to come in here, snap my fingers and get you to understand. Let me ask you for one thing. Can I spend some time with Grace? Just her and I, daddy and daughter, getting acquainted? I want her to know that I'm her daddy. Not just some guy that shows up once in a blue moon with a toy for her."

He watched her closely and saw a movie of expressions play over her face. In her heart, she was a good person, a loving person, and she wanted the best for their daughter. She would do the right thing, and allow him this small request, he just knew it.

She cleared her throat, blinked her eyes and said, "No."

"Wha—?"

She gripped his bicep and put her weight behind pushing him through the doorway. No small feat considering the difference in their sizes. But he found himself on the other side of the door, and before he knew it, a slam alerted him to the fact that she'd put an end to their visit.

He knocked. "Carly, please. Let me try again. I just want to say …" What? What could he say to make this better? Oh yeah, the one thing he hadn't said. The one thing he should've started with and had failed to. How did he feel about yelling it now through a closed … and locked, since he heard the deadbolt slide into place … door?

Lord, humble me to do your will.

"I'm sorry. I'm sorry, Carly. This is all my fault, none of it yours. I acknowledge that. I've been away too long. I want to try to make it right. Will you give me that chance? Please?" He stood in the hallway, so focused that he barely noticed that a person walked behind him. He glanced up and his face reddened while a man made his way down the hall, trying not to make eye contact with Ryan in this, one of the most humiliating moments of his life.

It didn't matter. This wasn't about him. His pride. His entitlement. This was about making up for past wrongs and getting Carly to trust that he'd do right by their daughter. If he had to get to his knees and grovel for her forgiveness, a position he definitely wasn't accustomed to, he'd do it.

"I'm sorry, Carly," he said again to the door.

And then, his heart jumped at the sound of the metal deadbolt sliding back in its casing. It was the sound of the doorknob turning. Carly was opening the door.

SO MUCH FOR THE BRICK wall she'd built around her heart. So much for the anthem ringing in her ears, "I am woman, hear me roar." So much for protecting herself and her daughter from Ryan's charms and his good intentions. So much for not doubting for one second that this was a temporary goal of Ryan's, and soon he'd tire of the responsibility and the reality of caring for a two-year-old.

His long-awaited apology had touched her. And she'd opened the door.

Of course, now that she had, and had seen his face transform from broken-hearted to relieved happiness in seconds flat, she would have to go through with it. She couldn't back down now.

"Carly, thank—."

She held her hand up. "I have rules."

"Of course," he said softly, as if she would change her mind if he spoke full volume.

"You can see Grace on Saturday for two hours."

His face beamed with an unfettered smile. "Awesome! Thanks, Carly."

"But." She paused until she knew she had his attention. "Not just Grace alone. I'll be there too."

"Oh." His eyebrows darted up at this news, but he didn't argue.

"You make the plans for how to spend two fun hours with our daughter, and you come here to pick us up. What time should we be ready?"

"Uhhhh," he stammered. "How about one?"

"One it is. See you then, Ryan." She looked down at the floor, knowing that she didn't want to see his eyes again. She didn't want to see his reaction to her ultimatum, whether positive or negative, didn't matter. She was in charge. And he was just going to have to accept that.

She shut the door, walked to the couch and sat down. Her life was changing. Drastically. New job, new work hours. Now this. How much change could she take all at once? She got up to start her homework.

He'd better not screw this up.

Chapter Two

Saturday at one, Ryan's deadline for planning a fun outing with his daughter was quickly approaching and he hadn't settled on anything yet. It was sort of like planning a date, but worlds apart. A first date with a woman was much easier than planning this outing with his daughter. A first date usually involved flowers, a reservation at a nice restaurant and dressing up in a suit.

On the other hand, Grace would just tear up the flowers, she wouldn't stop moving long enough to eat a meal, and he wouldn't be able to crawl around on the ground with her if he had on a suit.

On Friday evening he had dinner with his parents. Over a table full of roast beef and mashed potatoes, he said, "I'm going to see Grace and Carly tomorrow for two hours."

"Oh," his mother said, surprised. "What are you doing?"

"Don't know. I'm supposed to be planning it, but I honestly don't know what a two-year-old likes to do for two hours. Do you have any suggestions?"

His mother went motionless for a moment, looked over at his father, then back at him. "Sure. She loves to play on playground equipment. Ice cream. Coloring, painting. Listening to stories."

He nodded, absorbing his mother's list. Two hours was a long time with a toddler. Maybe he'd start with the playground, then have a combination of all the other ideas in his back pocket in case he needed them. He loaded up his fork and stuffed it in his mouth.

"When are you headed back to Chapel Hill, son?"

He looked up, swallowing. His mother's laser focus was zeroed in on him. He laid his fork down, his mind running while he tried to keep his face from reflecting his thoughts. Now wasn't the time to drop the bomb of his pending change in plans. At least not until he'd cleared it with the university and finalized his transfer plans. So, it wouldn't necessarily be lying to his parents if he didn't clue them in to the direction his current thoughts were taking him. Just omitting the truth.

"Chapel Hill semester starts after Labor Day."

"So, the visit with Grace and Carly is to spend a little time before you leave town?"

He considered that one. A positive answer would be a straight-out lie. "Just a fun afternoon before school starts." There, that was accurate, if not altogether honest.

The rest of the dinner passed uneventfully, and Ryan relaxed. When he said good-night and went to his room, he thought of the day, not too distant, when he'd need to break the news to his parents. He was leaving Chapel Hill and transferring to a college nearby, so he could be a full-time father to Grace.

The next day, he drove to Carly's apartment. His mother had helpfully packed a picnic basket full of finger foods that might appeal to a two-year-old: peanut butter and jelly sandwich quarters, potato chips, grapes, juice boxes, goldfish crackers. She'd included paper plates and a tablecloth too, explaining that if they found a picnic table they could cover it, but if not, they could spread it on the grass and sit on it.

He left the basket in the car, tugging it over to one side so that Carly could install Grace's car seat in the other. Checking the car clock – 12:57, he headed for the apartment. A gentle knock left him wondering what Grace's reaction to him would be. He'd last seen her nearly two months ago. No excuses, but he had stayed in Chapel Hill most of this summer completing summer classes and hadn't arrived in town until recently. Well, that type of lackluster fatherly behavior was over, starting today. Grace was his priority and he intended to make sure she knew it.

As he waited, a thought dawned on him. Would Grace adjust to calling him Daddy? When Grace's speaking skills first started developing, he and Carly had agreed that she'd know him as "Ryan." "Daddy" would only confuse her. They'd keep the two of them on a first name basis and not deal with the confusion of labeling him her daddy.

He hadn't minded it before now. But that was going to change too. Although he knew enough about the partnership of parenthood to know that he needed to speak to Carly about this before springing it on Grace. So, for today anyway, "Ryan" it was. Or, more accurately, "Why-n."

The door swung open and Grace stood in the doorway. A smile adorned her adorable face, which he hoped meant she was excited to see him. Where his daughter was concerned, he needed a second chance, big time.

"Hi there, baby doll." He squatted to be closer to her height, and opened his arms, hoping she'd run into them for a hug. She didn't. The smile stayed pasted on her face and she announced, "It's Why-n."

He reached out for one of her hands, squeezed and said, "So good to see you. You sure look pretty in your pink outfit."

Carly came up behind him, pushing a strand of hair behind her ear. "Oh yes, pink is our favorite color, isn't it Grace? In fact, we had a temper tantrum this morning when we realized that all our pink outfits were in the laundry basket."

Ryan glanced back at Grace with a mischievous expression, popping his hand over his mouth. "Uh oh. What'd you do, Grace?"

The little girl widened her eyes, offered him a shy shoulder. "I cried."

"Well you must've really wanted to wear pink today, huh?"

She nodded. With a laugh she turned and ran into the apartment, leaving Ryan to stand, looking down at Carly. She rolled her eyes good naturedly and motioned him inside. "I'm probably the worst mother ever, but it was either force her to wear red or blue, or just wash the darn pink clothes."

He smiled. "Pink it is!"

She nodded. "As a mother you definitely need to pick your battles. We do pretty well on the big stuff. She eats her meals, brushes her teeth, goes to bed. But she's really picky about her wardrobe. What am I going to do when she's sixteen instead of two?"

Ryan followed her into the living room, his mind racing with thoughts of parenthood. He should be here for the daily battles, so Carly wouldn't have to pick them all on her own. "You're not the worst mother ever."

Carly popped her head up from her task of packing a bag with Grace's supplies. She tilted her head, unsure about his delayed response.

"You're a great mother. Don't ever doubt that."

She went motionless for a moment, then shrugged and moved a small stack of diapers from the table into the bag. "How would you know?" Her voice was low, and her tone casual. But he knew there was a lot of emotion lined up behind the simple question.

He moved over to the table, wondering how he could help. "Look, I know you don't think I notice because I've probably never said anything before. But you are an awesome mother. I know it. Grace knows it. And you should know that too."

She sniffed and concentrated intently on her task. "You're never here long enough, or often enough to know if I'm a good mother or not."

What she was saying was accurate, and the slice it made in his heart was like a severe injury. But he couldn't blame her for telling the truth. So, he recovered and said casually, "I know. But my mom's here a lot, isn't she, and she tells me all the time what a great job you're doing with Grace." Lame, but true. His mother was very fond of Carly and had told him several times what a good mother she was. "And I want today's visit to be the start of me spending a lot more time with Grace. The kid deserves to have not only a great mom, but a good dad, too."

Carly's eyes went wide. He sensed her effort at holding in her words, biting her tongue as she contemplated his statement before she zipped the bag shut tight. The sudden noise made them both jump. "We'll see about that, Ryan."

Of course, she'd doubt his trustworthiness. Actions spoke much louder than words, and his actions so far, where Grace was concerned, had been crap. So, he'd keep his mouth shut and start letting his actions do the talking. He had all the time in the world. Any good mother would make him prove his worth as Grace's father. He expected nothing less than her suspicion.

He turned to Grace who was now twirling in little circles in front of the cartoon on the television. "Hey Gracie girl, do you want to go to the park and play on the playground?"

That caught her attention and she clapped her hands, the cartoon now forgotten as she jumped up and down, clapping. "Yaaaaaay."

Carly jumped into mommy mode, grabbing the diaper bag, throwing instructions at Grace and locking up the apartment behind them. When they got to the parking lot, she headed to her car while Ryan headed towards his. "Can you help me get the car seat latched properly into my backseat?" he called over his shoulder.

She kept walking and responded, "No, we'll take my car. The seat's already in place."

He bit his tongue and swallowed his disappointment. But it didn't matter. Carly was probably right. It was easier this way.

"Okay, I'll get the picnic basket and bring it over." Joining them at Carly's car, he laughed. "This is the same car you've had since I met you."

She gave him a pointed look. "Yes, Ryan. It was old then, and it's even older now."

He shut his mouth. Every time he opened it around her he was sticking his foot in it. Of course, she had the same car. How would she have bought a new one? While his expenses were paid by a combination of his academic scholarship and his generous parents, Carly had no such luxury. She was a truly self-sufficient single mother, working hard to raise her daughter and educate herself. She deserved his respect, not flippant comments about the age of her car.

He hated to admit this, but if their positions were reversed: if Carly had had their baby, then abandoned her – and him – and left him to the day to day care and financing of such a life, how would he be doing? How would he treat her? He'd be resentful, he could say that with certainty. Especially if she was off at college living life the way she'd planned, as if nothing had changed.

He glanced over at Carly while she drove. "Okay, baby girl, off we go," she chanted, a smile on her face. He couldn't look away. Staring at her brought him back to when they'd first met in high school, when they were connected at the hip and head over heels in love, either with each other, or at least with the idea of being in love. He was the forward on the basketball team, and she was the sole sophomore cheerleader on the varsity squad. She'd attracted someone's attention in the coaching staff with her athletic abilities. Her slight size made her a perfect candidate for the position of "flyer," and her fearless courage allowed her to be thrown high into the air, arcing gracefully and then being caught by her teammates before she went crashing to the wooden floor.

In early November, he realized that the cute little cheerleader with the strawberry blonde hair, the freckles and the tiny little fit body, was someone he wanted to meet. By Thanksgiving he'd asked her out on a date, and by Christmas he'd fallen, hard. He'd picked out a stack of presents for her and presented them to her one by one under the mistletoe. A kiss in exchange for a gift. It seemed like a great deal to him.

By spring break, they both knew she was pregnant, and by prom, she no longer fit into the dress she'd picked out. A different one was needed to accommodate her baby bump. And by the time Grace was born, he was well into his first semester at Chapel Hill, trying to forget what he'd left behind. By Christmas break, he had become so accustomed to college life, the normalness of it, he hardly spoke Grace's name to his friends. He'd get news of her occasionally from his mom. But it was so easy to pretend that it had never happened.

Easy for him. Not so for Carly.

Carly pulled into a little local park, the entire drive completed while his mind whirred over their past. Carly turned to him. "You mentioned a playground. Did you have one in mind?"

He looked around. "This is fine. I figured she'd enjoy the swings, a slide, whatever."

Carly parked the car and went around to the back to unfasten Grace. The little girl bobbed on her toes in excitement. "Grace, hold Mommy's hand."

Ryan pulled out the picnic basket, and hooking the handle over his arm, he joined the ladies. "How about you hold Mommy's hand, and Ryan's hand, both?" She nodded, and they walked, connected, over the expanse of lawn, up a small hill.

"Mommy! What's this?" Grace exclaimed. Her eyes took in the sight of an unexpected surprise: a carnival had set up at the park, complete with ponies to ride, a roller coaster, Scrambler and Ferris wheel, and even a selection of bumper cars.

"Cool!" he yelled, probably as excited as she was. "This'll be fun." He set the picnic basket down on a nearby table, and his gaze trained on the carnival, he swept Grace into his arms, and then up onto his shoulders in one swoop. She let loose an excited laugh.

He headed down the hill in the direction of all the fun. "Ryan," Carly said, then a little stronger, "Ryan, wait."

He came to a halt and turned toward her. "What?"

She shook her head. "I'm not so sure about this."

"Why?"

"First of all, it's expensive. There's an entry fee for each person, then once you're inside the gates, each and every ride costs extra tickets."

The money. Of course, she'd be worried about the money. He tried to set her mind at ease. "Hey, don't worry. My fun day with Grace, my treat." He gave her a reassuring grin and turned back to the carnival.

They went through the front gate and strolled around, seeing all the carnival had to offer. He couldn't see Grace's face, so he looked down at Carly. "Is she okay up there?"

Carly was studying her with apprehension, head tilted back, eyes narrowed. She paused before responding, "I guess she is. She's never been that high before. But I suppose if she was scared, she'd let us know." Then she directed her next words at Grace, "You okay, Grace?"

"I got her, Carly. I won't let anything happen to her."

Carly let her gaze land on his eyes and dwell there for a minute. She nodded briefly.

At the ponies, Grace squirmed and leaned down so she could yell in his ear. "Horsie! Horsie!"

He swung her off his shoulders and onto her feet. She took off like a bullet. "Grab her!" instructed Carly so he chased her and within two steps, covered the distance and grabbed her hand.

"Ride horsie?" she asked with such a cute little voice and face that he knew there was absolutely no way he could deny her. He wanted to give her whatever she desired, so it was his fervent hope that Carly wouldn't deny her this either.

He glanced over at Carly. "I'll walk along beside her, holding her in the saddle if you'd like."

Carly looked over at the children riding the ponies. The animals were small, short to the ground, wore saddles and stirrups for the children to hold onto, and best of all, they were slow. All that was missing was a seatbelt. And for each little child like Grace, either Mom or Dad was walking right alongside.

Huh. Maybe his paternal instincts were surfacing.

"Okay, but make sure she doesn't fall off. I don't want her getting hurt."

A laugh escaped him, and he looked at her with irony. She bristled but then laughed along too. "I guess I didn't have to tell you that, right?"

"It's okay." He knelt in front of Grace and said, "Let's go ride 'em, cowgirl."

She squealed, and they made their way to the horse line. "I'm a cowgirl."

"Yes, you are."

"Cowgirl hat," she announced, pointing at her head.

"Just like a woman," he said good-naturedly. "Always in search of a shopping opportunity."

They waited through two rotations, and then it was Grace's turn. "You're up, Grace." He took her hand and walked into the rink with her, approaching the pony they were directed to, a pinto named Patches. "Do you like this one?"

She gave a determined nod, her mouth clamped shut, eyes wide, looking up with a mix of excitement and fear. She wanted to ride, but she wanted to scream a little bit too. He helped set the tone by lifting her into his arms and going to the little horse's face, holding his palm out so the little guy could nuzzle his velvety mouth against it. "He likes me. He's giving my hand little kisses."

She let out a gasp and held out her tiny hand too.

"Yeah, palm straight out so he can't bite your fingers."

Back to fear, she darted him a look. *Ooops. Don't tell her worst-case scenario, Ryan.* "Not on purpose, sweetheart. Just by accident if you stuck your fingers in his mouth. He'd think you were giving him food and take a bite. So just hold your hand out flat like that. Good." The horse nuzzled her palm too and she let out a delighted giggle.

"Want to get on Patches' back?"

By this time, she was comfortable. She nodded excitedly. He swung her high so her legs cleared the pony's back and when she was in place in the saddle, he maneuvered her feet into the stirrups and showed her where to hang on.

"Don't worry, sweetheart. I'll be right here beside you the whole ride. You won't fall."

"Won't fall," she parroted.

He wished they'd sold little cowgirl hats on the carnival grounds because he would've bought her one and she would've looked adorable. The kid was so cute. A balance of her mom's fair skin and green eyes, and his chestnut hair. Features combined from both her parents to create one unique face. His heart welled with affection for their little family and he glanced across the ring at Carly. She was watching intently, of course, and he beamed a smile in her direction. She shifted her gaze from Grace to him, hesitated a second, then gave him a thumbs up.

He turned back to Grace. "Can you say, giddy up?"

"Giddy ...," Grace tried.

"Giddy up is horse language for 'let's get going.'"

She leaned forward in her seat and yelled, "Giddy up!" At that moment, the cowboy managing the ponies got them started. The one in front of Patches started walking, and so did Patches. Grace triumphantly grinned and held onto the saddle horn with white-knuckled excitement.

Five minutes later, the pony ride was done, and Ryan deemed it a great success by the way Grace jogged over to her mom and chattered non-stop about it. Carly knelt and gave Grace a hug. "I'm so glad you had a good time."

"What's next?" Ryan asked good-naturedly. "Bumper cars?"

"Yeah!" exclaimed Grace.

"No bumper cars," said Carly.

He missed the storm in her eyes and pushed it. "Why not? Bumper cars are fun. She can sit right in my lap and they'll put the strap over both of us."

"Bumper cars!" said Grace.

Carly came to a stop, which brought all of them to a halt as well. "Ryan, bumper cars are not appropriate for a two-year-old. This isn't a game, you know. I want Grace to have a good time, but I don't want her to end up getting injured. You're like another big kid that I'm now responsible for watching. I don't need or want any more responsibility."

Her harsh words were like a bat to his stomach. Why was she so angry? What had he done to cause it? "Carly …"

"I'm her mother, Ryan. I have final say on what I think is safe for her."

He stared, mouth open. Well, of course she did. And although he could argue that he was Grace's father, and should have an equal say, he decided to keep his mouth shut. Because he knew he didn't deserve that. Not right now. But if his plan worked as he wanted it to, he'd be a full-fledged dad, a constant in Grace's life, and a parenting partner with Carly.

Anger and fighting had no place here during their family day of fun. He knew that. He rested his hand on her shoulder. "You're a fantastic mother. I don't have any experience with two-year-olds. So, I will learn from you. And maybe soon I'll have some say on what's good for Grace too, as her father."

A storm of emotions crossed over her face and he watched them with interest. She was so torn, so battled. He'd done this to her with his return and his proclamation of wanting to become part of their lives. He was causing a huge change for them. But he couldn't give up now. It would be a positive change. They just had to get through the growing pains.

Tears filled Carly's eyes and she turned her back to him. She swiped her eyes and got herself under control, and when she turned back, she had on an iron face. A strong façade. This was why she could handle all the challenges life had thrown at her and still emerge a success. This personality trait, this determination that she had to be strong and achieve all her goals. Pride and admiration rose in his heart. Without second-guessing, he closed the distance between them and took her into his arms. She resisted for a few seconds and then she relaxed into his embrace. Her head buried in his chest, his arms surrounding her, pulling her close, his head bent, nose in her hair. It felt so right. It felt so good.

Together, they could do this. This is what God wanted for them, he was sure of it. He just needed to convince Carly. He needed to gain her trust back, and he needed to never forget why she didn't trust him to begin with.

One step at a time. A hug at the carnival. It was enough, for now.

The world disappeared as they stood motionless. He breathed in the scent of her hair, and he remembered. Her locks had always smelled like coconut. She loved tropical scents in her hair and skin products because she loved the beach and always had. Maybe on their next family outing they could go to the beach. He could dig in the sand with Grace while Carly got some much-deserved laying out time.

Then, like in a movie, the sounds and activity around them queued back in, and Carly pulled away from him, avoiding his eyes. She busied herself picking up Grace's bag, grabbing Grace's hand. "So, who's hungry?" she asked with a forced cheerfulness.

"Yeah, Grace, are you hungry?" he added. "Grandma Melrose packed us a picnic lunch. Do you want to eat it? Afterwards we can go pick another ride." He winked at Carly. "As long as Mommy thinks the ride is okay."

She agreed, and they headed off to the picnic tables.

THE OUTING ENDED UP taking way longer than two hours, as Carly had originally dictated. But Grace was having such a good time, and the carnival was such an unexpected treasure, Carly couldn't bring herself to put an end to it.

Grace had enjoyed the Ferris wheel, squeezed in between her and Ryan on the seat, all holding hands and screaming as it went high and then descended. She rode the children's roller coaster, really not much more than a train ride with a few dips and hills in the track, with her daddy beside her, his arm around her shoulders. They played some carnival games and Ryan won her three big stuffed animals which she insisted on carrying all by herself back to the car. Now, her yawns and droopy eyes were Carly's clue that it was time to go home. She was at least two hours past her nap time, and Carly knew that putting her down this late would result in a much later bedtime. But so be it.

Carly placed Grace's weary body into her car seat and snapped her in. On the way home, Ryan turned in his seat to watch their daughter.

"She sure had a good time today, didn't she?"

Carly nodded and murmured an "Mmm hmm."

Ryan went on, "It was such a beautiful day and what a great find, that carnival. I hadn't even seen anything about it in the paper."

Carly's eyebrows darted up. A surge of sarcasm went through her, which she managed to squash before it resulted in hateful words coming out her mouth. The surprise carnival, the ponies, the rides, the games, all contributed to making probably the best day of her young daughter's life. And he hadn't even planned it! Ryan was a golden boy, always had been. Everything always went his way. While she struggled and worked hard and barely made progress, everything came easy for him.

Straight A's in high school, star of the basketball team, every girl's dream. He led a charmed life. Scholarships to college, acceptance into his first-choice university. He'd never faced adversity.

Not like her. Her parents were blue collar workers. They didn't have money to send her to a prestigious university. She had to work and save money herself. And of course, she would've accepted this reality of her childhood without complaint, because her parents were awesome and provided her with a great upbringing. But then ... another monkey wrench, in the form of an unexpected pregnancy at the age of seventeen. She could just imagine the universe—an old man with a gray beard wearing a robe taking a few bolts of lightning in his hands—throwing them at her and cackling evilly, "Here, take this one! And this one!"

She sighed, and Ryan looked over at her. "You okay?" he asked, and his voice was so sweet and nice it almost brought tears to her eyes.

To be safe, she didn't respond verbally, in case her voice cracked with emotion. She nodded and tried to paste a smile on her lips. Hoping it didn't look like a grimace.

"Tired? Maybe you can take a nap this afternoon when Grace does."

Again, she bit her tongue. Although he had been a very neglectful father up till this point, she knew he was making an effort and she didn't have the heart to squash the happy mood today by retorting that as a single mom with a toddler, a full-time job, and four college classes, there was no way she had time to take a nap, today, or any other day.

"I can stick around and watch over her if you want to catch a few zzz's yourself."

She rolled her eyes while she drove, but otherwise didn't allow him to witness her reaction. "That's okay, Ryan. You've done enough today."

He cocked his head and she knew he was holding his tongue as well, trying to keep the peace with her. She knew her comment could be interpreted several ways, so she conjured up her nice side and clarified, "You gave Grace and me a really fun day. A great day that she'll remember always. Thank you."

She watched his tension roll out while he relaxed. His All American Boy smile seemed sincere when he said, "It was a great day because of you two, not because of me. But I agree. It was really fun, and I look forward to our next family day too."

He kept saying he wanted this change to be for good. That he wanted to be a permanent part of Grace's life, and therefore, of hers. But she'd trained herself for over two years to distrust him, to think the worst of him. Because, what choice had he given her? Just because he showed up now with a sudden desire to be a dad. It didn't work that way. Grace wasn't just a project he could pay attention to when the whim hit him. A child was a full-time commitment. One that she had made a priority for over two years, while he was off doing his thing.

But when she'd watched the two of them together today, it was hard to be mean. Not only was he a natural with Grace, his instincts about her safety (despite the faux pas involving the bumper cars) spot on, she easily recognized the look of pure love and adoration in the eyes of her daughter. Other than two grandpas, Grace had no men in her life. Ryan was a novelty, and she sure was soaking it up today. The way she looked at him, her eyes glazing over with adoration. The way she held on to his hair as she rode on his shoulders. The way she reached effortlessly for his hand whenever she was told to hold on while they walked.

Grace had it bad for her daddy.

Which, Carly couldn't help thinking, was bad for Grace. And for Carly.

She pulled into her apartment parking lot, the entire ride silent between her and Ryan while Grace slept in the back and Carly's mind whirred and whirred with implications. She parked, and Ryan popped out, circled around and pulled Grace gently out of the car.

"Careful ..." Carly whispered, but he nodded. He knew. Keep her sleeping and he could transport Grace right to her crib when they got in.

She grabbed the diaper bag and the picnic basket, and walked silently into the apartment. Ryan went into Grace's room and Carly watched him as he leaned over the rail of the crib and placed her gently on the mattress. Grace stretched and curled onto her side, stuck her thumb in her mouth, and kept sleeping.

"Score!" Ryan whispered with a grin. Carly couldn't help a chuckle. Yes, another win for Ryan. *Shock, shock.*

They went into the living room and Carly handed him the picnic basket. "Thank your mom for me for the lunch. That was very sweet of her."

Ryan brushed her thanks off with a shrug. "So, do you need anything from me? Any help? Want me to stay while you nap, or do you have any errands to run?"

His generosity overwhelmed her, and she shook her head. "No, we're fine. I have some homework to do so I'll try to get some of that done while she naps."

He paused, his eyes searching hers. He carried the basket to the door, then turned. She nearly bumped into him since she was seeing him out. She gasped lightly, and suddenly, his hand was on her cheek. A shudder traveled down her spine. His touch had always done that to her. Now was no different, even though two years had separated them from when they were in love.

"Carly, I know I hurt you. I was such an idiot, a total jerk. I'm sorry for how my selfishness hurt you. But I want to change. I want to do better. For Grace and for you."

She closed her eyes because she couldn't stand this close to him and absorb all the feelings he was causing in her. His touch on her face. His scent in her nostrils. His body next to her. She couldn't take the sight of his handsome face in her vision, on top of everything else. She'd fallen for him, first and foremost, because of his good looks. As she got to know him, she realized his good nature, his optimism and friendliness were lovable too.

"Will you give me a chance? I'm not asking you to be sure right now. I don't deserve that. But will you please just give me a chance to prove to you how sure I am about this?"

His voice, spoken in an intimate murmur, could talk her into anything. Obviously. Against all her good judgement and intentions, she'd lost her virginity to him as a teenager and paid the ultimate price for her decision by producing a child and being responsible for another human life. But even now, his voice had that same control over her.

She wanted to say yes. But was it the right thing to do? Was it right for Grace? Especially if he didn't end up sticking around? Grace's heart would be broken if she became close to him, relied on his presence, only for him to disappear again.

Not to mention, her own heart would be in jeopardy. Two years' time and space from him and she still thought about him regularly. Memories of their love. Visions of what life could be like if they'd never broken up. It would be so easy to fall again. Fall into those arms, those eyes, those words.

So, the best she could offer him right now was, "I'll think about it, Ryan. I'll really think about what's best for all of us. I can't answer you right now."

Disappointment flickered over his face, before he quickly restored it. "That's all I ask of you. Thank you, Carly. I'll be in touch about next time."

In the split second before he turned and left, she wondered if he was going to kiss her. He paused, gazed at her upturned lips, and then thinking better of it, he walked away.

RYAN LOADED INTO HIS car at six am, a travel mug of coffee in his cup holder, and set out on the familiar trek to UNC – Chapel Hill. He'd made the 200-mile drive many times over the last two years. The start of a new semester, the return home for a family vacation or holiday. He'd worked hard there; he'd done well there.

But this conversation would probably be the most difficult of all his interactions at college. He had to make some changes in his life, and this was a big part of it.

Because of his Grade Point Average coming out of high school, and his college prep test scores, he was highly sought after when he was selecting a college. UNC had been one of the top contenders, coming to the table with competitive scholarship offers, which, stacked one upon the other, made the school a much more affordable place to earn his education.

He watched the sun rise as he drove north, his mind occupied by the challenge in front of him. By the time he arrived for his 9 am appointment, the day was bright and sunny and warm. He found street parking near Jackson Hall, the Undergraduate Administration building and pulled in. He took a moment to glance into the rear-view mirror, run a hand through his hair to straighten unruly locks. He tugged on his tie. Wearing a full suit wasn't normally advisable in late August, but it may give him an air of maturity that he knew he'd need for this meeting.

He strolled up the cement stairway that led from the sidewalk to the older brick building, steeped in history, not only for the university but for the country as well. Everywhere he looked around this esteemed school, he knew the fabled stories behind its construction, or how it was used to support the country in various wars or historic events. UNC taught their students well, created a school pride that stayed strong throughout adult life.

He gave his name to the receptionist and sat only a moment when she announced that Mrs. Parker was ready to see him. She led him to the counselor's office. He held out a hand in greeting and lowered himself into the wooden chair in front of her desk.

"Mr. Melrose," she started formally, "I must say I'm curious as to the nature of our meeting today. You've already chosen and locked in your fall semester schedule, and school doesn't actually start for another ten days. How can I help you?"

"Yes, thanks for seeing me. I've reached a decision about my attendance at UNC and I have a couple of questions for you."

She nodded inquiringly.

"If I were to transfer to another university now, how much of my completed coursework would transfer?"

She frowned, her lips poking out. "Transfer? You're thinking of transferring? Why?"

He cleared his throat and tried to stop himself from squirming in his seat. "Personal reasons."

She stared at him, as if willing him to tell her more. He held his tongue. "Well," she said eventually, as though she knew he'd won the battle, "it depends on where you're transferring to. Is it a state university in North Carolina?"

"No."

She took in a slow breath like she was trying to control a sudden rise in blood pressure.

"Why don't we look generically at my courses since my transfer plans aren't finalized yet?"

She shook her head and pulled up his transcript on her computer, moving the monitor so he could see. "As you can see, you have successfully completed all the courses in the Accounting major expected of a sophomore. You've done extremely well, too, with a cumulative grade point of 3.85 out of 4.0. I assume you're going to continue an Accounting major?"

"Yes."

"Well, I'm not knowledgeable of other universities' Accounting major requirements, but I can assure you that UNC curriculums are high quality, well thought out and contain no fluff courses whatsoever." She folded her hands on her desk. "What I'm trying to say, Mr. Melrose, is that I can't imagine there will be any problem transferring what you've done here. But until I know where you're going, it's inadvisable to surmise."

Despite the seriousness of the situation, Ryan held back an amused snort. Did people really talk like that?

Maybe his expression revealed his thoughts because Mrs. Parker sat back in her seat and said, "Be real with me, Ryan. What's going on? Why would you give up all your scholarships and leave UNC when you're doing so well here? Do you realize that an Accounting degree from this school is a valuable commodity in your job search? We offer advanced Accounting degrees here too. You could just stay and continue on." She sniffed and for the first time he got the very real impression that she cared about him and his future. She wasn't objecting because he was a number and she didn't want her numbers to go down. She didn't want him to make a mistake that would impact his future.

"I'll be honest with you. I love UNC. A big part of me doesn't want to leave. But I've got responsibilities at home. I have a child, Mrs. Parker, and the mother of that child is working double time as a single mom. I can do more. I need to do more. I want to be a father to my daughter. And I can't do that from 200 miles away."

Her eyes softened as he spoke. "Well, in that case, you're doing the right thing, Ryan. I admire you for setting your priorities."

"Don't admire me too much, Mrs. Parker. Grace is two years old and I've been pretty much an absentee parent her whole life."

"It's not too late."

He met her eyes. "I hope you're right."

She pulled a business card out of a little display on her desk and handed it to him. "I can help you with this. Once you have your transfer plans finalized, give me a call. I will personally transfer your credits and if it's looking like the school is rejecting some, I'll discuss it with them on your behalf."

Her kindness caused a hitch in his throat. "Thank you," he croaked. He got up and walked to the door. Turning around, he said, "I appreciate your help and your generosity."

He walked to the car. This would most likely be his last visit to the campus. He was cutting ties with his past, full focus on the future. Fighting a desire to take one last tour to reminisce about all his good times there, he headed back to the highway to drive home.

ON FRIDAY, CARLY'S boss told her to leave two hours earlier than usual, since she had worked two hours on Wednesday night in a last-minute Admissions blast for procrastinators who hadn't yet registered for classes. She left the office with a light feeling in her heart and wondered what she should do with the unplanned freedom. She got in the car with her mind whirling over the possibilities, then she decided. She'd go visit Nora Ramsey at Dress for Success.

She jumped on Rt. 17 heading south and drove, watching the traffic lighten the farther she got from Myrtle Beach. If she had to pick one person who'd influenced her decision to change her life by putting the accelerator on obtaining her college degree, and working in a professional field instead of waitressing, it was Nora.

Through Nora's career guidance, Carly gained the confidence and skills needed to write her resume, strengthen her interviewing and organize her time to hold down both a full-time job and full-time student status. Since she worked at the community college and took classes there, she was able to fit both into a very busy day. But without Nora and her confidence in Carly, she'd probably still be waitressing at the steakhouse at night while taking a few classes during the day. Her whole life had changed for the better.

Carly made a left onto the obscure country road that led to a massive Victorian mansion that Nora had renovated to reflect its former glory. Beyond the house, a beautiful state-of-the-art horse barn stood which, in a former life, had housed a vibrant equine training and coaching facility, back when Nora's Aunt Edie had owned it. Nora had abandoned her career as a successful Philadelphia attorney when she'd inherited the property from Aunt Edie, and now she spent her days helping women prepare themselves for the working world.

Carly parked outside the mansion and went up to the front door. She rang the doorbell and waited. Soon, it swung open and there was Nora herself. "Carly! So good to see you."

"I hope you don't mind an impromptu visit. I got off work a few hours early and thought I'd take a chance and see if you were free."

"Absolutely." Nora stepped back and swung an arm in welcome. "Come on in."

They walked to the living room where clients normally gathered on comfortable couches to talk. Nora looked good. Always a pretty woman, her face looked calm and relaxed. She was in her element. Her hair looked longer than the last time they'd met, and her smile was easy and natural.

"Can I get you something to drink? Lemonade? Iced tea?"

"I'll have some if you do. If not, don't worry."

Nora chuckled. "I'll be right back."

While she was gone Carly wandered over to the Dress for Success showroom, a long room along one wall of the first floor that used to be a library and now showcased racks and racks of professional women's clothing, donated by Nora's business colleagues all over the country. Nora's franchise affiliate's purpose, first and foremost, was to provide women with a suit for that first important interview. When you looked good, it allowed you to present your very best self in an interview. Nora's career counseling, coaching and resume writing classes were value adds, showing that she truly cared about the professional success of her clients.

Carly located her size on the rack and let out a moan, fingering the soft silky fabric of a teal green dress. She pulled it out and held it up. The style was simple but classic. That's where Nora found her.

"Want to try it on?"

Carly smiled and looked longingly at it. "No, you already gave me my interview suit, remember?"

"Sure, but you're not limited to just one."

She looked over, surprised. "I'm not?"

"No. You're working five days a week, right? Wouldn't it be nice to have some variety in your professional wardrobe?"

Carly looked back at the to-die-for dress. With a wink at Nora, she carried it into the dressing room and came back out, wearing it. Nora reached for the skirt. "This is fuller than it looked on the hanger. I like that."

Carly twirled in a circle and watched as the skirt flared. "I do too."

"It's very flattering, Carly. And the color is great with your hair and complexion."

Carly studied herself in the mirror, optimism surging.

"Take it. Done." Nora sounded so sure. "Go take it off and bring it back out. I'll wrap it in plastic for you."

"I didn't come here to get another free outfit."

Nora chuckled. "I'm glad you came to visit. But if you had come to get another free outfit, I'd be glad about that too. You were my first real client and you'll always hold a special place in my heart."

Carly quickly changed. When she came out, Nora was in the living room, two glasses of lemonade poured and waiting.

"So, tell me about the job," Nora prompted and from then on it was twenty minutes of Carly chattering about the work, her boss, her co-workers, her students. When she stopped, Nora looked like she was bursting with pride.

"I'm so happy for you, Carly. Sounds like things are working out according to plan."

A sip of lemonade soothed her dry throat. She put the glass down and studied Nora. "One thing's not going according to plan."

"Oh, really? What's wrong?"

She smoothed out a wrinkle in her lap, avoiding meeting the older woman's eyes. Nora was her mentor and she didn't want to reveal the depth of her distress. "Do you remember I told you about Grace's father?"

"Yes, I do. You two were together in high school, but when Grace was born, he went away to college."

"Well, that's a very nice way of saying he abandoned the two of us."

Nora reached over and patted her hand.

"Ryan showed up at my office two weeks ago. He says he wants us to be a family."

You had to hand it to Nora. Her entire body froze, her eyes went wide but she didn't say a word. Such as, "You've got to be kidding me." Instead she said politely, "Excuse me?"

"Yep. You heard me. He shows up out of nowhere and tells me he's made a mistake and he wants to be a father to Grace and he wants us all to be a family. I have no idea where that puts me. I mean, families come in all shapes. Does he mean he wants us to be a couple and raise Grace together? I don't know."

"So how did you respond to this revelation?"

"I fainted."

Nora laughed out loud, and then must've felt bad about her reaction. Straight-faced, she asked, "Seriously?"

"Yeah. Right in his arms."

Nora settled for shaking her head back and forth. Then, "What are you going to do?"

Carly sighed. "No idea."

Nora steepled her hands and stretched her arms out, then rested them back in her lap. "Let me start with this question. Do you still love him?"

Carly shrugged but couldn't push out words. She let a moment of emotion pass. Nora waited. "This doesn't leave this room, right?"

"Of course not."

Carly waited till she could speak without emotion bogging her down. She had never revealed what she was about to say to anyone. But if she was going to tell someone, Nora was the perfect someone. "I think about him all the time. I've always daydreamed about what our lives would be like if we'd stayed together for Grace. And of course, in my daydreams, he's a devoted and loving husband." She clasped her hands and squeezed. "But I haven't forgiven him for what he's done. And I'm not sure I ever will. It's going to take a lot more than a fun day at the carnival to make me trust him."

"So, you've spent time together as a family?"

"Yes, a little bit."

"And how is Grace taking it?"

"My little girl has it bad for her daddy. You can just see it in her eyes. Although she doesn't know he's her daddy. Poor kid doesn't have any concept of what a daddy really is."

"Does Ryan want her to know him as her father?"

"Oh, I'm sure he does, but he's not pushing that right now. He just wants to spend time with her. And she definitely wants to spend time with him. Poor kid."

Nora blinked thoughtfully. "Do you think he'll disappoint you again?"

Carly paused. "That's the ten-thousand-dollar question, isn't it?" They sat looking at each other for several moments. "Can you give me advice? I have no idea what to do."

Nora's lips formed into a slight smile. "I know exactly what you should do."

"What?" Carly had guessed coming here was the right move. Nora knew everything.

"Yes." She reached out and took Carly's hands in her own. She bowed her head and closed her eyes. When she started speaking, Carly smiled and followed suit. "Dear Father, we ask for your help for Carly and Grace and Ryan. Open their hearts to your will. Help them to seek your answers in their problems and make it clear to them what your path is." She went silent and Carly tried to pray silently in her head. A little rusty at it, she didn't come up with anything except, *Help me. Please help me.* Then Nora ended with, "Amen."

Carly met Nora's gaze, then looked down. "I was hoping you had an answer for me."

"I did. My answer was to go to the one with all the answers."

Carly's lips tightened. "Thanks for praying with me. Now, do you have any opinions?"

Nora shrugged. "Pray about it. Be loving and kind. Don't put your heart on the line unless God answers that he wants you to."

"I just don't want to get hurt again. And most of all, I don't want Grace to get hurt."

"I get that. Life sure isn't easy, is it?"

They sipped in peaceful silence while Carly let Nora's words soak in. "Enough about me. Tell me about you. How's the business going? How do you like life at the beach? Do you ever miss the city life?"

Nora's expression was thoughtful. "I don't. I had enough traffic and car horns beeping and sirens blaring, and the rush rush rush of not only the city, but my whole lifestyle as a lawyer. This is much more peaceful, relaxed, easy. And yet, I really feel like I'm making a difference here, for others who need a helping hand."

"You sure made a difference for me. You educated me about how to get going on my new beginning, and you encouraged me when I thought it would be impossible."

Nora looked down at the folded hands in her lap. "I have a new beginning coming up myself." She looked up tentatively.

"You do?"

"I met a man."

Carly gasped. "Oh my! Tell me."

Nora laughed at her enthusiasm. "Despite my advanced age ...,"

Carly slapped her knee. "You're not old."

"You're too kind. Anyway, I have never had much luck at relationships with men. You know, falling in love."

Carly tried to resist an eyeroll. "It ain't easy."

"A few months ago, I started seeing a man named Shaw. A veterinarian who loved animals and worked hard and was so ... intriguing."

"And good looking?" Carly wanted to get to the good stuff, waggling her eyebrows.

Nora chuckled. "Yes, he looked good. Anyway, long story short, we began to see each other, and I think our feelings were mutual until I discovered a secret he'd been hiding. A lie, actually. A colossal one."

"Oh no!" This unexpected news truly devastated Carly.

"I'm not going to go into details because it's possible that you'll meet Shaw someday, and I don't want to color your opinion of him. But I couldn't trust him after his omission of the truth, so I ended it with him. I went on my life."

Carly put a hand on Nora's hand. "I'm so sorry, Nora."

"But as I said, I'm facing a new beginning. I'm trying to forgive him, to understand why he did what he did, and we're going to give it another try. Really, we're just going to get to know each other better. Take two." She smiled.

"Well. It sounds like the decision I need to make about me and Ryan. Can forgiveness restore the love we once felt for these men? Time will tell. I wish you the best, Nora."

"Thank you. It was great catching up with you. Stop by anytime."

Carly grabbed the teal dress, thanked Nora again and walked to the door. They hugged. Nora put a hand on Carly's cheek and said, "I'll be praying for you."

Chapter Three

Nora Ramsey woke, silence greeting her. Her white puffy comforter provided warmth from the early fall chill of air conditioning. South Carolina sunshine beamed in through the second story windows of her inherited mansion. Other than the distant sound of the ocean waves, and the immediate tart scent of the salt marsh, nothing seemed out of order. She settled back into the bed and exhaled a deep breath.

And yet, something was different today. Her life had changed. A happy smile formed on her face as her mind caught up with recent events. Ahh, yes. Shaw was back in her life.

She threw the covers back and stepped onto the wood plank floors of her bedroom. Stretching out the kinks, she grabbed a robe and headed for the stairs. Yesterday, she'd seen Shaw Flynn for the first time in months. Shaw, the man who had stolen her heart through an introduction by a black gelding, Thunder. The first man in her four decades of life she could honestly say she'd ever fallen in love with. The man who'd deceived her by not telling her about the unique circumstances in his life that meant they never should've been together in the first place.

The months of heartache, the miles of separation, her decision to move on with her God-intended life ... without him. He'd left a big hole in her life, as well as her heart, but she'd done it. She built this life that she could be proud of. A life of fulfillment, helping women develop their skills and attitudes for their dream jobs. She'd done it without him.

And yet ... God took her empty hole and healed it for her. Through life's circumstances, and through her own forgiveness, all things were new today. God had worked through her and helped her get over her anger and hurt at his betrayal and open herself up to a new beginning. New possibilities.

The simplest acts that she performed every day seemed fresher today, more fun. The ground coffee smelled heavenly as she loaded it into the filter. The English muffins sent out a delicious aroma while warming in the toaster, and the butter she spread over them was a sunshine-y yellow that put a smile on her face.

Shaw was back. They were starting over. They were putting past mistakes behind them and giving it another try. As she took a bite of her butter-soaked muffin, she closed her eyes and prayed for guidance, "Lord, guide us this time around. Help us be honest with each other, love each other, support each other. Let's see where this thing can go this time. Amen."

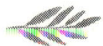

SHAW FLYNN WOKE EARLY the day after his wife's funeral, prepared himself quickly, and opened the calendar on his laptop. Grabbing a speedy breakfast of hard-boiled eggs, toast and coffee, he perused his appointments for the day, making mental plans. It would be a full one. They always were. Being a large animal veterinarian, caring for livestock as well as the occasional zoo wild animal, provided him with challenge and no shortage of patients. Driving up and down the coast was a normal part of his schedule, because his practice covered a large distance. Since he'd taken the whole day off yesterday, he also had some catch-up to do.

His daughter Sadie came into the kitchen and nodded at him as she moved to the cabinet where the breakfast cereals were kept. "Busy day today?" she asked.

"Yep."

"Well, take it easy on yourself when you can."

He pulled his gaze away from the computer and looked at her. "What do you mean?"

She shrugged. "I mean, you buried your wife yesterday. I know your marriage was far from typical, and I know you weren't in love with her, and I know her illness and disability dragged on for a long, long time. But. You still buried your wife yesterday."

His eyes lingered on hers a moment longer. "Yeah." He supposed in a normal love story, he wouldn't be rushing back to work after a day like yesterday. He wouldn't recover so quickly and so completely. But his wasn't a normal love story, and truly never had been. They'd rushed into a whirlwind marriage while they were young and impetuous, and it was fun. For a while. But eventually he started growing up, making plans for the future, his priorities changing. Not Melody. She was only interested in partying, traveling, drinking. The car accident that robbed her of her independence, her health and her life as she knew it, wasn't a total surprise to him.

He reached out a hand to the one treasure that had resulted from that marriage; his beautiful daughter Sadie. "How about we say a quick prayer for your mom?"

She grinned sadly. "Didn't we say enough yesterday?"

He gripped her hand and closed his eyes. "Lord, please welcome Melody into your kingdom and watch over her. She lived a hard life, but we pray for simplicity in heaven. Amen." He opened his eyes and gazed at her. "You having trouble dealing with this?"

She shrugged. "No, I'm really not. After she faded away, I prayed for her to go. Nobody wants to live like that."

"I agree."

"Best thing we both can do now is move forward and live our own lives. Be happy. Do what we were meant to do and live the lives we were meant to live."

He grinned at her, his heart full. "How'd you get to be so smart?"

She laughed. "I followed you around everywhere, don't you remember? I had to have picked something up."

Yes, he did remember, and he'd loved every second of it. He and Sadie were an unbreakable pair when she was a kid. Of course, as kids do, she started drifting from him when she got her drivers' license, forming her own interests, making her own friends. Her dad wasn't quite as important as he used to be. But that was okay, it was normal. They'd worked to stay close as she moved into adulthood.

She grabbed her book bag and headed for the door. "Well, have a good day. Oh and ... I bet I know someone who wouldn't mind a visit today." The door slammed, and he looked up. He knew exactly who Sadie was referring to: Nora. A warmth went through him as he thought of her, especially since he knew he had Sadie's approval about forming a relationship with her. Not that he required his daughter's support. But it sure was nice that he had it.

He got moving then, grabbing a paper printout of his calendar, and thinking about when he could fit in a visit.

The day passed quickly, as it always did. He delivered a healthy newborn foal, removed a fishing hook from a goat's hoof, and administered annual shots to a farm-full of cattle. Around three o'clock, his cell phone rang while he was driving to his next appointment in Georgetown. "Shaw, it's Phil Rosewood."

"Hey, Phil. How's Thunder doing?"

"I wish I knew. Disappeared again."

"What?" Shaw's mouth hung open as he puzzled over that one. Thunder was a beautiful black gelding who used to belong to Nora's Aunt Edie. He had been a vital part of Aunt Edie's Waccamaw Trails, held in the state-of-the-art barn on what was now Nora's property. Then, it had been a thriving equestrian training and show clinic. When Aunt Edie went into assisted living toward the end of her life, the Rosewoods bought Thunder. But the horse was the sentimental type, and had, on several occasions, jumped the fence and made his way back to Nora's property. The Rosewoods had added another three feet of height to their fencing to try to deter the escapes. What was shocking today, was how Thunder got over it.? "Phil, have you inspected your fence? Did that rascal jump over it again, or did he destroy a section and break through it?"

"I don't know, and I will do that. But I have to tell you, Jan's tired of this. She feels like Thunder isn't happy here if he's constantly trying to leave. She just wants a nice mount to ride when she feels like it."

"Sounds like you might want to find a new home for him, then?"

"Not new home – old home. Didn't you know the lady that bought Waccamaw Falls?"

"Yes. Edie Ramsey's niece, Nora."

"Would you give me her phone number? I'd like to talk to her about possibly buying Thunder back."

Shaw suppressed a smile. The wheels were turning. God was at work here. "Hey, Phil, I'm seeing Nora real soon. Would you mind if I said something to her first?"

"Not at all. We'd be willing to quote her a fair price. We just feel like we've treaded water with Thunder too long and we want to get a horse who wants to stay with us."

"Understood. I'll talk to Nora and get back to you." He broke the call, his heart feeling warm. He let his mind run over the words of one of his favorite verses of the Bible, from Psalms 37. It had gotten him through many, many despairing days. Kept his faith on track and him mindful of who he belonged to, who cared about him. "Take delight in the Lord, and he will give you the desires of your heart."

A desire that his heart had been dreaming up lately involved opening a new community service ... a ministry, really. A charitable organization that allowed children to ride: a huge selection of children who could benefit from a personal relationship with gentle horses. Physically disabled children, mentally troubled children, blind children, physically able children who had gotten into trouble with the law. He had done a whole bunch of reading about the benefits that horses provide. He was interested in starting a non-profit to offer equine-assisted therapy. All he needed was a horse ... and a place to ride. And some volunteers.

Nora had the place. Now a horse was becoming available. A good, reliable horse: a horse with a history. He could recognize a gift from God when he saw one. And, as an added bonus, it would be a project he and Nora could work on together. A way to spend more time together and help others while they were doing it.

He raised his eyes to the sky and silently thanked his Father and went on to his next appointment.

LATE IN THE DAY, THE sun was doing its beautiful low dip into the horizon in the west and Nora stepped outside onto her massive front porch with a glass of lemonade to observe and admire it. The sky treated her to a gorgeous light show of gold, purple and white as the sun made its final descent. As darkness began to settle, she took a sip, a smile on her face, a smile that said, she was happy here. She loved her life here.

So different than her previous life. Up until a few months ago, she'd lived completely differently as a real estate lawyer in a firm in Philadelphia, stayed in a high-rise apartment downtown, took limos to and from work. Her days were long, and her nights were lonely, but because she'd worked so hard to achieve it all, she was hesitant to give it up when Aunt Edie offered her this remarkable gift of an inheritance. This property—part pasture, part beachfront, containing a state of the art horse barn and a worn down Georgian style mansion. What on earth would she do here?

Despite her misgivings, she took the plunge. Her faith in God was untried at the time she needed him most, and as fate would have it, she grew to depend on him and his guidance while making this decision. Her belief in God was bolstered when she met Shaw, who included God is his daily decisions as if he was a friend, someone to talk to, to confide in. Spending a little time with Shaw helped her to see that she could have that kind of relationship with God too.

As she leaned against the porch railing, a big red pickup truck pulled in front of her house. She smiled as a long, lean, handsome cowboy jumped out and headed her way.

"Hey there, pretty lady," he said in a joking voice. She couldn't help breaking out in laughter. If someone in Philly had said it, she would've scoffed, but for some reason, in this setting, coming from this man, it was acceptable. Attractive, in fact.

"Hello yourself, cowboy," she teased. She felt light with him. He'd always taken away her business self and let the non-lawyer part of her come out.

He covered the distance between them and climbed the stairs. He leaned in close and she wondered for a moment if he was going to kiss her. Maybe he wondered too, but if he did, he thought better of it, and pulled back. Instead, he brushed her cheek with an index finger and let his smile linger. She took advantage of the closeness to take in a whiff of his essence. Hard working man, with an outdoorsy scent and an underlying aroma of the soap he'd used this morning in the shower. She loved his smell. It was so uniquely him.

She tamped down her disappointment at the lack of a kiss but reminded herself that they were starting over. Their past didn't count now. It was all behind them, and they'd both agreed to start off right this time. She'd look forward to a kiss when the time was right.

And maybe, just maybe, this time she'd determine when the time was right and not wait for him to do it.

She reached up and held his hand when it was close to her face and grinned her happiness at seeing him. "How was your day?" she asked and moved toward the front door of the house. He followed her in.

"Great. How about yours?"

She nodded. "Good too."

"Have a question for you. Have you noticed any unexpected visitors today?"

She paused, her eyes wide. "Not another alligator."

He chuckled. "No. Another black gelding."

"Thunder?"

He nodded. "He's missing from Rosewood Ranch again. The Rosewoods have about had it with him."

Shaking her head, she said, "No I haven't, but then again, I haven't been looking either."

"Want to take a ride and look for him together?"

"Sure."

They climbed into his truck and he drove over to the gate that opened to the 4-acre pasture. Nora jumped out and opened it, let the truck drive through, then closed it again. Jumping back in, she settled in and they took off, bumping over the grassy mounds. They drove slowly through the pasture, serpentining the width of the property, keeping a look-out for the horse. Eventually they made their way to the far side of the land, which bordered a salt marsh leading to the Atlantic Ocean. Nora's expanse of sandy beach was what had sold her ultimately on leaving her city life and moving here. Imagine, a beach lover like her, having her own beach to visit at any time.

They stopped on the sand and got out, their feet landing in softness. They walked toward the ocean and peered out at the waves. Nora took in a deep breath and let it out. Contentment overcame her, and she reached out and put her hand in his. His head turned, but she didn't break the moment by looking at him. She felt him smile and relax as they held hands.

After a few moments, she said, "So, we didn't see Thunder, did we?"

"No, we sure didn't. I'll need to call Phil and let him know he didn't show up here."

"I wonder where he made off to."

Shaw nodded. "I want to find out. In fact, I have something I want to talk to you about."

She glanced up and he gestured for them to sit on the sand. She joined him and waited expectantly.

"I feel like Thunder is a key ingredient to a new service I want to provide to the community. I had an idea and I've been mulling it over, and now I think the time might be right to start working on it. Here. Let me explain. Have you ever heard of equine-assisted therapy?"

Nora shook her head. "I don't think so."

"Horses have been shown to be very therapeutic to people who have a variety of special needs. Drug addicts, veterans with Post-Traumatic Stress Disorder, people with autism and cerebral palsy. Studies show that people working with horses experience decreased blood pressure, lower stress levels and reduced feelings of tension, anxiety and anger."

Nora thought about that. "I can see why. There's something about a horse. A huge, powerful animal, but in most cases, they're gentle giants who depend on their humans to love them and take care of them."

"Exactly. People gain the trust of this large animal, and it helps the human to gain feelings of self-esteem, empowerment, patience and trust. Add to that, a human with physical or emotional struggles to begin with, and this horse helps them overcome some very powerful problems."

Nora smiled. "Sounds wonderful. And right up your alley."

"There is an organization I'd join to learn how to do this therapy correctly. But since I'm a medical professional, I shouldn't have any problem getting certified. From there, we'd need the basics to get going: a horse, a place to house it, a place to ride, some volunteers and some clients."

"Thunder?"

"I'd been thinking about this project for a while now, but when the Rosewoods called and told me they were getting frustrated with Thunder always escaping, it started to dawn on me. I could buy Thunder and he could be the start of my equine therapy practice. And if you like the idea of this too ... maybe I could use your barn and front pasture to house the practice."

"Thunder was such a huge part of my Aunt Edie's training facility and she loved that horse so much."

"Yes, she did."

"It seems fitting that Thunder would come home, settle in and start a whole new purpose in life, helping people with problems get better."

He smiled at her.

"Maybe this is why Thunder keeps leaving his new home. He wants a greater purpose."

Shaw laughed. "That's a bit of a stretch, but you never know. I do think he misses your aunt, and he misses being here."

Nora stood. "Well then, we'd better find him." She reached out and pulled Shaw to his feet.

"Let's go over to the Rosewoods, see what we can find out."

RYAN MELROSE PULLED into his parents' driveway and turned off the car. He sat a moment, willing his racing heart to slow. He ungripped the steering wheel and took note of the shaking of his hands. An Admissions folder from the local college sat on his passenger seat. It was late in the game, but they'd accepted him. He'd lost two full classes from UNC, but he was still considered a junior. He could make those up later.

Now, he just had to break the news to his parents.

He cleared his throat and ran his hand absentmindedly through his hair. He pushed a breath out through loose lips and grabbed the folder. No time like the present. He entered the house and a whoosh of comforting smells reached out and grabbed him. Chicken and dumplings, white gravy and peas were his mom's offering tonight and his stomach instantaneously growled. He checked his watch. Twenty minutes till dinner time, etched into his routine since he was old enough to join his parents around the dinner table.

There was no way he'd be able to eat dinner with this news sitting on his conscience. He would have to break it now.

Shoulders back, he strode into the kitchen. His mother was sprinkling flour into a pan on the stove. "Hi, Mom," he said. "Where's Dad?"

She shrugged. "Where else would he be?" She gestured toward the TV room where his dad sat in his recliner, feet up, reading a newspaper while listening to the early evening news.

"Could you come into the TV room with me? I have something to tell you and Dad."

She used her shoulder to wipe a strand of hair out of her face. Still bothered by it, she pushed it out of her eyes with her hand, leaving a faint line of white powder. "I'm right in the middle of dinner, Ryan. Hold on and you can tell us when we sit down."

His confident facade was breaking down, and he knew it. No way would it survive if he had to wait. "No, Mom. This is important. Can you just stop what you're doing and come talk to me?"

She met his eyes, really looked at him. He had no idea what she saw there, but she narrowed her eyes, then reached over and turned the burner off. "Well, all right."

Ryan went straight to the TV set and turned it off. It took his father about ten seconds before he looked up and noticed them. "What's this about?" he said in a low voice.

"I have no idea," his mom said, her expression leaving no doubt that she was put out. "Ryan evidently has something so important to tell us that it can't wait till the dinner table."

His dad put the recliner upright with a clang and laid his paper down. "Well, then."

His mother sat, and Ryan stood in front of the TV. Certain that he now held their undivided attention, he wasn't sure he actually wanted it. He gripped the bright purple folder tightly in front of him, its brilliance an attempt to conceal its mediocrity. "I've been doing a lot of thinking. Soul-searching, I guess you could say. And ... I'm making a few changes in my life. In my future. I quit UNC and enrolled in Myrtle Beach College. Classes start next week."

The room was so silent, his ears hurt. The rumble of the high-pressure front in the small room was obvious to him, despite the lack of noise. Then, his mother said, "This isn't funny, Ryan."

"It's not a joke, Mom. I want to be close to Grace. I want to be a part of her life. I want to be her dad. I can't do that when I'm away at school."

His mother's eyes went wide. His dad said, "You did all this without consulting us?"

"Yes, because I knew you both would disapprove. This is my decision."

"But if you can't defend your decision to your parents who want the best for you, and you can't explain why you would willingly destroy your future, then you must know there's something wrong with your logic." His mother's tone was deceptively calm. He knew her well enough to know there was a hurricane of emotion simmering under the surface.

"How can being a hands-on father to my daughter destroy my future? How about Grace's future? How about Carly's future? I couldn't continue being so far away, neglecting my responsibility to my family."

"*We* help Grace. *We* help Carly. You're away working on your education. We're all doing our part."

Ryan exhaled. "I know Carly appreciates your support, and I do too. But no, it's not the same. I'm Grace's father and I need to start acting like it. By the time I was done with school, Grace would be almost six years old. She'd be in elementary school and wouldn't even know me. I don't want to be an absentee father. It's not right."

His mother rubbed her hands over her eyes. "What about your scholarships?"

"I gave them up."

"Do you realize how stupid that is?" his father asked, voice raised, just as his mother exploded with, "You had no right to waive your scholarships when they were so hard to come by!"

His parents looked at each other. Their angry words had all jumbled together and he probably didn't understand all of them, but he had caught the gist. His father shook his head, shoulders hunched. He spoke quietly, broken. "Do you know how many people would die for the opportunities you've had, and now just threw away?"

Ryan shrugged. "I'll make it work. Maybe after I go here for a while I'll qualify for some new scholarships."

"Maybe? You didn't research it before you pulled the trigger?" His father drew a hand down his face, his lower lip trembling. "You just don't get it. UNC has a reputation. A brand. A degree from UNC means something. Unlike a degree at ... what is it, Hodunk University?"

"A bachelor's degree is a bachelor's degree," Ryan responded, but even he could tell his voice was shaky. This wasn't about the quality of the degree as much as it was about doing what was right for Grace.

In his wildest dreams, he didn't anticipate this going well, and the longer he left the conversation open for his parents' feedback, the deeper he'd be dragged into trying to justify his reasoning. "Mom and

Dad, I made my decision. I'm an adult and I'm doing what I think is right. I would love to have your support, but I don't require it."

"You're making a mistake," his mom said coldly.

"You raised me to put family first," Ryan argued, even though he didn't fully believe it. He cleared his throat and went on. "I don't know how that can be a mistake."

She shook her head and looked away. His dad motioned to his mom and they stepped out of the room for a consultation. The room was silent in their absence, but the tension didn't dissipate at all. He stood still, but he felt like jumping out of his skin. He heard his heartbeat in his ears and took a deep breath to try to prevent a bodily catastrophe. After a few moments, they returned, a united front. "You'll be responsible for your own tuition and fees. You can live here, but we will have no part in financially supporting you. You say you're an adult with responsibilities. Start showing it."

Although it wasn't unexpected, nonetheless it was a punch to the gut. He schooled his expression to hide the distress rising up his esophagus. The chicken and dumplings aroma now made him nauseous.

He had put his new life in motion. It was up to him now to live it.

Chapter Four

In the truck, Shaw's phone rang. It was Phil Rosewood, Thunder's owner. "I found him. It's not good."

"Is he injured?"

"Yeah." Phil's voice was grave. "Best I can tell he tried to clear the fence with the extra height and didn't make it. He crashed through the new wood, splintering it, and he collapsed on the other side. He's lying there in the demolition."

Shaw closed his eyes tight, then opened them. "Where are you? I'm on my way."

"I'll meet you at my front gate and lead you there."

He glanced over at Nora and filled her in. "I just hope he hasn't broken a leg or severed an artery. About anything else can heal. Those two are usually life-ending."

Nora reached over and placed her hand over his as he drove. He nodded his appreciation, and then heard her praying. "God, help Thunder. Help him recover and be well to fulfill Shaw's new plans for his life. Amen."

The Rosewood Ranch was a dozen miles away. Shaw raced it as fast as he could without putting their lives in danger. When he arrived at the front gate, Phil opened it, letting him in, then he followed the other man's truck as he drove to the far west corner of his property. There, Shaw could see the damaged fence. He quickly parked, jumped out and circled to the back where he pulled out his medical transport bag and a large flashlight. All three people made their way carefully to the crash site. Shaw held his arms out. "Please be careful and keep your distance from hoofs and teeth. He could hurt you without meaning to."

He took the lead and hiked to the wood fence, now eight feet tall. Shaw reached the fence, pulled a few broken boards away and peered over the top. Thunder lay in the rubble, eerily motionless.

"How long's he been lying here?"

Phil shook his head. "I don't have an accurate time. Best guess is up to three hours. Maybe less."

Shaw needed to get closer. He hoisted himself up and over the fence and lowered himself carefully on to the ground on the other side, carrying his tools. He went immediately to Thunder's head. "Hey Thunder, how are you feeling, boy?" he murmured close to the horse's ear. The horse didn't flinch. Shaw opened Thunder's eye with his fingers. He was unconscious. He grabbed a stethoscope from his pack and searched for a heartbeat. Yes. It was there, and it was slow but steady.

He would need to rouse the big fella, but he took advantage of his stillness to do an examination. He ran his hands over Thunder's body, part by part, and mentally documented any abnormalities. There was a gash on his forehead, and judging from the blood on the ground, he had lost quite a bit already. However, the wound had clotted, and it appeared that the bleeding had slowed. Running his hands down the gelding's long face, on both sides of his neck, then on to his back, his ribs, then down each leg. Thunder's back right leg was bent at an abnormal angle. That's where the bulk of his injuries lay. The gash on his head was nearly stable, a few abrasions from crashing through the fence on his torso. But the leg.

He stood and faced Phil. "I'm not sure about this leg. It's going to need an x-ray to see if it's fractured. If it is, we'll have to see if it can be treated. But first we need to get him into a trailer, so we can transport him."

Phil frowned. "Horses can't recover from broken legs, can they? Isn't that an automatic euthanasia?"

Shaw shook his head. "Not necessarily. It depends a lot on where the break is, and if it can be set, and if we can keep him from putting weight on it."

"How do we do that?"

"First things first. You have a horse trailer, don't you?"

Phil nodded.

"Go get it and while you're gone, I'll work on creating a sling for that leg so it's up against his body and he can't put weight on it. Then we'll figure out how to get him up, and into the trailer on three legs."

Phil raced off.

NORA STAYED CLOSE TO Shaw, wanting to help but having no idea how, other than to provide moral support. She watched him rummage silently through his truck, mentally whirring through ideas about how to rig a sling for an injured horse using stray items that would hold once Thunder woke and started thrashing. Soft, calming, familiar voices would help the horse get over his fears and anxiety once he came to. She'd be there to help provide one.

Shaw moved from the bed of his pickup to his back seat, holding a few items he'd selected. He pulled a blanket from the backseat and got to work folding it lengthwise. He looked up at her. "I think this might work. This'll hold the leg up at the knee, then I'll tie it around his torso. I'll use this …" he held up a metal tool that looked like a clip, "to keep it nice and tight in place. I'll put Phil in the trailer with Thunder, both to keep him calm, but also to use his shoulder to help him balance on three legs for the ride."

"I could stand at his head and talk to him while Phil stabilizes his leg."

Shaw nodded. "Good idea. Let's get over there and see if I can get this thing on him while he's still down."

They jogged back to where Thunder lay. His eyes were still closed but Nora could tell he'd moved slightly, and his tail was switching. He was coming to. Shaw noticed the same thing. He went to his vet bag and pulled out a syringe and medicine.

"This will take the edge off the pain for him, but it won't sedate him. We need him to be awake to get him into the trailer. But I don't want him to be fighting me as I apply the sling."

Nora nodded and watched him work. He was so good at this. If there was anyone who embodied perfection at the field that was God's chosen work for a person, it was Shaw. He loved animals, he related to them, he wanted to care for them, and they trusted him. Nora hoped that Thunder would take comfort in Shaw, a familiar person, working on his injured leg.

The pain killer injection complete, Shaw moved to Thunder's leg. Nora stayed at Thunder's head, close by in case he awoke. Shaw took the blanket, folded accordion-style lengthwise and started maneuvering it around the leg, bending gently at the knee, keeping the harmed shin section safe from movement. He looped the blanket around the horse's torso and neck, tied a knot, then reinforced it with the metal clip. He leaned back to inspect his work.

Thunder shook his head, once gently, then a second time with more force. "Shaw, time's up. He's awake!" Nora tried to keep panic from her voice.

Shaw jumped to his feet and slipped a halter and lead rope onto Thunder. "You hold on to this and do your best not to let go if he starts to run. Of course, his ability to run will be limited with the injury and the sling. I'll be back here with his leg to make sure the sling holds when he stands up."

A rush of anxiety pulsed through her. "Wait, am I supposed to coax him up?"

"No coaxing needed. Once he's fully awake, he'll want to get up on his own."

Seconds later, several events all happened at the same time. Phil pulled the truck up feet away from Thunder, the horse trailer bouncing along behind it on the unpaved ground. Thunder awakened and hoisted himself up. Shaw grabbed the leg, held by the makeshift sling, and pushed his shoulder into Thunder's side, creating a substitute fourth leg. Nora stroked his head and neck and kept a running string of comforting words going.

All things considered, it went pretty well. But there was no time to celebrate their success. Phil jumped out of the truck and ran to the trio. Phil took hold of Thunder's lead rope and coaxed him up the ramp of the trailer while Shaw provided bodily support in the rear. Between the two men, they managed to get Thunder in place in the trailer.

"Phil, I want you to ride in this right stall and stay in Thunder's sight. Keep him as calm as you can."

Phil shook his head. "Why don't I stay in the left stall with him, and be fourth leg back up like you've been doing?"

"Too dangerous. If he gets nervous and starts thrashing, I don't want you in the way."

Phil considered. "What if that sling doesn't hold?"

Shaw shrugged, his mouth grim. "If it doesn't he'll try to put weight on the leg and change his mind real quick. He should be safe on the way to the clinic."

The three of them took their assigned places. Shaw took the wheel and did his best to cover the distance over the grassy pasture without bouncing the trailer around too much. Once on the highway, he made speed to get to their destination quickly: a veterinary co-op clinic that offered the use of big medical equipment to its participating vets. Shaw pulled the rig into a barn, parked and raced around to the trailer.

"I called ahead while we were on the road. They have an opening with the x-ray machine." As he finished the explanation, two people, a man and a woman dressed in lab coats joined him.

"Hi. This is Thunder. He fell through a fence that I'm guessing he was trying to jump over and misjudged the height. He landed and twisted his leg. I'm pretty sure the knee and thigh are okay, but I wonder about the calf."

They nodded and entered the trailer as Phil and Nora moved out of their way. Between the three veterinary professionals, they had Thunder out of the trailer and in place for the x-ray in no time.

"He did pretty well in the trailer, all things considered," Phil murmured.

"Yeah, I was proud of him. He's quite a horse," Nora responded.

Phil glanced at her, then focused on the medical entourage. "I know he's quite special to your family."

"Yep."

"We love him to death, but he just doesn't seem to want to stay with us. I feel terrible that he injured himself trying to escape so he could get back to your place again."

Nora put her hand on his arm. "Don't torture yourself. You can't assume that's what he was doing."

Phil shook his head. "He'd already escaped three times by jumping the fence and headed straight to your ranch. I added the extra height to the fence, assuming it would stop him and keep him in. But it ended up getting him injured."

A tear came to Nora's eye. "Poor Thunder. You realize it's not me he's running to. It's my Aunt Edie, who has passed. Thunder just doesn't understand."

Phil stayed silent for a moment. "He sure is loyal."

Nora nodded.

He turned to her with an urgency that surprised her. "Let's see what happens with Thunder. Hopefully he'll recover fully. But would you consider taking him on so that he gets to live at your ranch? It's obviously where he wants to be."

Her answer was immediate. "We'll do what's right for Thunder."

Phil nodded and set his full attention on the x-ray procedure.

THE X-RAY RESULTS WERE promising. Shaw sent a silent prayer of thanks upward when the technicians announced, "Hairline fracture. The bone's intact. Some ligament damage and just a tiny split in the bone."

"We can heal that," Shaw said softly.

"Yes, I believe so."

Shaw responded with a fist pump and a smile. He turned and looked across the open barn to Phil and Nora, and they immediately understood the good news and responded with smiles of their own.

They wrapped Thunder's leg with gauze and Ace-bandage type strips till it was tight and contained. "Just a second," Shaw said to the techs, and went over to where Nora and Phil stood.

"Great news. The fracture is very small and not entirely through the bone. The main injury is torn ligaments, which we can treat."

"Is he going to recover?" Phil asked.

"Yes. He's not going to be jumping over eight-foot fences, or even five-foot fences anymore. But he's going to be fine." Shaw ran a hand over his mouth, looking around the clinic. "I'm going to lease a horse sling apparatus from the co-op clinic here. It's a harness with a series of straps that connect to a hook installed in the ceiling of a stall. It allows the horse freedom within its stall but provides support while he's standing mainly on three legs for healing."

Phil said, "So you don't need to strap his leg up like you did with the makeshift sling?"

Shaw shook his head. "No. Because the leg hurts, and because we have it strapped, Thunder knows there's something wrong with it.

He'll keep it lifted naturally. I'll check him every day or two. I imagine he's only going to need to wear it for two weeks."

"That's wonderful!" Nora exclaimed.

"Here's the thing," Shaw said. "I happen to know Nora's barn has a stall with the metal hook installed in the ceiling."

"It does?"

"Yes. I worked with Edie to install it and we used it several times in the heyday of Waccamaw Trails." He looked over at Phil. "Would you give me approval to take Thunder there and do his rehab at Nora's place?"

Phil sighed. "Yeah, that makes sense. But at some point, we need to talk about Thunder's future and all the medical expenses he's incurring."

Shaw shook his head. "Don't worry about that. I have plans for Thunder. I'd be happy to cover all his medical expenses as part of a sales agreement to shift ownership from you to me."

Phil raised his eyebrows.

Shaw put a hand on his arm. "Let's not discuss it now. Let's put Thunder's needs first and get him healed."

CARLY STARTED THE WORKWEEK wearing her new teal dress. She took a little more care than usual on her makeup and hair, jewelry and shoes. Even Grace noticed. When Carly fed her breakfast, her daughter, normally focused on Cheerios and fruit juice, gave her the once over and said, "You pretty, Mama."

She leaned over the little darling's head and planted a kiss there. "Thank you, sweetie. You pretty too."

When she walked into the office and passed Haley's receptionist desk, the response was similar. "Girl!" Haley exclaimed, drawing out the word to last a few seconds. "You are looking good!"

Carly laughed. "Thanks, Haley. You too."

Haley rose and took Carly's sleeve between her fingers. "Is this silk?"

"Um, no, I'm pretty sure it's not silk." If it were, she would've made sure to put a coat over it while she was cleaning up Grace's breakfast mess and getting her into the car seat.

Haley winked at her and nodded approvingly. "I think I know why you're dressing up and wearing the new face and hair."

Carly chortled. "No, you don't."

"Oh, yes I do. It's that tall, dark and handsome hunk who's after you. You're looking your best, hoping he'll come back and visit you again. What's his name again?"

"His name is Ryan, and Haley, you have no idea how much history we have. None at all. Or else you wouldn't be pushing me into his arms."

Haley frowned, her forehead creasing with confusion. "Oh. That doesn't sound good at all."

Carly sighed. "It's a long story. I'll tell it to you sometime when we're not supposed to be working." She gave Haley a meaningful smirk, hoping that her message wouldn't be missed, and headed back to her desk.

"Lunch!" Haley exclaimed. "We'll go to lunch today at the cafeteria and it'll be my treat."

Carly chuckled, rolled her eyes and shook her head as she kept walking.

The morning passed quickly. Now that she knew how to do her new job, Carly felt a sense of confidence in her role helping students enroll in classes. She also took her job a step further and invited them to tell her their future career goals so that she could ensure they weren't missing any opportunities. It brought her a sense of achievement, a shoot of exhilaration at helping others and making a difference.

Before she knew it, Haley stood at Carly's desk, her finger pointing at her watch. "Let's go, babe. It's lunch time."

Carly grabbed her purse and joined her. At the cafeteria, they grabbed salads and found a table. Haley studied her as she punched her straw out of its paper wrapper. "So? Tell me all about this Ryan."

Carly wasn't usually forthcoming about her story, about Grace's story. She had no high school friends remaining. Not a single one. She harbored no ill feelings toward them. It's just that their lives didn't go the same way hers had. They all graduated from high school and went on to college. No one else had given birth to a baby and then had to work her arse off trying, not only support to Grace, but also to move forward with her own life and career as well. It wasn't the easy way. It wasn't the way she would've chosen for herself. On the other hand, she wouldn't change it for the world because she couldn't imagine her life without her daughter.

She needed a friend. A girlfriend. Someone to share her thoughts with, especially now that Ryan was evidently back in the picture, however short-term. And girlfriends weren't exactly banging her door down. Why not Haley?

"Okay," she said as she forked a tomato and put it in her mouth. "Ryan and I dated in high school. I fell for him hard. And well, I got pregnant."

That did it for Haley. She put her fork down and stopped chewing. "Oh my gosh!"

"Yep. It was stupid, what can I say? I like to think I was smarter than that but …"

"Well, no, these things happen," Haley said, her voice trailing off.

"Look, Haley. You can't tell me anything I haven't thought myself a million times. I'm not here to tell you how I got pregnant, or why I wasn't smarter. Suffice it to say that I have my daughter Grace who is now two years old, and she is the light of my life. Everything I do is for that little girl, and I love her to death, I really do."

"Do you have any pictures?"

"Well," Carly grinned, "of course I do." She pulled her phone out of her purse, pulled up a few pictures and handed it over. Haley ooohed and ahhhed over Grace's adorableness. She handed it back with a smile.

"Ryan abandoned us. It was such a shock when it first happened. I mean, all my plans for my future changed when Grace was born. Every last one. But his? Nothing changed at all for him."

Haley frowned. "What did he do?"

"He went away to college about a month before Grace was born. He missed everything. He never even saw her till Thanksgiving break that year. She was already two months old."

Haley gasped. "He wasn't in the delivery room with you?"

Carly shook her head. "A couple hundred miles away." Haley's reaction reminded her that Ryan's actions had been shocking. They were her reality and had been for a long time. She'd learned to live with his absence and his abandonment. She'd put her head down and focused on what she needed to do to raise this beautiful little girl. But still ...

"That's awful!"

"And he's been gone two years now. He just went off to college in North Carolina like he'd originally planned. Grace and I didn't change his plans at all." She looked down at her salad and suddenly didn't feel like eating. "I mean, don't get me wrong. I have help. My parents have been awesome about helping with Grace. They took her when I used to work at the restaurant. She goes to preschool now, but they take her in the evenings every once in a while so I can study. And Ryan's parents. They are in Grace's life too. They give me money to help meet bills, and they babysit when I need them. So, I don't want you to think I'm raising her alone, because I'm not."

"But Ryan ...," Haley started and then stopped.

"Ryan hasn't seen too much of her. It broke my heart Haley, it really did. It was so unlike the guy I thought he was, the one I fell in love with. I thought so much of him. He was my dream come true. But he never made Grace and me a priority. I couldn't go on loving him when he was breaking my heart every day." She was surprised that a tear came to her eye. Hadn't she cried enough tears over this man? Wasn't she long over him now? "Sorry," she said to Haley, grabbing her napkin and wiping it away.

"No sweetie, it's okay." Haley reached over the table and placed her hand over Carly's, squeezing it while tears filled her own eyes.

Carly shook her head, pushing out a chuckle. "I have no idea why I'm crying. This has been my reality for a long time. He disappointed me, but I've gotten over it."

Haley studied her for a moment. "But he's back now. With the Egg McMuffin and catching you when you fainted?"

"Yes. He's back. Would you believe he says he wants to be a family again?"

"He does?"

Carly grimaced. "No, of course he doesn't. He just says he does. He has no idea what that means. He has no staying power. Why would he track me down, just days before he has to be back at school and tell me he wants to give it another try? His timing is suspect."

"But Carly, maybe he's done some soul searching. Maybe he recognizes his mistake and wants you to forgive him. Maybe he wants to get to know his daughter better. Be a part of her life!"

A smile formed on Carly's lips as Haley spoke. The poor girl. She hadn't been jaded yet. She hadn't had her heart broken by some guy who told her one thing, got her to believe him, and then did the total opposite. Men were not to be trusted, at least not guys Ryan's age. But evidently Haley hadn't learned that yet. If she had to guess, she'd say Haley loved romantic movies and read romance novels and bought into all the Love Conquers All stuff. Heck, Carly had believed in it, once upon a time.

But putting your trust in a man who had the power to crush your heart, was just plain silly. The last thing she would ever do is put her trust in Ryan. Where he was concerned, she had built a stone wall around her heart, safe and secure so he could never hurt her again. No way would she give him the chance to chip away at it.

"You sound like you want to believe he's back for good. You sound like you want me to forgive him and let him back into our lives. But I can't do that, Haley."

"Why not? Just give him a chance?"

"Because. He already broke my heart. I can't allow him to do the same to our daughter."

Haley set her lips in a grim line. "I understand. It's just such a shame. He's so good-looking, and he seems so determined to do it right this time. But if you say he isn't trustworthy."

"Trust me, he's not."

Haley nodded. "You would know best, I suppose," although her voice held just enough doubt that Carly knew Haley thought she was making a mistake.

They changed subjects and spent the rest of the meal talking about the sale at Belk's.

Chapter Five

Ryan threw a swimsuit wrapped in a beach towel through his back window and got into the driver's seat. His heart was light, and he was excited that Carly had agreed to another fun family outing. This time, the beach. Growing up so close to the ocean, he was a beach lover. He'd spent his childhoods in the waves and on the sand. He wondered if Carly had, as well. They'd never been there together. Or even discussed the beach, that he could remember.

As a boyfriend, he'd sucked. As a father, he'd sucked. When they were together last weekend, he sensed Carly's hesitance to allow him access to her and Grace and had no doubt as to why. What had he ever done for her? Other than the obvious – he'd helped create their child. And then left her with all the responsibility and the day in, day out work of caring for her.

That was over. He'd been wrong, but his whole focus now was making it right. He would show Carly with his actions that he was turning over a new leaf. And he'd just hope that it wasn't too late. Carly had always been a reasonable girl. Hopefully that hadn't changed.

Words were one thing. Words were easy. It was only if you backed up your words with your actions, that you could be trusted. Believed.

He parked in Carly's apartment lot and closed his eyes a second, grounding himself, focusing in on his intent for the day. Fun. Conversation. Build relationships. Get to know each other better. It was enough, for now.

Carly opened the door to his knock and looked at him, a dubious expression on her face. That's okay. He'd push through it.

"Hi!" he said enthusiastically. "It's a beautiful day."

"Why-n!" came a happy voice from inside the apartment.

"Grace!" It did his heart good that she recognized his voice and was happy to hear it. Her little feet pounded the short distance from the living room to the door. He knelt and held his arms out and this time, she bounded into them. "Urgh," he groaned playfully as he let himself fall backward, laying on the floor now, holding tightly to Grace on his chest while she laughed hilariously. "You're so strong you knocked me over, little girl."

"Oh, Why-n," she giggled deliciously.

He glanced up at Carly who looked amused but guarded. Her eyebrows revealed tight lines and her mouth twisted at the corners.

"All right, let him up Grace."

Grace scrambled to her feet and held her hand out helpfully. Ryan grabbed it and pretended that she was pulling him to his feet. "There we go. Thanks, Grace." He walked with her to the living room and put his hands on his hips. "Do you want to go have a fun day together? Grace, Mommy and Why-n?"

Grace gave an excited leap into the air. "Yes!" she yelled.

He knelt again so they were closer, face to face. "I was thinking we'd go to the beach today. Have you ever gone to the beach, Grace?"

"Yes!" she yelled again. He grinned into her smiling face but couldn't ignore the puff of exasperation from her mother. He turned his attention to Carly who had crossed her arms in front of her chest and was rolling her eyes.

"Um," he stammered. "Bad idea?"

She gave an exaggerated exhale and shook her head. "Beach day? Why didn't you tell me, Ryan?"

He smiled uncomfortably, eyebrows up. He was positive he'd messed up, but he had no idea why or how. "Uh, I really just thought of it this morning. Why? Is this bad somehow? We don't have to go to the beach. We can do whatever you want to do. What would you prefer?"

"No ...," she started, and was interrupted by the wail of a two-year-old thinking she'd been promised one thing, only to have it ripped from her hands.

"Beeeeeach!" Grace wailed.

Carly didn't move from her angry stance, just moved her eyes towards him. Then, she raised her eyebrows in an unspoken challenge. He had caused this outrage somehow; it was up to him to fix it.

"Oh sweetie," he soothed, bringing the crying Grace into his arms. "It's okay, it's okay. Don't cry now, sweetheart."

Grace started sniffing and blinking, pulled back to look at his face and asked in probably the most adorable voice he'd heard in his life, "Are we going to the beach?"

The girl was good. He could learn a lot about persuasion from this little one.

One sure way to get her to stop crying would be to say yes. But that wouldn't remove the pissed-off look on her mother's face. So, what to do, what to do? He looked at the little girl, held up one finger in her face and said, "Before I answer that, wait just one minute, okay?"

She nodded warily but withheld judgement.

He got to his feet and took Carly's arm and led her into a huddle in the kitchen. If he'd learned anything from his own parents about parenting, it was that they always presented a united front. He gazed into Carly's eyes and thought he saw just a tinge of softening there. He murmured, "Did you not want to go to the beach today?"

She shook her head. "It's not that. It's just that if you'd told me your plans ahead of time, I could've gotten all the prep work done before you got here."

"Prep work?"

She stared at him, her eyes widening in disbelief. "You really don't have a clue, do you, how much work it is to take a toddler to the beach."

Ryan thought of the towel and swimsuit he'd thrown into the backseat. "Um, no, I guess I don't."

"Look, I don't want to put a damper on this outing with Grace, but you're gonna have to work with me here."

"Yes, of course," he agreed. "What would you like me to do?"

She gazed over at Grace, watching them intently. "You entertain her while I start gathering everything that we'll need."

"Sure. I'd love to." He took a step toward Grace, then turned back. "I'm sorry if I messed up here."

Then her whole face transformed. The anger drained, the tightness of her eyes and forehead fled and for a moment, it was just Carly. His Carly, the one who had made his senior year in high school the absolute best year of his life. The one he could be himself with, the one he could share his dreams with. The one who used to look at him like he was the center of her world.

That Carly was gone now. But it did his heart good that he'd seen a glimpse of her, if only for a moment. And all it took was a sincere apology from him.

"Thank you for that. And thank you for being willing to handle this together. You could've just made me out to be the bad guy to Grace."

A relieved smile formed on his lips. So, he had done something right after all. He'd take each small victory he could get. "You're welcome. And thank you for being patient with me while I come up to speed."

A kiss on her beautiful lips would've been the perfect way to express his gratitude but of course he didn't do it. He wouldn't even allow himself to think of it. Not right now.

He went back to Grace, then turned to Carly. "What do you say, Mommy? Do we have an answer for this pretty girl?"

"We're going to the beach."

Grace exploded with happiness. Her smile was pure and happy and unfettered. She jumped up and down in a circle like it was the best news she'd ever heard. His heart exploded along with her. This is why he'd made so many changes in his life. This moment. Right here.

Carly disappeared, and he could hear her making noises in the back of the apartment while he pulled out a coloring book and colored with Grace. Minutes passed, and then it dragged into tens of minutes. Her voice, muffled from the distance and walls separating them, floated in the air but he couldn't make out her words.

"Carly? Do you need some help?"

"No," she answered. "I'm getting there."

He looked back into the light green eyes of his daughter. She resembled Carly so much, with her mom's complexion and fairness. "I wonder what your mommy is doing."

Grace shrugged and went back to her picture.

Another ten minutes passed before Carly reappeared. She had put her longish strawberry blonde hair up in a ponytail and wisps had escaped the binding, brushing her face. She carried a huge bag and dumped it on the floor. He came to his feet. "Do you need help?"

She gave him an ironic look. He guessed that she did, indeed need help. "Here, let me help you."

She shook her head. "You're entertaining Grace, remember?"

He looked back at the little girl. She was absorbed in her artwork. "At least with the heavy lifting."

"I've about got it. Although I will let you carry it to the car."

She went back into the bedroom and came back with another load. When she left again, he began to study the pile of stuff. A big rolled up straw beach mat, a beach bag filled to the top with large multi-colored towels. An umbrella to install in the sand, and an anchor to allow for easier digging. Another bag containing diapers, swimsuits and about a million different varieties of sunscreen. A cooler, which he guessed she would begin filling with items from the kitchen. Another beach bag, which, when he peered inside, contained several pairs of flipflops in Grace's and Carly's sizes, and several cotton cover-ups.

She entered the room again, carrying a hat her size and one Grace's size. He glanced at her, his eyes wide. "What? All this?"

She put her hands on her hips, panting slightly. "Do you see anything here that we don't need for a day at the beach?"

He looked back down and after a perusal decided, no, there was nothing extraneous here. Then she snapped her fingers, said, "Chairs," and headed back to the bedroom. There must be a closet the size of a warehouse back there. Where was she storing all this stuff?

She returned with three reclining beach chairs and added them to the pile. Just as he expected, she headed for the kitchen and leaned into the refrigerator, digging around for lunch items.

"How about I start loading this stuff into my trunk?"

She looked up. "Start with the heavy stuff. I still need to get her suit and sunscreen on her."

He nodded and started lifting, grateful for the chance to be useful. He could see now why she was irritated when he just showed up and expected a fun day on the beach. What was he thinking?

It took two trips to get the trunk filled, and there were still several items left on the pile in the apartment. When he returned the second time, Grace was outfitted in a cute orange bathing suit and Carly was trying to keep her still long enough to coat her with sunscreen. She looked up and blew a hair out of her face. "Here, why don't you do this, and I'll go get my own suit on." She held up the lotion. "Just don't be in a hurry. She's very fair, so if you don't get even application, she'll burn in streaks."

He took the lotion cautiously, apprehensive about being trusted with this simple job. He didn't want to be the reason his little girl got a painful sunburn. On the other hand, he needed to prove himself to Carly as a competent parenting partner. He could do this.

"Hey, little girl. Stand in front of me here and I'll get your back first." Grace hopped into place and he began rubbing lotion on her back, shoulders, under her arms, backs of her legs. Then he twirled her around and he started at the bottom and went up: feet, shins, thighs, hands, arms, shoulders. He was just wondering how to do her face without getting it in her eyes, when Carly returned wearing a sundress.

"Oh, here," she said, bent and dug in one of the bags. She pulled out another sun product and tossed it to him. He caught it and looked at it. Special face formula.

"Thanks." He squeezed some out on his hands and carefully applied it until he was confident that he had covered every centimeter of exposed flesh on the kid.

When he was done he looked around and saw that Carly had finished packing the cooler and had quieted, staring at him while he'd been working on Grace. He met her eyes and wasn't sure what he saw there. Affection? Admiration? Probably directed at Grace, not him. Maybe she was simply pleased with the thorough job he'd done with the sunscreen. No need to get his hopes up.

"You can put her cover-up back on her. Looks like you did a good job with the sunscreen. At least for a couple hours when it'll be time to reapply it all again."

He smiled. "Thanks." He fumbled with the tiny cotton dress with a lightness in his heart.

Eventually it was time to go. Glancing at his phone, Ryan saw he'd arrived over an hour ago. Lesson learned: there was no quick pick up and go when it came to preparing a toddler.

They drove south to beautiful Huntingdon Beach State Park in Murrells Inlet. It boasted not only a three-mile stretch of protected beachfront, but it also had nature trails in case Grace wanted to stretch her legs. He paid the fee for the three of them, drove on the causeway over the salt marsh, and made it to the large parking lot. He parked and started pulling everything out of the trunk while Carly got Grace out of her car seat.

"Where's your bathing suit, Ryan?" asked Carly.

He pointed into the back seat with a thumb. "It's right there. Once I carry all this stuff out and get us set up, I'll just hop over to the locker room and change."

She nodded and started studying the best way to transport all their stuff to the beach with only one trip. She hoisted a few of the lighter beach bags over her shoulders and held out a hand to hold Grace's.

"I got all this, don't worry about it," Ryan said confidently before actually establishing how he would carry it all. He glanced toward the boardwalk that led to the beach. They had quite a walk. Oh well. He was young and fit. He'd manage. The important thing was that the ladies in his life wouldn't have to become pack mules.

They waited, watching him while he tried a variety of options, and ultimately, he managed to get every last parcel on his body. He looked up with a smile and a thumbs up. "Ready to go."

They walked slowly to the beach. Normally, he'd want to stride as fast as he could, so he could dump his load and relax. But again, you don't do anything fast with a toddler. Grace stopped and studied everything along the way. The boards on the path. The vegetation growing in the sand. The sign displaying a picture of a turtle. The yellow flag indicating moderate waves today.

Carly was so good with her. Patient and kind and encouraging of her questions. Ryan could learn a lot from her. So, he strolled at a snail's pace as they elongated the walk to ten times its normal length.

They finally arrived on the sand and he let Carly select the perfect location to set up. Thankfully it was late summer, and it wasn't as crowded as it would've been earlier in the season. He unloaded the beach mat, set up the umbrella and chairs, and laid out the towels. While Carly dug out the bucket and shovels for Grace to start digging, he grabbed his suit. "I'll be right back," he said, motioning with the garment.

Carly nodded and went back to playing with Grace.

He covered the distance to the locker room in a jog, put on his bathing suit, then back to the car to throw his clothes in the back seat and grab his towel. He'd never really messed with sunscreen; his complexion was responsive to sun and he'd never burned, despite his lack of care. He headed back to their spot on the beach and when he approached his two ladies, he went breathless for the first time since he'd started the jog. However, it wasn't due to his run.

It was the sight in front of him.

Carly kneeled in the sand, reaching for a shovel while Grace filled a small plastic bucket with sand. The sight of Carly on her knees, stretching and reaching and extending her beautiful petite figure to grab the shovel, slammed the breath out of his lungs.

He came to a stop about twenty yards away, so he could breathe normally again. And continue to observe her.

Carly grabbed the shovel and came back to sit on her haunches, knees bent while she dug with Grace. Carly wore a purple two-piece suit. Not a bikini exactly: not a revealing garment meant to entice and show as much skin as possible. It was more like an athletic suit. High-waisted bottoms that looked like the shorts an Olympic track star would wear, paired with a sports bra on the top, exposing her midriff. Functional. Utilitarian.

She looked beautiful.

Her body looked different than it had when he last saw her exposed to this extent; when they were dating in high school and in their youthful ignorance, were exploring each other's bodies. She was leaner then, thinner, more of a girl. Now, she was a woman. Her body had plumped in all the places that a woman's body needed to be plump. She had luscious curves and her shape was perfect. Still petite, not an ounce of fat. Just ... perfect.

His breathing returned to normal, and still he lingered at a distance, watching her, admiring her. The unmistakable attraction he felt filled his head. He liked what he saw. But no. No, no, no.

Bad idea. He couldn't, shouldn't. He forced his eyes away from her while he worked with his mind. He couldn't allow his physical attraction to Carly, which had always been there, from the very beginning of their relationship, distract him from what he was trying to do. This was about Grace, first and foremost. Sure, in a perfect world, it would also be about Carly. The three of them together. A family. But he'd done such damage to Carly, he didn't even harbor a hope that she'd be open to that. The very worst thing he could do was to reveal his physical attraction to Carly and make her think, that's all this was about.

He had a higher purpose. A higher goal. He wanted to be a hands-on father to Grace. If it meant that someday he could also have Carly, great. But until then, he had to focus on his daughter.

"Ryan?"

Her voice came to him on the breeze. He shook the thoughts out of his head and glanced up. She was looking at him with a frown. "What are you doing?"

Shoot. "Oh," he called, mind racing. "I dropped something." He bent over and scanned the sand, filling his hands, looking for a missed item that didn't exist.

"What is it?"

He straightened, kicked the sand and began to walk toward her. "Oh, just some coins I had in my pocket. No biggie." Making his way over to her, it disturbed him how easily the lie had come, and he made a mental promise that he'd never lie to her again. He'd already betrayed her and their daughter by being an absentee father. The last thing he wanted to do was lie to her as well.

He approached their set-up and Grace gave him a distracted wave from underneath her beach hat. She also had on tiny sunglasses that made him smile. Carly really did think of everything.

"Everything okay?" Carly asked.

"Yep. Sure is." He sat on the sand beside them and played.

CARLY RECLINED ON HER beach chair, then scooted it to the right a little bit so she'd get the perfect angle from the sun. She closed her eyes and breathed out her stress, then positioned her hat more fully over her face. Darn her fair complexion. What an irony God had handed her – to make her absolutely worship the sun yet give her skin that burned at the drop of a hat. Severely. Painfully. And then, despite Ryan's DNA combining with hers, their daughter got Carly's exact complexion.

She sighed and peered at Ryan from under her hat brim. She didn't think he used an ounce of sunscreen, yet his skin tone was at least two notches darker now than it had been when they'd arrived three hours ago. She could literally see him tanning. It was ridiculous.

Her gaze rested on him as he lifted Grace, swung her up onto his shoulders and trotted to the water. Grace was laughing and giggling, of course. She always did when she got attention from him. She bathed in his responsiveness. She was madly in love with him.

He was a great ... playmate. She wouldn't make the mental leap that he was a great father ... yet. Spending an afternoon occasionally entertaining a child and keeping her in good spirits was not the same thing as parenting. There was a lot more to being a parent than being the fun guy every week or so. What about the non-fun chores? Bathing her, feeding her, waking her up in the morning, getting her dressed and ready to walk out the door by seven thirty? Where was Ryan for all those activities? Well, he was away at college, of course.

But she could admit that the two of them enjoyed their time together, and because of that, she got a little bit of relaxation during their outings. Right now, for instance. When could she ever rest in a chair facing the sun with her eyes closed when she took Grace to the beach? Never. She was the one digging with her, holding her hand, taking her to the water's edge, preparing her peanut butter and jelly sandwich, reapplying sunscreen. She was determined to take advantage and savor this break in responsibility if he was going to hand it to her.

She sighed and closed her eyes, but way too soon, opened them again. Yeah, that was the problem. She couldn't just drift away when Ryan was around. Because she wanted to watch him.

He was a good-looking guy; he always had been. Feelings that should've been squashed long ago, simmered just beneath the surface. Which meant that when Ryan Melrose was mere feet away from her, wearing nothing more than swim trunks, she was going to look. She had no choice.

He was in constant movement because of Grace. Reaching for a shovel, getting up and following her when she wandered, lifting her up, his muscles moving gracefully under his skin. He was beautifully fluid.

And those eyes. Those unique, wonderful brown eyes the shade of a cup of hot cocoa. She'd always loved to gaze into them. Occasionally, she'd shift her gaze from his body to his face and see that his eyes were locked with hers. Could he know she was studying him or were her sunglasses shielding her eyes? And why was he watching her? Then her face heated, and almost certainly she blushed.

No. Having Ryan around definitely was not conducive to peaceful rest.

The hours passed pleasantly with a break for lunch, several swims in the waves, sandcastle creation and a short walk up the beach. It became clear that their day was over when Grace's mood shifted to ornery and irritated. Naptime. Carly was gratified to see that she didn't have to explain this to Ryan. He seemed to understand when she announced that it was time to go, and although Grace started crying, he supported her decision with an enthusiastic, "Time to go, Grace," and a concerted effort to start loading up all their stuff.

Grace fell asleep a minute into the drive home, and Ryan's instincts must've told him to stay silent in the car and let her sleep. All he did was look in the rearview mirror, then motion to Carly with his head and wink at her. The gesture made her smile, and yet her heart hurt. When Ryan was like this, she could picture them together, facing the joys and challenges of family life. They could be raising Grace together. A real family. The three of them.

But then she pulled that guard back up and reminded herself that a few fun family outings were not real life.

He parked and turned to look at her. "Why don't I carry her up and put her right into her crib?"

She considered, then shook her head. "As tempting as it is, I don't want her to take her nap yet. She is covered in lotion and sweat, and she could still have sand in uncomfortable places. You can carry her upstairs, but I need to give her a bath before I let her sleep."

He gazed at her a moment, his face a mystery, before he nodded. "You're amazing, you know that?"

She let out an embarrassed laugh. "Why?"

"You are such a good mother. You really are."

She shrugged, then got back to business. "You carry her up and I'll bring the bags, then you can come back down for the heavy stuff while I bathe her."

"Yes ma'am," he joked, and they sprang into action.

Later, when Grace was bathed, dried, and changed into her shorts and t-shirt, Carly was in her room, trying to convince her to take her nap. She kept asking for "Why-n" and although Carly assumed he hadn't left yet, she hadn't seen him in a while since she'd been tied up with Grace. "If I let you say good-bye to Ryan, will you settle down and take your nap?"

The little girl nodded and gave her a determined, serious look. Carly smiled at her. "Okay, go ahead and call for Ryan and ask him to come in here."

Grace sat and let out a loud "Why-n? Why-n?"

Carly heard Ryan's voice from the living room, "Yes, Grace?"

"Will you come in here?" she asked in her adorable little girl voice. Who could resist that? Certainly not Ryan, because he appeared in the doorway about five seconds later.

"Yes?"

"I told her she could say good-bye to you and thank you for a fun day at the beach," she eyed Grace with a nod, "if she promised to settle down and take her nap."

Ryan's face transformed with a happy smile. "Oh, okay," he said, and stepped inside. On uncertain ground, he came to a halt in the middle of the room and looked around. Grace patted the mattress and he looked at Carly as if for permission. She nodded and scooted to make room for him. He squeezed his tall body onto a crib mattress beside her, so he could give Grace a kiss good-bye, making Carly chuckle.

"Thank you, Why-n. And good-bye."

His heart melted; Carly could tell by the look on his face. He leaned forward and kissed Grace on the forehead. "Thank you for spending a fun day with me, and good-bye till next time. I love you, Grace."

He traced a knuckle across her cheek and was starting to get up when Grace said, "You do?"

Ryan froze and looked back at her. "Huh?"

"You love me?"

Ryann swallowed but met her gaze directly. "Yes, I do, Grace. I love you, and your mommy loves you, too."

Carly could feel her pulse start to race, wondering if this revelation was going to lead to additional questions from her daughter that she was nowhere near ready to address. But fortunately, his explanation seemed to suffice for now. She nodded and closed her eyes. Ryan locked eyes with Carly, then got up to leave.

She stayed with Grace through a few lullabies and left the room about fifteen minutes later. She walked by the mound of beach supplies and started with the towels, getting them ready to put in the washer. She assumed Ryan had left, but he was sitting there in the living room.

"Oh," she said.

"Sorry, I didn't want to go into your bedroom to put all that stuff away, but I'd be happy to help you now."

"That's okay. It'll be just as easy for me to take care of it myself."

He nodded. "Carly, I have something to tell you."

Why did those words make her blood run cold? Why did he have this power over her? He was taking off again. His semester was starting, and he needed to leave. What else could it be? "You do? What is it?"

He patted the couch beside him, just as his daughter had earlier. She went over and sat next to him, frowning. "Relax," he laughed. "It's good news. At least I hope you think it is."

She schooled her expression to release her tension. "What is it?" she said again.

"I quit Chapel Hill. I'm starting school here in town to finish my degree."

She stared at him. Her mind was blank. What did this mean? He'd actually quit UNC? This was monumental. "Why?"

He considered the question. "When I said I wanted to be a hands-on dad, I meant it. I can't do that from hundreds of miles away." He looked at her, probably waiting for some kind of reaction. But she was frozen. Turned to stone. She wasn't even sure if she was breathing. He took her hand in his. "I'm serious about this, Carly. I've never wanted anything more in my life."

Chapter Six

Carly felt like she was stumbling through her life. Case in point, she got out of her car at work and tripped over a cement parking barrier. Thank God she didn't fall and skin her knee. She really needed to shake out the cobwebs in her brain in order to do her job.

But Ryan's confession had thrown her for a loop. She couldn't think of anything else. It was so much in the forefront of her mind that when she walked into the office and saw Haley, she told her, "Ryan quit UNC," before she even allowed the woman time to say hello.

Haley blinked. "Uh. What?"

Carly shook her head, then held out her hands, which were suddenly tingling. "Sorry. Ryan withdrew from his college in Chapel Hill and he's going to school here in town. He starts classes today."

Haley let her mouth drop open. "And this means ....?"

"He wants to be a hands-on dad to Grace. So he says."

Haley came out from around her receptionist desk and took Carly into her arms in a warm hug. "That's fantastic!" But she must've noticed that her friend was not reciprocating. Carly was limp, standing there with her arms down. Haley pulled back and studied her with a frown. "Isn't it?"

"I have no idea." She stumbled back to her desk, Haley following her.

"What could possibly be bad about it?" Haley's smile was a little too big for comfort.

"Oh, let me see," Carly deadpanned while she unlocked her desk, removed her purse from her shoulder and sat in her desk chair, "he could start showing up and get Grace so hooked on him that when he decides he doesn't want this after all, she'll be totally destroyed." She halted her non-stop activity to stare wide-eyed at Haley.

Haley stared back. "Maybe he won't change his mind," she said in a small voice.

"You don't know Ryan. He's never had to sacrifice. He's always gotten what he wanted. He was the star of the high school basketball team. He got straight A's. Tons of friends. Won scholarships to one of the best schools in the country. I'm sure he earned great grades there, too."

"And ...?" Haley asked, confused.

"He gave all that up ... to be Grace's father. He's now living with his parents, taking classes at an ordinary college so he can see Grace regularly."

A smile burst back onto Haley's face. "That's great!"

Carly shook her head, the threat of tears overwhelming. "You don't get it. How long will that be enough for Ryan? He walked away from so much to do this. How long until he gets tired of it, and wants his old life back?"

Haley squatted in front of her, took her hands and squeezed them. "Ahh, sweetie. Maybe he won't. Maybe you just need to trust him in this."

Carly let her eyes drift closed and whispered, "What has he ever done to make me trust him?"

IN CLASS WAS WHERE it all made sense.

When he was in class, he knew what he was doing. He could learn and study. The numbers were always consistent. There was one right answer when it came to the numbers. It was either right, or it was wrong.

The problem was everywhere else in his life.

He was forging a brand-new path, a path that was foreign to him. Living back under his parents' roof, even though he'd only been gone a couple of years, was difficult. Would it be difficult if they weren't so openly angry at him? Maybe, maybe not. But their anger didn't make it any easier.

They glared at him when he came into the room. He tried to be pleasant in conversation, but his efforts weren't reciprocated. They were mad at him, he got that. They felt he'd made a grave mistake. But he knew that wasn't true. The mistake he'd made was two years ago. Now he was just trying to rectify it.

His parents' priorities were different than his own. He'd blindly followed their lead for too long. He'd finally realized that he needed and wanted to put Grace first, despite his parents being against that plan. But he was sure. He was certain. Despite how difficult it was without their support.

A few days of classes in, it became clear to him that he needed to find a job. If he was bringing in money, he'd be able to reduce the debt he'd have to repay when he finished his degree. And maybe, just maybe he could find a cheap apartment which would get him out from under his parents' roof. Life would be much less complicated that way.

His schedule allowed him hours during the day that he could be working. Take today, for instance. He had a 9 AM class, and then not another one till 1 and 2 PM. He could work four hours in between without even impacting his study schedule, which was usually at night.

He stopped in the kitchen, grabbed a quick bowl of cereal and while he was standing at the counter, shoveling it in with a spoon, his mother appeared, wearing her lab coat. *Kill her with kindness,* he thought.

"Good morning, Mother," he declared in a cheery radio announcer voice.

She jerked her head up. Her deep-rooted plan to ignore him other than directing a glare his way was now interrupted. "Hello," she mumbled, and moved to the coffee pot.

"I made a big pot just how you like it. I thought we could share the coffee." His cheeriness was exaggerated, and he knew his mother knew what he was doing. He couldn't help sending a big smile in her direction.

She just shook her head and rolled her eyes.

Finishing the cereal, he dumped the extra milk in the sink and loaded the empty bowl in the dishwasher. "I'm off to my Statistics class. Oh, and it's going just fine, thanks for asking." He gave her a brilliant grin, kissed her on the top of the head and reached the door. "You have yourself a wonderful day."

The sight of his mother annoyed with him for having the nerve to be happy, despite throwing his life away, sustained his good humor for the entire drive to school.

After Statistics, he was walking through the small campus, so much smaller than he was used to, and he passed the Student Life building. On a whim, he went inside. There was a snack bar and he ordered a Coke. The guy working behind the counter filled his order and took his payment.

"Hey," Ryan said, "do you know if the snack bar is hiring anyone?"

The guy picked up a towel and started wiping down the counter. "No, we're not, but have you looked at the bulletin board over there?" He pointed to a large board hanging on the wall a few yards away. Ryan glanced over at it. It was covered with a few long sheets of paper pinned up, as well as at least a dozen index cards.

"Thanks."

He took his Coke and went to check it out. Sure enough, there were job opportunities posted, lots of them. He'd never had a job during school before, just the occasional summer job when he was younger. His parents always wanted him to focus on his studies, never wanting him to be distracted by working for money. Well, times had changed.

He ripped off the flaps on the bottoms of a few posters containing phone numbers. No time like the present. He made phone calls, discussed hours and pay, and before he knew it, he had a job.

CARLY SAT IN THE QUIET of her living room, glancing at the text Ryan had sent a half hour ago. "Stopping by to see the princess?"

The wording made her nervous on a number of levels. First, he didn't say when he was stopping by. Not to mention, thought it was punctuated with a question mark, he wasn't leaving her with a choice. He may as well have written, "I'm stopping by to see the princess. Drop everything to be there."

And by the way, the princess? A stab of despair hit her heart. Ryan calling Grace his princess irritated her. If Grace was anyone's princess, she was Carly's. He had no right to call her that.

But on the other hand, shouldn't she be happy for Grace that her daddy finally recognized her as the princess she rightfully should be in his eyes?

Her endless mental wavering was driving her crazy. Why couldn't she just relax and take this cool? She let out an aggravated scream and was feeling just a tiny bit better after the release ... until the doorbell rang. She heard Ryan's voice, "Carly? Are you okay in there?"

Her timing couldn't be worse.

"Yeah," she said, then got up and went to the door. Opening it, she brought him into full view. "Yeah, I'm fine."

He wore shorts, a soft, worn out oxford button down shirt, heavy socks and work boots. He was covered, almost every inch of him, with some combination of dust, dirt and grass. He held what looked like a t-shirt and pair of gym shorts in one hand. She couldn't remember a time she'd ever seen him not looking clean and put together. "What on earth?"

He looked down at his clothes and shook his head good-naturedly. "Yeah, sorry about this. I was wondering if you'd mind if I took a shower here. I didn't want to go all the way home."

She frowned and stepped cautiously aside, wondering if he'd emit a cloud of dirt wherever he went, sort of like that *Peanuts* cartoon character.

"Why do you look like that?" she asked, pushing the door closed behind him.

"Oh, I guess I haven't told you. I got a lawn care job on campus. It's really cool because all their workers are students, so they're used to accommodating crazy schedules. I can fit my work hours in between my classes. There's a job board with all the work that needs to be done each hour. When you're free to work, you just look for where the crew is on campus, and you join them there." He brushed his sleeve. "I did mostly weed whacking today. It's a little messy."

She shook her head. "Back up. You're working?"

He looked at her, eyebrows up, and shrugged. "Yeah. My parents cut me off and I had to take out a ton of loans, so my free ride is over." He smiled again, and it dawned on her that nothing ever brought the guy down. He'd just executed a major life change, one his parents were not supportive of, and he'd lost literally all their considerable financial support. But he didn't seem to mind. He took it in stride. He just enrolled in a local college, got a job mowing grass, and he was happy as a clam.

Why couldn't she take life as it came like Ryan did? She could learn so much about life from him. If she would only let herself.

"Where's Grace?"

Carly jerked her attention back to the present. "Oh, sorry. She came home from preschool exhausted because they swam this afternoon. She fell asleep on the way home and I laid her down till dinner."

"No problem. Would you mind if I used your shower? I promise I won't leave a mess."

She blinked. Ryan Melrose in her shower? Her mind jumbled with all kinds of reasons why this was not a good idea. She didn't want him taking her for granted. She didn't want him making himself that comfortable around her and Grace. She didn't want him feeling at home here. It wasn't right. She was being a protective mother, and protective of her own heart as well.

It had nothing to do with having Ryan in a totally undressed state standing under the stream of water in her shower.

No. It had nothing to do with that.

She glanced up and he was studying her carefully. "There's no way I could even sit on your couch, as dirty as I am."

"All right," she grumbled with irritation. She stomped off down the hall, reached in the closet, grabbed what he'd need for a shower. Spinning around, she crashed directly into his broad chest. "Ooof."

He looked down and their eyes met and held. His revealed confusion and amusement. "Hey, take it easy there."

She was standing so close to him, his aroma floated to her nose. Far from smelling bad after working hard and sweating all day, he actually smelled good. Like sunscreen and grass and working male. She took a moment to calm her racing heart. Their closeness was out of place. He didn't belong here, in her tiny apartment, in her bathroom ready to shower and he certainly didn't belong, within smelling distance. It implied an intimacy she wasn't comfortable with.

Yet, it *was* familiar. He was close enough to her to reach out and hug. She could put her arms around him and pull him in and savor his strong chest. She remembered. She remembered what it was like to be in his arms, and it was always a good, safe, warm place to be. She liked it.

She loved it.

How easy would it be to step back into his arms now, to allow herself to fall deeply back into the excitement and thrill of being with Ryan? Of loving Ryan. He was right here.

She wrenched herself backward, away from him, away from the temptation her mind was serving up. She held out the towels and slammed the gate down on her heart. Because she wouldn't do this to herself again.

"Here you go." She gestured to the open door of the bathroom. "Pretty self-explanatory."

He chuckled. "Thanks."

She squeezed past him in the narrow hallway and was a few steps away when he said, "Hey, uh, Carly? Were you screaming when I first came to the door?"

Her cheeks heated with a flush of embarrassment. He knew she was screaming. He'd only phrased it as a question to give her an out. But taking the out would be lying, and she refused to be a liar. "Yes, I was. I'm not proud of it, but I was."

She looked up to find his expression was one of unqualified concern. "Can I help you with anything?"

Her eyes flicked across his face, landing on his lips and cheeks, then moving back to his eyes. "No, not really. It just gets hard every once in a while, you know?"

He nodded. "I do know. And that's something I can help you with. I'd like to make your life a little bit easier. At least as far as Grace is concerned."

Then he stepped into the bathroom and closed the door.

If she'd had a hard time keeping her heart under control when she stood in close proximity to a dirty, sweaty Ryan, ten minutes later she got to test that theory by standing close to a clean, sweet-smelling Ryan. He emerged from the shower, his brown hair damp and curling up slightly at the ends, his skin smelling like the feminine soap she'd given him, and yet on him it smelled masculine. Everything on him looked and smelled masculine. It couldn't help but do so. He was one of the best-looking males she'd ever known.

"Thanks, Carly. I feel so much better. Can I steal a plastic bag from you to put these in?" He held up his dirty clothes. She walked past him into the kitchen, handing him an empty grocery bag.

"Unfortunately, Grace is still out like a light. I guess it was a wasted trip over here." She needed him to leave, and hoped she was making that clear without being rude.

"No, no, not at all. In fact, since she's sleeping, we have a minute for me to ask you a question. Something that's been on my mind today while I was mowing." He grinned, and she looked away and tried to ignore how his smile made her pulse race through her veins faster than usual, leaving her with a tingly feeling.

He headed for her couch like he owned the place, and sat down, looking up at her expectantly. She sat on the chair on the other side of the room.

"What do you think about sitting down with Grace, and telling her together, as her parents, that I'm her daddy? And encouraging her to call me Daddy instead of Ryan?"

What did she think? What did she think? She thought it was a bombshell that she in no way was prepared for. Her mouth fell open and her eyes went wide, and her heart was racing so fast that she felt dizzy. "Are you insane? The answer is no. The answer, in fact, is no way."

He studied her, his mouth falling open, a frown putting a crease between his eyebrows. She could tell his brain was whirring, figuring out how to respond. "Too soon. Okay, I get it. You think it's too soon."

She took in a deep breath. "I don't think it's too soon. Let me make this clear. Whether it's today, or next week, or next year, it's not going to happen."

"Carly, be reasonable here ..."

"No. I'm Grace's mother and I decide what's best for her."

"It's best for Grace to have two parents, a mom who loves her and protects her, and a dad who does the same. I know I've been lacking in the dad department her whole life. I know she's had an awesome mom and you've done a great job of being mom and dad both to her for two years. But that's over now. I'm here. I'm finally here. And I want to be her dad."

As much as she wanted to be strong and ferocious, she was furious when her voice betrayed her and cracked with emotion. "I have to do what's best for Grace, and telling her that you are her father, and allowing her to get close to you and fall in love with you, is not the best thing for her."

"Why not?" In the heat of the discussion he stood and paced the room, twirling around to look at her. "That's exactly what I want her to do."

"Because. You are a flight risk, Ryan. You left us before. You'll leave us again." Unwanted tears filled her eyes and she wiped them away brusquely with the back of her hand. "I can't let her get destroyed." *Like I was destroyed.*

She didn't say it. She didn't want to say it. She didn't want him to know he'd had that much control over her to break her heart when he left.

But he knew. She could tell he got her meaning. His expression softened into a tenderness.

He came to where she sat and kneeled in front of her. "I'm sorry, Carly. If I say I'm sorry every day for the rest of my life, it won't be enough to make up for what I did to you. But I want to try. I want to be there for you now. For Grace to understand what the love of a father is, and to rest in the assurance that I will be there for her, every day for the rest of her life."

He reached out and took her hands in his, tentatively, until he discovered if she'd let him touch her. "It's not too late, Carly. You've done an excellent job with Grace for two years, but I'm back now and we can work together to be her parents. She deserves the absolute best. She already has the best mom she could have. Now I want to be the best dad."

She closed her eyes and let the emotions cascade over her like a crashing waterfall. Should she believe him? Should she let go of all the resistance and mistrust and believe that he was being honest with her? What if he thought he knew what he wanted, only to bail when the going got tough? It wouldn't make any difference to Grace. It would still mean giving her heart over to her daddy, only to have him leave, good intentions or no.

She needed to think. She needed to consider her options. And she sure as heck couldn't do it when Ryan Melrose, fresh from a shower, was less than a foot away from her, holding her hands and speaking sweet, loving words to her.

"You need to leave," she mumbled, looking up at his expression of hurt. "I'm not saying forever, but you have to give me time to think. I'm so confused." She sighed and pulled her hands out of his. "I don't know what to do."

"It's simple. Give me a chance. I swear you won't be sorry."

She stood, brushed by him to the door and opened it. "You need to leave," she said again.

She couldn't watch as he dropped his head and stumbled to the door. He stopped in front of her, like he was thinking of something else to say, some last appeal to make her change her mind. She didn't want to hear it. She shook her head, turned her body so she didn't have to look at him, and he left.

RESTORATION

THUNDER WAS A VERY good patient. Maybe the comfort of being back in the Wacccamaw Trails barn brought him calming memories. Shaw installed the sling in the stall, led Thunder into place and wrapped the intricate grouping of straps and pads around him. He could walk a step or two front and back, could reach his hay, oats and water easily. But most of all, he kept the weight off that leg, so it could heal.

Life at the ranch went on as normal, from Nora's viewpoint. She continued to operate her Dress for Success business; she took on appointments of women needing help with their career plans, their resumes, their interview skills and their wardrobe. Shaw stopped by whenever he could to check on Thunder. And whenever he did, he also stopped by the mansion and knocked on the door.

Every time he did that, it put a smile on Nora's face.

"Would you like to come in for a drink?" she asked one day when she opened the front door to him.

"Love to," he said with a smile. A smile that caused her heart to beat a little faster, and a rush of adrenaline to her belly. He always had that effect on her. Was that normal, she wondered? Not having much experience in the falling in love department, Nora had to wonder if that feeling was one of the tell-tale symptoms.

He followed her to the kitchen and watched her as she prepared two iced glasses with a combination of tea and lemonade. She handed him his. "Want to go sit on the porch?"

"Sure do. And thanks," he added, saluting her with the glass.

They walked comfortably to the porch and settled into the wooden Adirondack rocking chairs Nora had set there. Rocking like an old married couple, surveying their land, Nora mused. She tried to hide a chuckle, but he noticed.

"What?" he asked with a smile before he took a huge gulp of the drink.

She almost denied it but at the last minute she said, "I was just thinking that we're like an old married couple rocking on the front porch at the end of the day."

He gave her an odd look. "Part of that I like. I like that you're thinking of us as a couple. But let's revisit the old part."

Nora laughed.

"I don't think of myself as old, and I certainly don't think of you as old."

Nora gazed at him. No, the man was not old, not by a long shot. He was tall and strong and vibrant. Sure, in years, he was about her age, late forties, maybe fifty. But his life of working with animals had given him lean muscles and a fit physique. He'd taken good care of himself, and it showed.

"Thank you for the compliment. I certainly feel younger out here on the ranch than I did in the city working twelve hours every day. My whole life consisted of riding to work in the darkness of the early morning, working in the office all day long, riding home at night, eating a microwave meal and pulling out my email to do before bed."

"That was no way to live."

"You're absolutely right about that." She knew her affection for him was evident in her face, her eyes, her smile.

"So, here we are." His words were tentative and a little awkward. But she knew what he meant. They hadn't gotten started on their relationship do-over before Thunder's injury. Now that the horse was healing, maybe it was time to focus on themselves.

"Yes, we are." She smiled wide, giving him a message.

"I'd like to take you on a phenomenal start-over date."

She giggled, which, much to her dismay, sounded to her own ears like a love-sick teen, not a woman with her years of experience and stature. "That sounds good to me."

"Do you like music?"

"Hmmm," she considered, frowning as she thought. "Yes, I do. I like oldies from my childhood. Sometimes when I'm working I put on my headphones and listen to instrumental music with no lyrics to distract me. It helps me to relax."

"How about live music?"

"Never been to a concert, believe it or not."

"Well now, you leave it to me. I'm going to plan a musical night out that will be life-changing."

"Wow, that's a big promise there, cowboy." She reached over and put her hand in his. He squeezed and there went that adrenaline shooting through her veins again.

"Stay tuned," he said with a grin. They went on to talk about other things: Thunder's progress, his day, her day, until the sun had set over the coast and it was time for him to go.

Chapter Seven

Ryan's days were jam-packed, and yet they passed slowly. From class to lawn-mowing back to class, to the library for studying, grabbing an occasional meal and only returning home to sleep. One endless period of activity, of purpose, but there was a huge piece of his day that was missing. The whole reason he was here, in Myrtle Beach, instead of Chapel Hill. The whole reason he'd made such great changes in his life.

Grace.

She was absent and had been for almost a week. And he felt the loss. He missed that little girl. He wanted to fit in time to see her every day, or nearly every day. He wanted to continue to build their relationship. He got such a kick out of seeing her smile when she saw him and hearing her laugh when she delighted in something he'd done.

Carly had put him in isolation while she mulled over his suggestion. A part of him wished he'd never brought up the idea of telling Grace he was her father. At least then Carly would still be tolerating his visits and he'd get to see his little girl. And yet, another part of him was certain it was the right thing to do. Because he wasn't just some big male playmate for Grace, showing up once in a blue moon to play with her and make her laugh.

He was her father.

He could certainly understand why Carly was hesitant to trust him. But he had to somehow regain her trust so he could prove to her how committed he was to being the kind of father that Grace deserved.

So, he waited. And he went to school and he went to work, and he studied to keep up his grades. Waiting for the day he could see Grace again.

One morning, he was in the kitchen making himself some breakfast. His mother walked in, and when she saw him, she came to a stop. Pain and distress were etched into the lines of her face as she looked at him.

"Good morning, Mom," he said softly.

Her eyes wandered over his face. "Hello." She pushed past him to get to the cereal cabinet. She stopped and turned her head slightly, not quite enough to see him. "How's your semester going?"

"Good."

She sighed and turned the rest of the way around. She looked up at him and then pulled him into a tentative hug. Ryan put his arms around her and held her in place. "This isn't what your dad and I wanted for you. None of this is what we wanted."

Ryan nodded. "I know." The teenage pregnancy, the baby, the release of his scholarships, his enrollment into a less prestigious school. "But you can make all the plans in the world, and sometimes life doesn't go according to plan."

She sniffed, her head against his chest.

"I'm doing what I think is right, Mom. I hope you and Dad can recognize that, and maybe even support that decision. Even if you don't agree with what I'm doing, maybe you can try to understand why I need to do it."

There was so much more he wanted to say to her. He could sit down for an hour and get her caught up on his classes, his professors, the few friends he'd met at Myrtle Beach College, his job, the days he'd spent with Grace, and his argument with Carly. But the time wasn't right. Maybe someday it would be.

His mother didn't say any words, but she pulled back from him, gave him a shaky smile and placed her hand on his cheek. That was her way of saying that she loved him still, and although she didn't agree with his direction, she wasn't as angry about it. He finished his cereal in silence, placed the bowl in the sink and left with a "Have a good day, Mom."

Midway through the day he got a text from Carly, "Could you come over tonight?"

His first reaction was to smile, a whoosh of relief going through him. Then he reconsidered. Maybe his optimism was premature. After all she didn't say what her decision would be. So, he typed back, "Sure. About 5:30?"

The afternoon dragged while Ryan checked the time every fifteen minutes, but he finally finished his schedule and headed over to Carly's apartment. She answered the door to his knock, and this time, Grace stood beside her mother, and began to hop up and down in place, her excitement at seeing him erupting. His heart rushed as he leaned down and swept Grace into his arms, swinging her high, while she giggled and beamed.

"Hi sweetheart, how are you today?"

She was laughing so hard she couldn't respond, but he got the message.

He glanced at Carly. She watched the two of them, her face a blank mask of interest. He stepped into the apartment and Carly gestured to the living room. Sitting on the couch, he lowered Grace onto his lap. She bounced up and down like she was riding a pony, then her mother said, "Grace, you jump down and play in your room for just a minute. Mommy and Ryan have something to talk about."

Grace looked at her, then at Ryan. He smiled at her encouragingly. Then she did as her mom said.

"So," Carly started, "you gave me a lot to think about the last time you were here."

He nodded earnestly. She'd taken close to a week to think about it, and now evidently, she was going to deliver her decision. He just hoped it would go his way. If it didn't, he wasn't about to back off his desire to be Grace's father. However, it would be so much easier if the two of them could agree.

"I kept thinking about what you want, and how nervous I am ... scared, actually, Ryan ... that this will be a total disaster."

He started to interrupt her, but she held a hand up. "Anyway, I kept going back and forth, not knowing what to do, and then the wise words of a good friend popped into my head. If we don't have answers, go to the one who has all the answers. And that is God."

He nodded, surprised. He'd never really known Carly to have a strong faith in God. In fact, he hadn't really either. Other than taking him to church on Christmas Eve and Easter Sunday, his parents hadn't placed a high priority on faith either.

"So, I prayed. And I prayed again. Again and again until I got it all out. And I looked up verses about fatherhood and parenthood in the Bible. I wanted to make the decision that God led me to. I finally got there."

"You did?"

"Yes. God values families. God developed the idea of a family, with a mom and a dad and the kids. Although I have been raising Grace largely on my own, and could continue to, I think God's direction is to let you into Grace's life and show her a father's love."

A smile jumped onto Ryan's face. "Thank you, Carly. This is great. This is awesome."

"But."

Of course, there was a but. And there should be. Carly wouldn't be half the mother she was if there weren't guidelines and rules.

"You have to show up, Ryan. When you say something to Grace, you have to follow through. When you promise something, you have to do it. You can't decide today that you want to be her daddy and decide next month that you're tired of it. This is a life-long job."

"Yes. I know that."

"But do you?" She looked at him intensely. She wasn't trying to be insulting, he knew that. As much as he didn't like hearing her lecture, he knew he deserved it.

"Yes, I do. I promise you, Carly. This isn't a passing whim. I have made a lot of changes in my life, so I could be here close to Grace. I am ready to be her father." He leaned closer to Carly, and in his heart, he felt the urge to seal the deal with a kiss. His lips were just inches from hers. But that wouldn't help his plea. This wasn't about him and Carly. It was about them and Grace. Instead, he whispered, "Please trust me."

"I'm going to put my trust in you, for Grace's sake."

He felt like whooping for joy. Instead, he brought her hands up to his lips and kissed them. "Thank you. You won't regret this, Carly. This is definitely the right decision."

His happy gratitude made her face crack into a smile for the first time. This had been a huge weight on her, and now she could relax. "Ready to tell Grace?"

A surge of nerves went through his veins, but he was ready. He was more than ready. "Yes. Are you?"

She looked a little surprised that he asked. "We'll see, won't we?" Her laugh was tinged with tension. Then she looked at Ryan and winked. That wink meant solidarity. They were in this together. They were a team.

Carly walked down the hallway, returning with Grace holding her hand. His heart bulged with love for this little girl who was now and would continue to be the center of his life. Carly lifted Grace and sat her on the couch between the two of them.

"Grace, Ryan and I have something important to tell you. Something exciting." The little girl turned to look curiously at each of them. Carly took a deep breath and went on. "Ryan is your daddy, Grace."

She looked over at him and studied him closely. "He's my daddy?"

Ryan nodded while Carly said, "Yes." Grace's face went still while he was sure her brain was whirring, trying, in her two-year-old fashion, to process this news, to make sense of it. She turned back to her mom.

"Daddy?" she asked, uncertain.

"Yes, sweetheart. Ryan is your daddy, and he loves you very much. He wants to spend more time with you, and if you want to, you can call him Daddy."

She turned back to him. Her eyes flickered all over his face. He needed to help, not just sit here silently and let Carly do all the work. "Yes, sweetheart. Do you want to call me Daddy, or would you rather just call me Ryan?"

"You live with me?" Her big green eyes blinked at him.

"No, sweetie. You'll still live here with your mommy and I will come and visit just as often as I can."

"But you're my daddy." Her mind had been presented with a brand-new concept and she was trying to understand something that she'd never had before. How many of her friends had fathers? Had she ever seen them in a family setting? Did she even know what this meant?

"Yes, baby. I'm your daddy and I love you very much."

"I call you Daddy." Her mind made up, Grace got up and took his hand, pulling him down on the floor to play with some plastic animal toys she had in a basket in the corner. He raised his eyebrows at Carly, who shrugged.

"I guess that went well," she said.

He guessed so too. At least he hadn't done too much damage to his baby girl on his first official day on the job.

"Have you eaten? I was going to order a pizza."

"Yeah, great." He dug into his back pocket for his wallet and pulled out a twenty-dollar bill. "Here, let me get it." It was sort of nice to have spending money and be able to buy things for his family. Carly glanced at it for a minute, then took it. He was glad she hadn't argued.

AN HOUR LATER, RYAN said, "I have an idea. Let's go to the car."

Immediately, Carly frowned. She didn't want him to come up with the ideas. Because she may not approve of them. On the other hand, she'd followed Nora's example, and prayed about this. God had led her to give Ryan his full chance to be Grace's father. She couldn't get suspicious and resentful every time he suggested something. Parenthood was a dual job. So, with a quick silent prayer in her head, *Help me, Lord*, she forced a pleasant expression onto her face and said, "What's your idea?"

He laughed as he stood. "It's a surprise. You'll find out when we get there."

She sighed with comic exasperation and he laughed. "Grace, do you want to find out what Daddy's surprise is?"

Of course, she did. She jumped up, hopping excitedly. *Make me a little more like Grace*, Carly added to her prayer, and they headed out the door. Ryan led the way to his car, but Carly headed toward her car. "We need to move the car seat, Ryan."

He shook his head at her. "No. No need."

She bit her tongue. What was he doing? "She's not allowed to ride in a car without a car seat. It's state law." She rolled her eyes behind his back. If he were a real father, he would know that without her having to tell him. What had she done?

Ryan arrived at his car and opened the back-passenger door. He gestured like a host on a game show. Curious, she walked closer.

There, positioned in his back seat was a toddler's car seat. She leaned her head in. It was the latest model on the market; in fact, she'd coveted it on more than one occasion herself. She wanted this model for her own car but hadn't had the funds to buy it. "You bought this?"

"Yes. I figured we needed a car seat in both of our cars, so we can each transport her safely."

Knowing how much this model cost, she had to admit she was impressed with his willingness to invest in it. She should've just been happy about it, but she had to ask, "Did your parents buy this for you?"

He chortled. "No. My parents cut me off, remember? No funds for Ryan."

She stared at him. "What? Why?"

"Oh, I never told you about that. My parents, shall we say, are making known their displeasure with my recent life changes."

She would've asked him more, but Grace started talking and trying to climb into the car seat by herself, so Ryan lent her a helping hand. Carly stared at him. So, his parents didn't approve of his decisions, but he still was here. Their financial support was something he'd had his entire life, something she was sure he'd taken for granted like it would always be there. He's always been the pampered only son of their high-performing family. And now that was gone. How was he dealing with that?

Well, he'd gotten a job and he was paying his own way. And he was showing up for Grace.

She double-checked his installation of the seat, and buckling Grace into it, she gave him a thumbs-up and a smile. A genuine one, because he was truly starting to impress her now.

He roared his old engine to life and started driving. He turned his head slightly and said, "Grace, I want to take you somewhere that your mommy and I know very well."

"What is it?"

"It's a surprise, baby girl. You'll just have to wait and see."

Carly felt a little churn in her stomach, wondering as well, but soon Ryan pulled into the parking lot of their high school. Then he drove around to the gymnasium and parked. While Carly got Grace out of the seat, Ryan went around to his trunk, pulling out a basketball. "This is where your mommy and daddy met, Grace."

"Here?" she asked.

"Yes, right here. We went to school here. I played basketball right over here, and your mommy was a cheerleader. Did you know that?"

Grace fairly trembled with excitement, and she shook her head. "What's a cheerleader?"

"Well, come right on in, and we'll show you." Ryan tucked the basketball under one arm and reached for Grace's hand with the other. Carly grabbed Grace's other hand and they walked to the gym, swinging her between them.

"It's probably not open," she said.

Ryan smiled. "I made a call. It's open."

Sure enough, he reached the door and the handle turned and let them in. He looked over at her, "I still have contacts." He laughed.

They walked into the big open gym, crossing the wooden floor carefully. Ryan disconnected and went into the corner and suddenly, the entire gym was bathed in brilliant light. Grace clapped her hands and giggled.

"Do you know what this is, Grace? This is a gym where we play basketball. Imagine a team of five basketball players in uniform on the floor, running around, throwing the ball, another team wearing a different uniform color trying to stop them from making baskets. Over here," he gestured with his arm, "your mommy and a bunch of other pretty ladies are shaking pompoms and yelling for us, trying to get us to play harder. And here," he waved his arms to encompass all the seats in the arena, "people are sitting and watching, and yelling and cheering and booing, depending on the play." He kneeled in front of her and took her head in his hands. "Can you see it, Grace? Can you hear it? Can you feel the excitement?"

Grace closed her eyes and Carly could see her trying desperately to absorb all that Ryan was telling her. A smile filled her daughter's face as she imagined this magical game that brought together all the people Ryan had described. "Yes."

Ryan rose to his feet. "Yes! I knew it! You're going to be a part of it someday, Grace. You're either going to play basketball, or be a cheerleader, or watch from the stands, but you are going to come to this very gym and be a part of it." He bounced the basketball, its sound echoing throughout the empty gym. "You hear that, Grace? That is the absolute best sound in the world. That's the sound of fun, competition, winning. I used to practice bouncing this ball for hours and hours every day. Shooting it, dribbling it, running, passing. It was a big part of my life."

Grace opened her eyes. "Let's see!"

Ryan was more than happy to show her his basketball skills and he demonstrated his shots, his dribbling, through the legs and twirling around, running while bouncing. Grace enjoyed every second of it. She was truly enchanted.

Ryan came over, panting slightly, rubbing the ball with his fingers as if getting to know an old friend again. "Do you want to see what a cheerleader does? Do you want to see your mommy cheer?"

"Yes!"

Carly rolled her eyes good-naturedly. She was out of practice and hadn't even thought of cheering in well over three years. That was a part of her past that had been buried ever since Grace, or the pending arrival of Grace, had entered her life. Leave it to Ryan to bring it back in such epic fashion. She'd loved this stage of her life. She'd loved being a cheerleader, going to all the games, helping her school's teams and leading the fans in cheers. And watching Ryan play. That was the best part.

Well, her life had changed now, but she could thank Ryan for bringing back this tiny little reminder of their past together. And introducing to the daughter they'd created, how and where they'd started. It was ingenious, really, when she thought about it. She'd told Grace that Ryan was her daddy, but the poor little thing had no frame of reference for that term in her two years of life. What did a daddy do? Where did a daddy come from? She'd told Grace – Ryan was showing her.

Carly walked to the middle of the gym floor, facing Ryan and Grace. She cleared her throat and put her head down, thinking for a moment. Maybe it was like riding a bike, and it would just come back to her.

"Raiders, let's go. Be aggressive! B-E aggressive. B-E A-G-G-R-E-S-S-I-V-E!" Somehow, the hand motions and the kicks came back to her, right when she needed them, and she managed to execute a pretty basic cheer. Feeling empowered, she went ahead and did a cartwheel before she talked herself out of it, and waved her fists up in the air, pretending she was holding pompoms. Grace went crazy, running over to her, laughing and clapping. Sure, the kid had no idea what the cheer said, since she couldn't spell, but she had gotten in the spirit that Ryan had initiated. Grace threw her arms around Carly's legs, hugging where she could, and Ryan finished the family hug, pulling Grace and Carly both into an embrace.

"Great job, Mommy. Great job, right, Grace?"

Grace nodded and yelled, "Yes! Great job."

When they pulled apart, Ryan handed the ball to Grace and spent about twenty minutes chasing the big ball that Grace attempted to throw but actually rolled. But they were playing together, and they were building memories and Carly couldn't remember a time when either of them was that happy.

Let him stay. Dear Lord, please make him stay. The words made a continual loop in her brain. This decision seemed so right. So right

RESTORATION

for Grace. But she didn't even want to think about the total disas
it would be if he left again.

Chapter Eight

"You don't have to knock each time, you know. If it's unlocked, just come on in." Nora stood in the open doorway, taking in the sight of Shaw in the early evening, the autumn sunset showcased behind him, his cowboy hat on and his face fatigued from a long day.

He shrugged. "Not sure about that."

"Why not?"

"Doesn't seem right, somehow. This is your place, not mine."

She grabbed his hand and pulled him inside, standing on tiptoe to plant a friendly kiss on his cheek. His face flushed a little, then he recovered enough to pull her closer and return the kiss ... on the lips this time. They stayed that way for a few long seconds and then he pulled back. Nora's heart raced. She loved the way his kisses made her feel. And truth be told, she was glad he wasn't rushing her for more intimacy than she was ready to offer him at the moment. There was something about making a new start that caused them both want to do everything right this time. Premature intimacy would definitely not fall on the "right" list.

"Okay. Then you can still knock, and I'll answer, and some day maybe you'll feel comfortable walking right in."

They walked into the sitting room and only then did Nora realize he held a big brown bag with corded handles. "What's that?" she asked.

"It's a gift. Something for our concert date."

A rush of emotion went through her. The fact that he was planning a fun, exciting night for the two of them. The fact that he'd brought her a gift. There was something very appealing, dare she say, sexy about both those facts. "My curiosity is piqued."

He grinned and moved the bag to the coffee table in front of her. "Open it."

She pulled a shoebox out of the bag, bigger than average. Square. Inside was a pair of beautifully crafted leather cowboy boots. A medium brown color, embroidered lines tracking through the leather, a slight heel. "Oh my gosh."

"Do you like them?"

She opened her mouth to answer, but the words that immediately popped to her mind were not ones she wanted to speak. She didn't want to taint the pleasant evening. She couldn't put her finger on it, but the gift made her feel odd. "Um, they are beautifully crafted," she said tentatively, tracing an index finger over the stitching.

"When you get to the concert you'll see that a lot of the women wear western clothing."

She stared back at the boots. "Shaw, I've never worn a pair of cowboy boots in my life." She looked up at him, and sensed an attack of tears forming. "Do I need a hat too?"

He chuckled. "Cowboy hats are not mandatory, but I'd say the boots are. They'll help put you in the country mindset." His light hearted mood came to an end when he noticed her emotion. He placed a calming hand on her shoulder. "Nora. What's this? Are you okay?"

Nora shook her head. "I'm feeling a little weird about this gift."

"Why?"

"Because. How do I say this? It comes across as a little ... pushy. Like you're trying to dress me up to be more like you." She looked up at him, her heart rate racing. If she couldn't be honest with him about her true feelings, then they had no chance in the world of making this work. And she wasn't about to accept the gift without telling him how she was internally freaking out over it.

"Wait." He pushed the boots away and concentrated on her. "You think I got you these boots so I could transform you into a country girl?"

"Well, yeah. That's not who I am, Shaw. My background is very different than anyone who grew up here in the Low Country. No matter how you dress me up, you're not going to change that." She sniffed. "Can't you accept me for who I am?"

He ran his fingers through his hair, leaving it looking distressed. Leaning close, he said, "Of course I can. I love who you are. I love being with you, not because you're the same as the others, but because you *are* different. I just enjoy being with you." He rubbed hands over weary eyes. "Nora, I'm out of my element here. I truly want to start over with you and do it right this time. I messed up big, the first time. I know that. I don't want to mess up again."

Her heart began to melt. "Shaw, just ... don't try so hard. I want us to be together, too. To be easy and comfortable and get to know each other better."

He studied her and she could tell his mind was whirring. "How about this? Let's take everything at face value for now. I invited you to a concert of my favorite country artist because I wanted to share that experience with you. Not because I won't like you if you aren't a fan of his too. Not because you're a city girl and I'm trying to push you into being a country girl. But because it's something I wanted us to do together." He gave a sad chuckle. "I'm really a simple guy, Nora, and I very rarely do anything with an ulterior motive. But then again, you don't really know that about me, do you?"

Had she been suspicious of his intention because of his past mistakes? Were the lies that she was determined to forgive him for inching their way back into their new start? Was her city background causing her to mistrust him, when his intentions were clean?

"Let me see those boots."

He gave her an eyebrows-up expression.

"I want to see them." He picked up the box and placed it on the seat beside her. She slipped her foot into one and it slid right in, a perfect fit. "How'd you know what size I wore?"

He stared at her for a moment, then fessed up. "I checked the size of your shoes that were sitting around."

She slid the other boot on, got up and walked around. "They're amazingly comfortable."

"I'm glad." He watched her appreciatively. "I'm almost afraid to mention this now, but here goes nothing. If you want any wardrobe advice, Sadie has offered her services."

She glanced over at him. "She did?"

"Yep. Only if you want it. Not pushing. Really, anything you wear, you'll look amazing." He brushed her cheek with his finger. "You always look amazing."

A warmth spread in her chest, brought on by his compliment. "So what do women wear to country concerts?"

"Anything. It really runs the gambit. Whatever you wear, make sure you're comfortable."

She nodded, the concern in her chest easing. "I think I will talk to Sadie. Thank you. Very thoughtful."

"Great. I'll have her call you. Meanwhile, I've gotten tickets so put that date on your calendar."

"Who is it again?"

"It's Radley Ray. He's my favorite country artist and I've seen him at least three other times. He's coming to Charleston."

His enthusiasm was contagious, and she listened while he explained that Radley Ray was not only a talented singer, performer and songwriter, but he was also one of the most accomplished guitar players in country music. Not to mention, he had a sense of humor, which he showcased in his lyrics, as well as while talking to the audience between songs. After a few minutes, Nora was excited to be going.

Later in the evening, when Shaw was on his way out, he held up a finger and said, "Wait just a minute." He ran out to his truck, rummaged around before closing the door and jogging back to her door. He handed her a CD. "This is Radley's Greatest Hits album. If you have some time, listen to it before the concert so you're familiar with his music. It'll make the concert more fun for you."

She gave him a grateful, close-mouthed grin. She was glad she'd brought up her concerns, and he'd addressed them. "Thanks, Shaw."

"Thank you for being open with me. I just need you to be patient. I'm doing the best I can." He gave her a long, tender kiss, and with a wave, he departed.

SEVERAL WEEKS LATER, Carly was at work, head down, plowing through her extra-long To Do list when her desk phone rang. She ignored it for a second, long enough to finish a student's schedule on her computer and press Enter, then she picked it up with a flourish. "Admissions Department, this is Carly, may I help you?"

"No, but there's someone here who wants to help you." She recognized Haley's voice, hushed but tinged with laughter. She instantly stood and looked across the big room in her friend's direction. Not only did she see Haley on her feet, phone to her ear, facing in her direction, but standing on the other side of Haley's receptionist desk was Ryan. Her heart melted when she saw him. He was dressed for work in his khaki shorts and worn t-shirt, but he appeared clean, like he hadn't started mowing yet. He'd spotted her. A beautiful smile graced his face and he raised a bag at her with eyebrows up.

"He says he won't stay long." Then she put her hand over the receiver and whispered, "Although I'm sure you could think of some reason for him to stay longer." And she made a hilarious sound like a cat meowing.

Carly chuckled. "I'll be right up." She waved at Ryan as she hung up the phone.

"Hi," he said, moving his mouth close to her ear and brushing his lips there, causing a shiver to run down her spine.

"Hi. What are you doing here?"

"You told me you'd be too busy to eat lunch today. So, when I was buying mine, I went ahead and got two. Hope you don't mind."

God help her, no, she didn't mind at all. In fact, she was happy to see him. He put a spot of handsomeness in her day. "When did I tell you that?" she asked, trying to remember.

"Last night."

She shrugged. She didn't even remember telling him, but he sure remembered hearing it. And acting on it. "This is so sweet of you." Not just sweet. Downright thoughtful. Sure, the guy was turning out to be a rock star father to Grace. He came over regularly, sometimes just to hang out with Grace while Carly studied in the evening. Sometimes they all three went out together for outings that built memories, and once or twice, Carly trusted him to take Grace out all by himself.

But this. This nice gesture had nothing to do with Grace. This could be a sign that he cared for *her* as a person.

"It's no big deal, Carly. It's just a hamburger and fries."

She grinned. "Well, it's the thought that counts." Maybe to him it was no big deal. But other than her parents, she hadn't had anyone in a good long time who was watching out for her. Thinking of her needs. She'd been alone and responsible for herself for a long time.

She was just about to ask him to sit down and chat with her while she ate when he said, "Well, I better run. My work shift starts at 12:30. See you tonight."

She waved and was about to respond when he held a hand out to Haley, who was watching their exchange unabashedly. "I'm Ryan, by the way. Nice to actually meet you." He grinned at Haley, then at Carly, then he was gone.

Haley waved a hand in front of her face. "Oh. My. Gosh. He's so cute. He's a hunk, lady. You realize that, don't you?"

"I ..."

"And how sweet was that, bringing you lunch as a total surprise out of the blue?"

"Yeah, I wasn't expecting that."

"I know you've had your doubts about him in the past, but yowza. That boy's turned over a new leaf."

Carly grinned a closed mouth smile. "I have to admit you're right. He convinced me that he's committed to Grace. We went ahead and told her Ryan was her daddy. She calls him Daddy now. That was a big step for me."

Haley came out from around her desk and pulled Carly into her arms. "I'm so happy for you, girlfriend. Life is working out just right, now, isn't it?"

Carly giggled, then quieted. "It's absolutely fantastic that he is building a relationship with Grace. But I ... I have no idea how he feels about me."

"What do you mean?"

Carly sniffed. "I mean, he thinks I'm a good mother, I know that. But whether or not he wants us to get back together as a couple, and raise Grace together ... I have no idea."

"Are you serious?"

"Totally serious. Between us, there seems to be a chemistry, but maybe it's just me. He is a perfect gentleman around me, which is great, don't get me wrong. But maybe he just has platonic feelings towards me. I don't know."

"Well, I know how to get him to show his feelings. Put a big fat smacker right on his lips and see what he does. You'll know one way or another, now, won't you?"

Carly shook her head. "I can't do that. We have to be on good terms for Grace's sake. What if I told him how I felt about him, and he doesn't reciprocate my feelings? I'd feel so awkward around him. Like such a loser. And I'd still have to see him every day because of Grace. No. I want him to make the first move. If he doesn't, I guess we just stay friends."

Haley was studying her, a thoughtful expression on her face. "You realize the flaw in your logic, don't you? If Ryan is thinking the same thing you are, you two are at a stalemate. Neither one of you wants to make the first move because of the chance of rejection."

Carly shook her head. She doubted Ryan was thinking anywhere near the same thing. Ryan Melrose? Afraid of rejection? The man had never faced rejection in his life. Everything always went his way. She doubted he even knew what the sting of rejection was.

Maybe being platonic friends and effective parents to Grace was enough. Maybe the whole 'fall back in love, get married and raise Grace together' fantasy was way out of reach. She'd better be happy with what she had ... like a greasy bag containing a cold hamburger ... and keep moving forward.

"WHAT ARE YOU DOING on the 20th?"

Carly was talking to Ryan on the phone, trying not to notice the effect the deep timbre of his voice in her ear was having on the rest of her body. Like her heart, pumping noticeably faster, and her hands, tingling from the increased pulse rate.

Why did his voice do this to her? What was wrong with her lately?

She found him constantly on her mind. The more she saw him, the more she wanted to see him. Ridiculous. She needed to put a clamp on her emotions and accept things for the way they were. Ryan making a concerted effort to be a father for Grace. This had nothing to do with his feelings for her.

"The 20th?" she repeated absentmindedly.

"Yeah, my cousin is getting married. My parents and I are invited to the wedding and I wondered if I could bring you and Grace as my guests."

"What?" Her focus was laser sharp now. He wanted the three of them to go to his cousin's wedding? As a family? "Why?" she managed.

"Why?" he said and laughed. "I don't know. It's a family event, and you guys are my family. I just thought it would be nice to go together."

Nice for who? she wondered but didn't ask.

"Grace could meet more of her extended family and see the Melroses in action."

Carly brought in a slow, cleansing breath, trying to slow her heartrate. "Would you just like to take Grace?" Why would he want the three of them to go, when he could take their daughter and let her be the center of adoration for the evening, introducing her to the relatives who probably didn't realize he was back in his daughter's life?

"Well," he started, and she recognized that he was measuring his response carefully, "I mean, I would take Grace with me if you wanted me to. But I really pictured the three of us going together. My relatives haven't seen you for ages. In fact, some of them have never met you at all."

Carly's heart stopped for a moment. Sure, some of his aunts, uncles and cousins never met her because she was the teenaged mother of Ryan's unplanned, unexpected child who came way too early in his life to be welcomed and celebrated. She was the girl who Ryan got pregnant, the one who could've potentially ruined the future of their golden boy.

Talk about awkward introductions.

She exhaled a frustrated breath. "Ryan, spill. Why is it important for me to go to your cousin's wedding?"

She was putting him on the spot, and she knew it. But she wanted to hear his answer, what was truly on his mind. A moment's pause and then, "I want to introduce you and Grace to my family and I want them to know how important you are to me." He cleared his throat and Carly thought she could hear him rubbing a hand over the stubble of whiskers on his chin. "Will you please go with me? It would make me very happy."

Even if his tone hadn't been sincere and humble, even if he didn't sound like taking her and Grace to the wedding was the very most important thing in his life, she probably would've said yes anyway. Just because he'd asked her so nicely. When she did finally say, "Okay, Ryan, we'll go to the wedding with you," his happiness surged over the phone line and put a catch in her throat and a beat in her heart.

"Oh Carly, that's fantastic. Thank you. This'll be great. I'll tell you all the details when I see you tonight."

"Is it a dressy wedding?" she asked, wondering if she could find something in her closet that would be appropriate attire.

"Yeah, you know, dresses, suits."

They ended the call and Carly was happy to have made his day. He was so transparent in his emotions, especially his happiness. It didn't take much to make Ryan happy, but his delight over this was unmistakable.

She'd been cleaning the apartment when he'd called and she went back to it, trying to avoid the inevitable line of thought: *why* was he so happy that she'd agreed to go with him? Why did he want to introduce her to his family so badly? Did he see a future with her? And if he did, why had he never talked to her about it?

She had no idea. And she wasn't about to ask him. She needed to protect her heart as much as possible.

Instead, she pulled out the Comet and a sponge and headed for the bathroom, ready to scrub her aggressions out.

AFTER THREE WEEKS OF rehab, Shaw took Thunder out of the sling apparatus. Free in his stall for the first time, he stood completely still, gazing at Shaw and Nora, as if asking for direction.

"Come on, Thunder, come over here, boy," coaxed Nora. The horse stood with his injured leg slightly bent, avoiding putting any weight on it.

Shaw went to him and placed a gentle hand on his halter. Applying subtle pressure, he pulled Thunder's head while murmuring soft words in his ear. But instead of taking a few steps, Thunder simply extended his neck as far as he could without moving his legs.

"I want to see him try to put weight on that leg. I'd rather be here so I can make adjustments if he's still in pain."

Nora nodded. She wondered if the healing was complete. "So, you think he's ready to walk without the sling?"

"It's a trial and error approach. If he still favors the leg and I think it's because he's in pain, I'll take him back to the clinic for a follow up x-ray. If I think it's because he knows in his head that it used to hurt, and he's still favoring it to avoid more pain, then I can use some techniques on him to make him forget about that for a while and see if he can actually walk."

Shaw slid open the stall door. "Come on buddy, want to go outside? You haven't been out for a long time."

Thunder perked his ears and lifted his nose, sniffing the incoming breeze. Although he looked interested and tempted, he stayed still. Shaw watched him for a moment, then went over to Thunder's feed bin and grabbed a handful of oats. Walking back to the open stall door, he held his hand out. "Here you go, buddy. Want some oats? Come over here to get them."

Poor Thunder. He looked tempted, and he seemed to know exactly what Shaw was trying to get him to do. But he stubbornly stayed still in his spot.

"How about a carrot? Or an apple? He loves those treats," Nora suggested.

Shaw shrugged. "I'm willing to give it a try."

"I'll be right back." Nora jogged out of the barn, and into the mansion, coming back with the treats. Unfortunately, they didn't work either.

Shaw went back to the horse, running his hands down the leg, pressing to catch a reaction, searching for swelling or problems. He straightened. "The leg feels good, and Thunder didn't show any pain. I think his head's getting in the way. Not unusual for animals. As long as they remember something painful, they're not going to put themselves in that position again." He patted Thunder's shoulder and left the stall. "I think he'll be fine in here, even if he does put weight on it. But if you notice him in trouble, just call me. I'll drop everything to come over."

Nora nodded. "I'll check him whenever I have a break in my day."

A FEW DAYS LATER, CARLY stopped by Haley's desk. She seemed like the kind of girl who owned some dressy dresses. Maybe Carly could get some advice. "I need some help. Some wardrobe advice."

Haley looked up with a smile. "You sell yourself short! You look nice. I like the dark pants and white button-up blouse. Only thing you might want to add is a clunky necklace and earrings for a splash of color."

Carly chuckled as she looked down at her plain outfit. "No, actually, I wasn't talking about this outfit. But thanks for your expert critique." She reached out and patted Haley's hand when she blushed at her faux pas. "I need something to wear to a wedding."

Haley recovered, looking interested. "Whose wedding is it?"

Carly shrugged. "A cousin of Ryan's."

Haley's eyes went wide, and her jaw dropped. "He invited you to a family wedding?"

"Yes. Well, me and Grace."

"Oh. My. Gosh."

Carly really didn't want to get excited. She gave a restrained grin. "Now, don't get crazy."

"Why not? He wouldn't invite you if he didn't have feelings for you. Told ya! Told ya!"

"Haley, I don't ....," her voice trailed off.

"Okay, follow me home after work and you can look in my closet. I'd recommend a cute cocktail dress. Something with lace and a little bling, shows a little skin, but not too much."

"You have something like that?"

"Of course!"

"You really are a life saver."

At the end of the work day, Carly followed Haley home. She couldn't help but notice what an upscale complex Haley lived in. Covered parking stalls to protect from the elements, beautiful palm trees and tropical floral landscaping, unobscured ocean view. They both parked, and Carly caught up with her. "Beautiful place, Haley!"

"Oh thanks," she said dismissively.

They walked up a flight of stairs to a second-floor apartment. Haley unlocked the door and led Carly into an impressive open floor plan apartment about four times the size of her own. She couldn't help a gasp of admiration. "Haley," she breathed. "This is gorgeous. Absolutely gorgeous."

Carly took some mesmerized steps over the light-toned hardwood floors straight through the living room to the sliding glass doors. A balcony overlooked a swimming pool with a swim-up bar, and farther on, the ocean. "It's like living constantly in a vacation resort!"

Haley nodded. "Yep. It's my parents' rental unit. But when I started working, I convinced them that it was stupid for me to find a cheap, scruffy little apartment that fit my budget, when they were continuing to rent this place out to vacationers. So, I pay them rent, probably much lower than it's worth, and I get to live here."

"Oh, how wonderful." Carly tore herself away from the view. She'd love to live in a place like this, but she'd never get anything done. The sound of the waves, the gulls flying overhead, and the kids and adults vacationing on the sand below would be way too distracting for normal life.

"Want to see my closet?" Haley asked, and they went to her bedroom.

Forty-five minutes later, Carly made her selection. That is, after trying on half a dozen dresses of varying colors and styles, all of them perfectly suitable for a dressy wedding. A tinge of envy hit Carly's heart as she perused the selections in Haley's chock full walk-in closet, almost as if she were at Nora's Dress for Success showroom.

But she finally selected a peach-colored pastel with cap sleeves, a lacy V-neck bodice, and an embroidered skirt that fell to about an inch above her knee. It was beautiful: simple but classic. Better than anything, it was comfortable and flattering.

"Thank you so much, Haley. I can't tell you how much you've saved me here."

Haley smiled. "No problem. Although we're not exactly the same size," she tapped her bodice with an index finger, indicating that hers was much fuller than Carly's, "we're about the same height and for the majority of dress styles, we can share pretty easily."

Carly pulled her friend into a one-armed hug while clutching the dress covered in plastic. "You are so nice and so generous. I can't thank you enough. Thanks for being my friend."

Haley smiled happily. "My pleasure. I'm a sucker for happy endings, and I'm determined to make sure you get yours."

Emotion rose in her throat and she blinked away a tear. Not quite trusting her voice, she waved, gestured to the dress, and left.

Chapter Nine

Thunder didn't move from his spot on Day Two. On Day Three, Nora visited him three times, and by the third, he had moved to the far corner of the stall. He must've decided to give walking a try. She slipped into the stall and approached him quietly, her hand out for him to smell. He was comfortable with her, so she went to his leg, running her fingers down it as Shaw had. However, her fingers didn't have the magic touch his did, so she had no idea what she was looking for. She was happy that Thunder didn't flinch at her touch.

Shaw came over later in the day and Thunder had moved yet again. They held a private celebration in the stall, rewarding the gelding with a carrot and an apple and lots of pats all over. Shaw clicked the lead rope onto his halter and led him out of the stall into the barn aisle. Although he needed to be encouraged to leave the stall, he eventually complied and took a short walk up and down the aisle before Shaw let him back in the stall.

"He's looking good. He's favoring it slightly but no limp. I'm happy with what I see."

As they were leaving the barn and closing up for the night, Shaw said, "Tomorrow morning I'll be over to take him out to the pasture, see how he does there." He grinned and pulled Nora into an embrace, her body pressed against his. "We got lucky. Thunder's a very special horse."

"Yes, he is," she said. She tilted her head back, and they touched lips for a kiss.

NORA'S CELL PHONE RANG while she was wrapped up in paperwork for her not-for-profit. Glancing at the screen, she saw it was an unknown contact. "Nora Ramsey, may I help you?"

"Hi Nora, it's Sadie Flynn."

Nora looked up, leaving the paperwork behind. Shaw's daughter. "Hi Sadie."

The girl's voice filled the line. "Dad tells me he's introducing you to his favorite country artist, Radley Ray."

"Yes, that's right."

"Are you a fan too?"

"No. In fact, I know nothing about country music. I'm sadly behind the times."

Sadie laughed, a happy explosion of sound. "That's okay. He mentioned he gave you a CD to listen to. That'll help you get familiar with his music."

"Yes, and I have been listening. I've found his songs very easy to listen to. Very sing-alongable."

"Great! You'll be able to sing at the concert too."

Nora didn't know about that. Singing in public was definitely not in her comfort zone. Sadie continued, "If you're going to be around, I have some things to drop off. Dad said you might need a few wardrobe choices to go with your new cowgirl boots."

They discussed sizes and found that Sadie had a few things to share. "That's very nice of you, but let's just say our age difference could keep me from looking good or feeling good in your clothes. Can't I just wear my blue jeans?"

"Of course! But maybe just a few tops and skirts to give you some options."

They agreed on a time and hung up.

A few hours later, Sadie arrived, right on time, with a short stack of clothes on hangers draped over her arm. Nora let her in and chuckled. "Not very often that someone gives me clothes to wear. Usually it's the other way around."

Sadie smiled and gazed over at the Dress for Success showroom. "Yeah. I'd love to browse over there sometime." She turned back. "But first things first. Dressing for a country concert is across the board. You can wear usual clothes – jeans, t-shirt, shorts, whatever. But you can also wear stuff that you'd never wear anywhere else. Like a costume." She pulled out a few plaid cotton tops in various colors. "Plaid is always a nice option to wear with denim. I brought a couple to choose from to see what you like the best. And I will say that although you can certainly wear jeans, a short skirt or shorts would really showcase the boots."

Nora sighed. She was nervous but decided to try everything on. Who knows? It was all about keeping an open mind, like she promised Shaw. Maybe there was a hidden gem in this stack. She swiped them all up and headed for the dressing room in the showroom. "Keep your fingers crossed."

Inside, alone behind the closed door, she was relieved to find that Sadie was right; these were flexible styles that could be appropriate for a woman her age. She tried on all of them and finally settled on a denim skirt that wasn't too mini – it fell almost to her knee. She paired it with a red and blue plaid shirt that she could tuck in. She could even put a tank top on underneath it and leave the top few buttons open. If she thought of it as a costume, she didn't feel so ridiculous. Gathering her courage, she wore it out to where Sadie sat waiting. Her response was immediate, and positive.

"You think?" Nora said, her forehead scrunching with doubt while Sadie raved about her appearance.

"I know! You look fantastic. Perfect for a Radley Ray concert."

Nora looked down at herself and brushed her hands over the skirt. "If you say so."

"Better yet, I know my dad will think you look fantastic." Sadie beamed her approval.

Nora supposed that was the important thing. She was leaving her old Philadelphia lawyer life farther and farther behind. Now she was wearing cowgirl boots, a denim skirt and a plaid top to a country concert and her date was a cowboy veterinarian. Not to mention, her cowboy's daughter cared enough to loan her concert-worthy clothes.

Who would've ever thought?

Nora changed back out of the clothes. "Thanks so much for bringing these over. It's really sweet of you, Sadie."

The girl shrugged. "Just want to make sure you two have a good time."

The affection Nora felt made her pull Sadie into a hug. Patting her back, Nora whispered, "I think we will."

THE REST OF THE WEEK passed by quickly and soon, it was Wedding Day. Carly provided sufficient pampering to her two-year-old in her preparations: curled her hair, painted her nails and slipped a beautiful red dress on her. "Oh baby, you look beautiful," she exclaimed with a smile.

"Mommy wear?"

Carly whipped the plastic off the peach dress with a flourish and slipped the dress on.

"Oh!" Grace gasped.

"Do I look pretty?"

"Very pretty. Like a princess."

Carly chuckled as she finished her preparations, her hair, makeup and jewelry. One final look in the mirror and she declared herself done. She hadn't spent this much time on herself since before Grace was born.

Funny how priorities like that changed once a little one was around.

Just on time, a knock sounded at the door. Grace giggled excitedly and ran to open it. "Daddy!"

Carly's heart twisted just a little. Her daughter was so excited to call Ryan her daddy, and the fortifying wall Carly had built to protect her heart let loose one more brick. Poof, gone.

Ryan knelt in the doorway to be face-to-face with Grace. "Well, darlin', don't you look pretty?"

Grace smiled and blushed and twirled in a circle, giving him a chance to see her beauty from all angles. "Hi Daddy," she said softly, with a tinge of shyness. She plunged herself into his open arms for a hug and he chuckled. Gripping her tight, he came to his feet and took her along for the ride, bringing on an excited squeal.

"Oh, but wait. Wait just a minute, Princess. You have competition. Who's the most beautiful girl in this room?"

"Me!" Grace said through a smile.

"But look at your mama. She looks beautiful too, now doesn't she?"

Grace tore her eyes away from Ryan so she could look at her mother and generously nodded her head: wild, energetic nodding in agreement. "Mama beautiful, too."

"Oh my, well, there's no way I could choose between the two of you, so I guess I'll just thank my stars that I'm the luckiest guy at the wedding with two beautiful girls."

A giddy happiness filled Carly's heart. It was so silly, this exchange, and she knew he was doing it for Grace's entertainment, but Ryan looked so handsome in a dark suit with white shirt and tie. And he'd cut his hair back to his high school short look; he was clean-shaven and there was not one inch of him that didn't look delicious. His mood was light and carefree, and she let herself soak in the sentiment. They were a young, happy family, off for a day together without a care in the world.

At least, that's the way it would look to the wedding goers. She'd worry about the underlying motivations and assumptions later and just let herself have a good time.

"You look very handsome yourself, doesn't he, Grace?"

Their daughter smiled and planted a kiss on his cheek. "Yeah!"

Ryan looked pleased at her compliment. He came close, and while still holding Grace in one arm, he put his other around Carly's waist, pulled her in and kissed her. He placed his soft lips on hers and let them linger there. She was so taken by surprise that she didn't quite know what to do. But if truth be told, she didn't want to pull away.

A few short beats later, he ended the kiss and Carly turned, unwilling to meet her daughter's curious gaze, and hoping to God that Grace didn't start asking questions. It was the first time they'd kissed in front of her, or displayed any type of affection whatsoever, for that matter. Later. Tonight, at bedtime, she would answer any questions Grace had about the kiss, or their relationship or their potential future. But for now, they'd have fun.

They piled into Ryan's car and he drove the short distance to the church. Carly had given her daughter a brief rundown of who the players were, since she had no experience in the concept of weddings. The bride, the groom, the minister. Fancy dresses and suits. Vows taken and the love the married couple shared. So, in the car, Grace was full of questions.

"Who is the bride?" she asked.

"The bride's name is Jessica," Ryan explained.

"Who is the groom?"

"The groom is my cousin Charlie."

"Why are they getting married?"

"Because they love each other, and they want to spend the rest of their lives together." Ryan winked at Carly and she knew he was pleased with his answer to Grace's interrogation. Until the next question came.

"Why?"

Ryan's brow wrinkled. Carly snorted. He probably didn't realize yet, but "why" was Grace's go-to question in any conversation. When she couldn't think of what else to say, she'd fill the empty space with "why?" It took Carly herself a few months to realize that Grace wasn't necessarily expecting a coherent answer to this question. But Ryan hadn't figured that out yet. So, she smiled sweetly at him, raised her eyebrows as if she, too, were waiting for an answer and let him fluster.

"They want to be man and wife," he attempted, probably praying to himself that it would be sufficient.

And it was. For now. Grace nodded her head hard enough to flip her carefully created curls around her shoulders and looked out the window.

Ryan looked at Carly and gave her an exaggerated expression of relief. Carly chuckled. "Life with a two-year-old."

Ryan nodded, then smiled. "A two-year-old with a birthday coming up."

"Yeah." Grace's birthday was several months away.

"Let's throw a party." He said it with such enthusiasm that Carly wanted to simultaneously thrill in his excitement and shush him, so he wouldn't get Grace's hopes up for a party that might never take place.

He'd always been like that. His upbringing allowed him to follow his interests, whatever they might be. His parents had encouraged him to try new things. But in the case of fatherhood, he not only tried new things – college – but he'd abandoned his "old thing."

"Awww, what's going on?" His concerned words cut through her unhappy thoughts and she turned her head to look at him.

"What do you mean?"

He shifted his eyes from her to the road, a worried look on his face. "We were having such a good time, and you looked so sad just now. What were you thinking about?"

Her first impulse was to brush it off. "Nothing, no. I'm fine." She managed a fake smile.

"Aww now. You can tell me."

His sweet smile made her heart rush with sentimental feelings she knew weren't healthy for her. She sighed and decided to be at least part-way honest with him. As much as she could without opening herself up to total heartbreak. "I'm just getting used to our new reality, Ryan. You and me and Grace. Doing stuff together. Her knowing exactly who you are. It's just new to me. It was me and Grace for so long."

His face turned sad, a crease between his eyebrows, a look of shame taking over. "And you don't know if you can trust me, right? Because I did such a bad thing when Grace was first born. I left you on your own with her and went off to live my own life as if I wasn't leaving you guys behind."

She stared at him. "Yes," she said, surprised at his depth of exposure.

He nodded and then, looking in the rearview mirror, found a spot to pull over. He stopped the car and turned in his seat to look at her. He sat still for a long moment, then pulled her hands into his and said, "I did a terrible thing. I made a huge mistake. But I am sorry, and I'm doing everything I can to prove to you, Carly, that I'm back. I want to earn your forgiveness and your trust. I want you to believe in me. I want to make things right."

A whirring filled her ears and the car's silence morphed into a dizzying windstorm. She shook her head to clear the sound and looked straight at him. The watering of her eyes could've been caused by the sunlight pouring into the window behind him, or who knows, it could've been his words. Words she'd wanted to hear for years. Words she wanted to believe, but her heart couldn't quite let go of her resistance.

"And listen, don't you let me off too easy, now." He smiled that beautiful smile that had first made her lose her heart to him when she was a young teenaged girl. That same happy smile that radiated a light all around him and made him special. "You make me earn it, you hear?" He laughed as if everything in his life was going great, going fine, according to plan. There was nothing that could destroy this guy's optimism. "Because when you fall back in love with me, I want to know that I did my darnedest to win you back, and it's going to be forever this time."

Her eyes popped open wide. "Wha...?"

"I still love you, Carly. I always have. I just lost my way for a bit. But I'm back."

Carly frowned and shook her head. "For Grace."

He let his eyes wander into the back seat to their daughter, then back to her. "Yes, absolutely, for Grace. But not *just* for Grace. For you, too. I want us to be a family."

She stammered, because regardless of how empty-minded it made her sound, she had to know the truth of his intentions. "You want us to be a family because it's best for Grace?"

His eyes rested on hers. "I want us to be a family because it's best for all of us. I want us to start now and do this thing right this time. I want you to love me as much as I love you."

"You love me," she whispered. She hadn't known. Had she missed it? Had he told her, and her heart was so clamped shut against him that she wouldn't listen? Or was this a new revelation? "You love me?" she said out loud.

"Yes, darlin', I love you."

Well. Now she knew. He wasn't back just to be Grace's father. He was back to be with her too. At least that's what he was saying. Now the question was ... what did she want?

BEING AT A MELROSE family event on the arm of the crowned Prince Ryan was an experience Carly had never had. He had jokingly called Grace a princess this morning, but sure enough, her daughter was definitely living out her wildest royal fantasy. Everyone flocked around her, and her daddy made sure that everyone got an introduction and a chance to say hello. Ryan's hand found its way to Carly's lower back and stayed there all day. Occasionally he would take her arm or entangle his elbow around hers. His possessiveness was sweet, in a way. To anyone's watchful eye, they appeared to be a young couple in love, a young family with nothing but happiness in their future.

Carly hated her skepticism, abhorred it, but doubtful thoughts ran through her mind ... why now? Was all this affection and commitment just an act to impress his family? Or was it true? She just didn't know, and she couldn't allow herself to fall unguarded into the depths of his adoring gazes at her. As much as she admired her own resolve for protection, she hated it too. She wanted to allow herself to fall in love with him again. But she couldn't forget what had happened the last time she'd done it.

Her daughter, on the other hand, had absolutely no trouble playing the part of Prince Daddy's adored princess. Always a happy little girl, Carly observed a more ecstatic side to Grace that was new. She was positively blossoming under the attention of this big Melrose clan.

They stood in line to shake Charlie and Jessica's hands at the reception. A little bit of shyness took over Grace, and she turned away from the bride in the big white dress. Ryan swooped her up into his arms and said gently, "Grace, this is your second cousin Jessica Melrose. Doesn't she make the most beautiful bride?"

Grace turned and nodded shyly.

"Someday you'll be a beautiful bride and I'll be there to walk you down the aisle, just like Jessica's daddy walked her down the aisle."

Grace let out a little smile and held out her hand for Jessica to shake. "Congratulations," she attempted, the difficult word stumbling out over her lips. But the bride and groom chuckled and leaned in to give her kisses on her cheeks.

Ryan and Grace moved on past, and Carly held out her hand, ready to offer her own congratulations to the pair. She was surprised when they both gave her a personal message. "Carly, we want you to know how happy we are that you and Ryan are back together. He's never looked happier or more content, and we know that you and Grace have done that for him. Congratulations."

Carly paused, her mouth open before she recovered with a quiet, "Thank you both." She nodded at them as she moved on. It wasn't really their business that she was confused about her and Ryan's relationship, and that it was only just today that Ryan had made clear his feelings about her, and his vision for their future. That she wasn't there yet and would need to search her feelings and her heart to determine the right thing to do.

On the other hand, it sure was an exciting prospect.

RYAN SAT AT HIS SPOT at the table of the reception hall, waving off a wandering waitress with a tray full of champagne for the bridal toast. He knew Carly wasn't old enough to drink legally, and he wasn't going to put her in an uncomfortable position. Instead he asked the waitress for sparkling grape juice for the two of them.

"Everyone, stand for the bridal toast." He smiled at Carly. They'd found themselves alone since one of his relatives had nabbed Grace.

The little girl was the hit of the reception, second only in popularity to Jessica, the bride. As it should be. His little girl was soaking in the love and affection of her extended family, in her deserved place at the center of attention.

The sparkling juice arrived just in time and he handed one to Carly. They raised their glasses, along with the rest of the guests, and he slid his hand into position along her back. He loved touching her. He loved that she allowed him to touch her. He hoped beyond hope that it wasn't just the novelty of the wedding day that encouraged their closeness, and that it would continue into their daily lives. It was a start.

The toast delivered, they clinked their champagne glasses and drank. He couldn't help himself; he leaned in and captured her mouth with his own and kissed her, tasting the sweet juice on her lips. He pulled back and studied her, wanting to see her honest reaction. She smiled up at him and his heart jumped. His beautiful Carly.

The DJ started the music and he took her hand. "Will you dance with me?" She looked hesitant, and he continued, "Grace is taken care of." He scanned the room and pointed over to one corner. "My grandma has her."

Carly looked and then nodded. "Okay, let's dance."

They danced fast to the beat of a 90s pop song, and then the pace changed to a slow song. He pulled her into his arms and placed his chin on her shoulder, his nose in her auburn hair. Breathing in, he smelled the scent of her shampoo, an apple scent, and it made him smile as he pictured her getting ready for this day ... for his family ... for him. "You smell so good, Carly," he murmured and under his hands he felt her shiver. He wanted to tell her again how much he loved her, but he held back, knowing she wasn't there yet. Knowing that she was smart to be hesitant in believing his words of commitment, knowing he hadn't earned that yet.

It would happen. He would get her to love him again, and they would be happy. They were both hard workers, and although they were a little behind schedule at the moment, they would both earn their degrees, get good jobs, and have a good life. He knew it.

"Ryan." His mother's voice came from nearby and his head jerked up.

"Mom."

"May I cut in?" she asked.

Carly immediately stopped dancing and pulled back, but he held her tight. "Mom, I'll come find you for the next dance. This is Carly's and my dance." He didn't know what his mother was up to, but there was no way he would cut Carly loose and make her walk all by herself back to the table.

"No, that's okay," Carly said with an uncomfortable expression. "You two go ahead and dance." And she backed out of his arms. His mother moved closer to him. He had to move his head to see Carly as she backed up. "Carly, are you sure?" he asked.

She nodded and just like that, she was gone. He sighed and took his mother's hands in his.

"Nice wedding," she remarked.

"Yes, it is."

"Jessica is such a nice girl. Masters degree in Accounting, got her CPA. Has a job offer waiting for her in Charleston."

Only his mother would confuse being a nice girl with having a killer resume and paycheck. But he didn't want to get into a debate with her now. "That's nice."

They danced in silence for a few beats and Ryan hoped beyond hope that the conversation was over.

"Dad talked to Chapel Hill yesterday."

Ryan went motionless and his heartrate went motionless as well. "What? Why?"

"He wanted to know if they would take you back and transfer your credits from this junior college."

A flash of rage raced through him and he took a moment to gain control before he opened his mouth. "It's not a junior college, Mom. Myrtle Beach College is a four-year institution. And I'm not going back to Chapel Hill."

She sniffed. "They said they'd take you."

"Well, of course they'd take me. They didn't ask me to leave. It was my decision."

"The worst decision of your life."

He clamped his mouth shut and fought the urge to grind his teeth together. "That is your opinion."

Another few beats of music passed before she continued. "You would find a suitable young lady at Chapel Hill. Someone you could spend your future with."

Her frame of mind was so frustrating, Ryan couldn't continue the charade of a friendly mother-son dance. He stopped dancing, let go of her and walked off the dance floor. She followed him closely, her words loud in his ear. "One of the most important decisions of your life is picking the right mate. Another important decision is picking your career. You're making a total mess of both of those."

He spun around to face her. "That is your opinion, Mother."

She came at him, shaking her head and raising her voice in anger. "It's not an opinion. It's a fact. You got a teenaged girl pregnant in high school. Big mistake, but we were helping support her while you got away and got a good education at a prestigious school. Now, you gave up everything we worked so hard for, and you're back. With her, it appears. Why? Why on earth would you ruin your future like that?"

"Because I love her." His words were strong and firm and loud, and just happened to coincide with the end of the music. He'd shouted those words at his mother during a lull and everyone had heard.

Including Carly. She stood not too far away, and she'd not only heard his declaration. She'd heard his mother's hateful words. From the look of horror on Carly's face, and the tears budding in her eyes, she'd heard all of them.

Everyone was staring at the three of them. During that moment of silence, mother and son had become the spectacle of the entire reception. Carly spun and ran out of the ballroom. Ryan took just a second's hesitation to spit out, "See what you've done?" then chased after Carly.

She was enough steps in front of him that he watched her disappear into the ladies' room. He raced up to the door and pounded on it. "Carly! Carly? Come out here. I need to talk to you." Silence met him. "Please? Please come out, I want to talk to you."

When she didn't respond, he swung open the door. The restroom had a small foyer containing a couch and a vanity and a huge mirror and Carly sat there, sobbing. She looked up, surprised at his presence. She reached for a nearby tissue and wiped her face. "Ryan, you can't come in here."

"I can if it means I can comfort you. I don't want you in here crying by yourself." He kneeled in front of her and pulled her into his arms, against his chest, tucking her head close to his heart. She pulled back and whimpered, "I'll get your suit wet."

"I don't care."

"I'll get makeup on it."

He scoffed. "I don't care."

He held onto her while her shoulders shook, and her tears fell. Eventually she calmed, and her stream of emotion stopped. He continued to hold her, willing his strength and resolve to reach her. They could get past this. He wouldn't let his mother's terrible words impact their budding love affair.

He couldn't lose her over this. He just couldn't.

"I'm sorry," he whispered, and she shook her head. "No, listen. I'm sorry that you had to hear that. What my mother said. She had no right to say that. Or if she did, she had no right to say it in front of you."

Carly sniffed and pulled back from him, and he instantly felt her loss. It pained him to see her face streaked with tears, painful tears brought on by his mother's awful words.

"She's wrong," he said firmly.

Carly shrugged. "What if she's right?"

"No." He gripped her shoulders. "She's not right. She's wrong. I love you. And I know you may not love me again yet, but I know we have a future together. You are my choice. You are a wonderful person. Hard working, ambitious, smart. And you're an awesome mom. You've done a great job with Grace, and I feel so blessed that you're letting me take part in her life too."

"But I'm not ..."

"You're not what?" He studied her face, unwilling to let her put herself down.

"I'm not ... the type of person your mother would approve of."

He let out a frustrated explosion of breath. "Do you think I care about that? I don't! I don't care a lick about what my mother thinks. My father either, for that matter." He straightened, ran a hand through his hair, and joined her on the couch. "My mother is missing the point. I love you. I want you. I choose you. It's not up to her who I pick for my wife. It's up to you, Carly."

Carly slumped back in her seat. "I don't know," she mumbled.

"I do! I can see it. You, me, Grace. We become a real family and work hard for our futures. And then, when we become successful, it won't be because my parents handed it to me. It will be because we worked hard, together, for it."

She squinted at him, listening.

"We can be very happy, Carly. I love you. And as soon as I convince you that I'm here to stay, I think you can love me too. I'll work every day to make you happy. To make you glad that you took another chance on me."

The door swung open and a wedding guest walked in. "Oh!" she exclaimed. Fortunately, Ryan didn't know her. "Excuse me, ma'am," he said. "We're having sort of a family crisis here." She nodded and went through the door to the bathroom stalls.

He looked back at Carly. She straightened. "I can't do this to your family."

He searched her eyes. "What do you mean?"

"I can't cause this kind of riff between you and your parents."

"Carly, no, listen ..."

"Your parents will never approve of me. They'll never accept me as an appropriate wife for you. They love Grace, and that's fine, but they'll never love me. Admit it."

He shook his head, he didn't want to admit it, and his head took on a life of its own, shaking back and forth, faster and faster. "No. I don't admit that. They'll see how happy we are together. They'll see what great parents we are. They'll see us succeed in business and they'll grow to love you and love us both as a couple."

"Oh Ryan, you're living in a fantasy, only saying that because you want it to be true. You can't possibly believe that." She stood, facing him. "I can't be the wedge that drives you and your parents apart. I think the best thing I can do is move on."

He came unsteadily to his feet. He couldn't believe what he was hearing. "What do you mean, move on?"

"I can't love you, Ryan. I can't imagine a future with you. It's over between us."

"No. No, Carly." He couldn't accept her decision. He reached for her and pulled her in to him. He rested his lips on hers and kissed her, willing her to return his passion. His hands slid into her hair and he gave her the kiss of his life. If he couldn't appeal to her with words, with reason, with explanation, maybe his passion and his love for her would convince her.

She didn't pull back, he was relieved to discover. She was just as engaged as he was, and as his breath came to a timeless halt, he could only hope that she was breathless too. This was love, this thing between the two of them. How could she deny it? How could she walk away from it? He'd done his best to explain what he felt about her. Maybe his actions wouldn't fail him.

When he finally pulled back, he kept hold of her beautiful face in his hands. He waited, hopeful that he'd gotten through to her.

"Will you go find Grace and bring her to me?" she asked, barely audible.

"Yes," he said uncertainly. "Sure." Unsure why, but grateful that she hadn't continued with talk of a break up, he stumbled from the ladies' room and returned to the reception area. Music and conversation continued, as if everything were normal, as if his whole life hadn't been torn apart in the last twenty minutes. He moved past tables, searching for his daughter, ignoring calls of "Ryan! Over here!" that floated over him. Finally, he found Grace on the dance floor. Two of his aunts were teaching her the Hokey Pokey and she was enjoying herself. Not wanting to drag her away, he forced himself to join them for a round. When the song ended, he took her hand and said, "Let's go find Mommy."

Fortunately, the little girl agreed good-naturedly, and he headed back to the ladies' room where he had left her.

But Carly wasn't in the ladies' room. She was standing in the hallway and she'd gathered Grace's bag full of supplies. She looked ready to go. Standing beside her was her friend Haley.

"Here we go, little Grace," Carly called out in a cheerful voice that betrayed the messy look of destroyed makeup on her face. "Time to go home now. We had a good time, didn't we?"

Because her mom sounded so cheerful, and because she had, indeed, had such a fun day, Grace didn't realize anything was amiss and appeared to go willingly with her mom. "Daddy?" Grace asked.

"Oh, Daddy has to stay here and help clean up," Carly lied blatantly, but of course Grace knew no better. "So, I called my friend Haley to give us a ride home."

Ryan held his tongue, looked angrily at Haley. But Haley gave him a sad, regretful expression and he knew instantly that Haley was here because Carly had called and asked for help, not necessarily because she agreed that this was the right thing to do. "Would you watch Grace for just a minute while I have a word with Carly?"

Haley nodded. "Of course," and she got Grace interested in something a few steps away in the hallway.

Ryan turned to Carly and couldn't help letting the full blast of his emotions appear on his face. "Please don't do this. Don't leave. Can we talk about this?"

Carly stared at him for a moment, and her eyes ran over his face, as if she were trying to memorize it. "I just don't have it in me, Ryan. I don't have the strength. I can't fight against your mother's hatred of me."

He shook his head. "She doesn't hate you. She doesn't even really know you. But what I want to say is, it doesn't matter. I'm an adult. I make my own decisions. I love you. Who cares what she thinks?"

Carly shook her head, her forehead creased with concern. "Do you know how hard it would be for the two of us to work out if your parents are against us from the beginning? I don't want to come between you. But I also don't want to try to start with two strikes against us. Strike one – you got me pregnant and then left me for two years. Strike two – you finally come back and want to make it work but your parents are against us. It doesn't take too much to know that strike three isn't too far behind: we fall apart under the weight of it all."

"No. No, Carly. I love you."

She went on as if he hadn't spoken. "I can't do that to Grace." She sniffed and wiped her eyes. "And I won't do that to myself."

Before he could stop her, she turned and rushed down the hallway towards Haley and Grace. He stayed where he was. Because she'd finally gotten through to him.

Maybe she and Grace were better off without him.

Chapter Ten

Haley's little car was going entirely too fast out of the hotel parking lot, and Carly bit her tongue on her advice to slow down.

"So, what on earth happened in there? You've got to tell me."

Carly raised her index finger to her lips and shook her head, gesturing at Grace.

"Ohhhh," Haley said in a drawn-out syllable. "But when I get you home can you tell me?"

Carly turned in the seat and looked at Grace, who was having trouble keeping her eyes open. "If I can get her to go to bed I'll tell you the whole story. In fact, I need your advice, so I don't do something really stupid."

"Hmmmmm," Haley murmured. They got home, walked into the apartment, took Grace's fancy dress off and laid her down in bed, where she curled up without hesitation. Carly went back to the living room where Haley waited.

"I have to say that dress looks hot on you," Haley remarked.

Carly scoffed. "Thanks. Just don't look too closely at my face." She pointed at her streaked mascara and stained cheeks. She took a few minutes to give Haley the Readers Digest Condensed Version of the Carly and Ryan story, and then quieted, waiting for her reaction.

"So, he finally laid his heart out on the table."

Carly frowned. "Yeah, I guess."

"And you carved it like a Thanksgiving turkey."

Carly winced. "Geez. Don't hold back, will ya?"

"I'm sorry. It's just that ... I'm a romantic. And when I hear about a sweet, gorgeous, smart, gorgeous and great guy who falls head over heels in love with one of my friends, I really want it to work out. Oh, did I mention? The guy's gorgeous."

Sighing, Carly looked down at her lap. "Let's put aside the fact that he's gorgeous."

"Do you agree?"

"Of course, I agree! I'm not blind! I always thought he was gorgeous. But his looks have no place here. I have to focus on what's important."

"Like he's madly in love with you?" Haley asked.

"Like his family doesn't approve of me."

"Yeah, I get that. But is that a show-stopper? Really?"

Carly felt the sting of tears in her eyes again. "I don't want to break apart his family."

Haley grimaced.

"What?" Carly asked.

"That sounds awful noble of you. But he's a grown up. Doesn't he get to choose what he wants to do?"

"You're saying I don't have a choice in the matter?"

"Of course, you do! But you have to consider two people only: you and Grace. Don't try to accommodate him or his mother. Someone else can worry about them." Carly nodded. "So, let me ask you this: do you love him?"

"Yes," she said without hesitation. "But ..."

"No buts. You love him. You just said so."

"There have to be buts," Carly pointed out. "Forget his parents who don't approve of me. I don't know if I can trust him. You know what happened before. Once life got tough, he fled. Why should I believe he's in for the long haul now? You know it's going to be tough again."

"I don't know. I just believe in him, Carly. I see him when he looks at you. He's crazy about you. He worships you. Not to mention how he feels about Grace. And now he's actually told you he loves you. This is a good thing. You need to take it and run."

Carly shook her head. "I just can't. I'm too afraid nothing has changed."

Haley looked at her with pity in her eyes and took her hands. "Oh sweetie, that's where you're wrong. Everything has changed."

THE DAY OF THE RADLEY Ray concert arrived. Shaw asked Nora to be ready to leave by three in the afternoon, so she scheduled her last appointment for noon. When it was over, Nora took her second shower of the day, taking care to moisturize her skin and style her hair and make up her face. She wanted to look good.

She went about her preparations with a nervousness in her heart. Then she slipped into her concert costume. She looked in the mirror and her first reaction was *no way. I'm far too old to be wearing this. I'll be a laughing stock.*

But then she turned back to the mirror. Really considered, trying to be subjective. How did she actually look? Different, yes. But honestly, she appeared comfortable and southern and a fan of country music. Although none of those things were particularly true, why couldn't she relax and enjoy a different type of night out?

She'd be with Shaw. And he'd make her feel at ease. He always did.

At three, Shaw came to the door and when she opened it, she watched for his reaction. It started in his eyes. They popped wide, then he squinted, then it spread to his mouth. A smile formed, first closed-mouthed, spreading across his whole face: a happy grin. "You look great, Nora," he murmured as he reached for her hands. Pulling her close, he wrapped his arms around her and she breathed in his aroma. He smelled clean and showered and absolutely irresistible.

"Thank you. You look great too." Enjoying the shot of adrenaline rushing through her core, she let out a chuckle. Oh, it was going to be a great night. He was dressed in perfectly worn jeans covering his long, lean legs, a comfortable denim shirt buttoned over a red t-shirt with just a trace of the color at his neck. A newer pair of cowboy boots than the ones he wore for work, and the cowboy hat she'd occasionally seen him in.

He looked delicious.

Eventually they pulled apart and she stepped back so he could come in. He walked by her but turned his head, so he could continue to observe her. "That skirt looks great on you. And the boots." He made an "A-OK" gesture with his hand.

She couldn't help a flirty giggle. "Sadie was a huge help."

"She gave me a hint that you looked awesome. She really likes you, you know."

Well, wasn't that interesting? "I like her too. You did good with that one, Dad."

"Would you be interested in coming over to the house and spending some time together, the three of us?"

"Yes, I would." Of course she would. Sadie was a huge part of his life. Nora wanted to become a bigger part. So, getting to know Sadie better was definitely a good thing.

They got in his truck and made the easy drive south to Charleston. They parked in a garage near the amphitheater and walked a few blocks. Nora had been to the city before, but strolling along with Shaw, holding his hand and hearing about the history of the charming buildings from him made it an enchanting experience. It was all new with Shaw beside her.

They stepped into a tavern that dated back to the late 1700s, sat and ordered a drink. Shaw ordered an ale and Nora chose a glass of chardonnay. They chatted easily about a range of topics: the city, experiences Shaw had had here, Thunder, and both their jobs. Drinks done, Shaw checked his wristwatch and said, "We've got reservations for dinner at Circa 1886. Have you ever heard of it?"

Nora shook her head.

"It's in the historic section of the city, housed in a building that dates back to ... take a guess?"

"Um, circa 1886?"

"You got it! It's got great reviews and it's very quaint. I've always wanted to eat there and then we can take a cab to the concert."

He'd really put thought into this. She was both impressed and touched by his kindness and care.

The restaurant was magical. The building wore its history like a beautiful coat, but it was tastefully modernized too. Nora enjoyed the top-rate service, and when she perused the menu, she had difficulty deciding. Usually when she sat down at a restaurant, a glance at the menu resulted in one item jumping out at her, begging for attention. Not this time. At least five selections intrigued her. Finally, she settled on the scallops appetizer and the wedge salad.

Over dinner they talked about Radley Ray. A huge country music fan, Shaw placed Radley Ray at the very top of the list. They discussed their favorite songs in his playlist. Nora was able to contribute to the conversation because of Shaw's thoughtfulness in lending her the CDs weeks ahead of time. They made a mental list of the songs they most wanted to hear, and Shaw shared some stories of past Radley concerts he'd attended.

Then he reached over the table and put her hands in his. "But this will be the best concert of all. Because I'm sharing it with you."

Tears appeared in her eyes and she blinked. Nothing like dampening a tender moment with tears. But honestly, how could she resist this man? She liked just about everything about him. He was one of a kind. She lightened the mood with a joke. "Yes, and because when I run up on stage, I'll be pulling you with me."

When they stepped onto the sidewalk out front, Shaw put his fingers to his mouth and did one of those loud whistles that could probably attract the attention of livestock miles away. He raised his hand, attracting the attention of a rickshaw driver. A young man in a shorts and t-shirt uniform pedaled a vehicle whose front half was a bicycle, but the back half was a seat wide enough to accommodate three people. "Have you ever ridden in one of these?"

"No."

They climbed up onto the seat and Shaw gave the driver the name of the amphitheater. He put his arm around her shoulders and pulled her in tight. Nora looked around. Between people walking, riding in horse-drawn carriages, and in rickshaws, not to mention the cars, the streets of Charleston were quite active.

Although the pace generated by the driver's pumping legs wasn't particularly speedy, Nora rested her head on Shaw's strong arm and enjoyed the breeze blowing through her hair. She rolled her head to look up at his face. Excitement rushed her heart and she said softly, "Thank you for this."

He leaned down and touched her lips with his. A brush turned into a kiss and then a deeper one. Her pulse raced through her veins, creating a delicious breathlessness. He drew back, looked into her eyes and murmured, "You're welcome."

He made her feel special. He made her feel desirable. While continuing to gaze at him, she let her mind say a silent prayer of thanks to God for placing him in her life.

They arrived at the theater and slid off the wide rickshaw seat. Shaw pulled some bills out of his pocket and gave them to the driver before grabbing her hand. He sported an excited smile that was contagious.

They stood in a long line outside the venue, then after passing through a metal detector and another line where Nora handed over her purse to be manually searched, they went inside.

"This guy has a lot of fans," Nora commented, watching the mass of people walking all over, standing in line for refreshments, waiting for the restroom, or heading for their seats.

"Maybe he'll have one more after tonight?" he replied, grinning at her.

Nora couldn't help but notice that other women were dressed just like her. Sadie had done well. This concert costume was exactly right.

Twenty minutes later, they were in their seats watching the opening act. Nora wasn't familiar with the group, but she enjoyed the music, and she especially enjoyed sitting close beside Shaw, sharing in this activity he loved. She gave him a fond smile.

"What?" he said with a grin.

"I'm just glad to be here with you."

"Well, I'm glad you're here with me too." Shaw hesitated, his thoughts flickering across his face, then leaned in close to her. The noise level was so high, he put his mouth right up to her ear to speak, which caused a shiver to flit down her spine. "Shortly after I met you, I knew I wanted to get to know you better. I knew I wanted you in my life. I handled it badly. I messed it up and I lost you. But God handed me a second chance. I'm not messing it up again. I'm doing it right this time."

She sat motionless, soaking in his words. She didn't want anything to spoil the magical moment.

"You're special, Nora. Let me think of some words to describe you: kind, smart, beautiful and caring. I want to see where this goes between us. And I never want you to forget how I feel about you."

"I won't. I promise."

When Radley Ray hit the stage, it didn't take long to see that he was quite a showman. From the moment Radley appeared, everyone jumped to their feet and stayed there for two straight hours. A carefree spirit ran through her and Nora felt young again, dancing in her spot, holding onto Shaw's arm, singing along and cheering. He not only performed his fun peppy songs, he also did his sentimental ballads, and he kept the crowd firmly in the palm of his hand. Thanks to Shaw, she knew his music and had the time of her life.

Late into the night, the huge lights of the theater came on, bathing the tired concert-goers with neon light. Shaw grabbed her hand and led her down the steps, through the crowds of people and outside, where they headed for the parking garage. "So?" he asked her.

"Best concert ever. Radley is my new favorite country act."

He stopped her in the garage, pulled her into his arms and gave her one of those kisses that she was coming to know and love. "And you're my new favorite country concert partner."

They jumped into the truck, and thanks to the warmth, the darkness, and how safe she felt with him behind the wheel, she was asleep before they hit Route 17.

Chapter Eleven

Life settled into yet another new routine for Ryan. As if he hadn't gone through enough change already. Now, he could only show his love for Grace, not Carly. He could no longer strive to convince her of their future together. Because as far as Carly was concerned, there was no such future. At all.

Of course, he was still Grace's father. And he always would be. And thankfully, Carly still considered it important for him to have a relationship with his daughter. So, between the two of them, they worked out a visitation schedule. He would come over and pick up Grace and spend time with her. But not with Carly. Never with Carly.

No more family fun days. No more stolen kisses. No more confessions of love. No more striving for a life together.

Still he tried to count his blessings. As deep as his disappointment at being cut out of Carly's life ran, at least he still had Grace. He was determined to be the best father he could possibly be for her. That was enough. For now.

He and Carly spoke briefly at the beginning of each week to determine what days he'd have his daughter, for how long, and other specific arrangements. He held his tongue with Carly. He didn't want to put her on the spot or make her feel uncomfortable speaking about the two of them. Because she'd made it very clear. When it came to the two of them, there was no relationship. No romance. Nothing.

IN THE LUNCHROOM AT work, Carly opened her brown paper bag and pulled out her meager lunch. This morning, she'd made a peanut butter and jelly sandwich and bagged some potato chips. She really hadn't been hungry lately, but she knew with her schedule she needed to uphold her energy level with protein. She took a bite and chewed, forcing her mind to go empty, and just stared at the table top in front of her.

"Hey, chickie," she heard and looked up. It was Haley. She sat at the table and pulled out her own lunch bag, an insulated zipper kind. She pulled out what looked like leftovers from last night's dinner and walked to the microwave to warm it. A ding later, and she was back, stirring it around. She took a bite and then glanced at Carly's lunch. "Awwww. Want to split mine?"

Carly had to smile. She should probably be insulted at being pitied, but it was Haley. She only meant the best. "No thanks. I like PBJs."

Haley raised her eyebrows doubtfully. "If you say so." She took another bite, then smiled at Carly. "What's on tap for tonight?"

"What do you mean?"

"What are you doing?"

Carly shrugged. "Ryan's picking up Grace and having her spend the night at his parents', so I'll be home alone."

"Then I say the two of us need to go out together. Have some fun."

Carly automatically rejected the suggestion. "No, that's all right ... I don't ..."

"You don't go out. I know. But that's because you usually have a little almost-three-year-old and all the responsibility that goes along with it. Tonight, you won't have that. Besides, you've been a gloomy Gus ever since the wedding and I'm going to take it upon myself to make sure you have a good time. What do you say?"

Carly sighed. A night out would not be a bad thing, now that she thought about it. But she knew she'd have to lay some ground rules first. "When you say going out, what do you have in mind? Because I'm not interested in going to a bar and being propositioned by a loser guy who is only interested in one thing."

Haley nodded. "Definitely not. How about we go to a classy bar, have a glass of wine, maybe some dinner, and then entertain the idea of a movie. Just us girls."

It sounded good, and Haley was offering her the perfect therapeutic evening. Tears welled up.

"Oh sweetie, look at you. You're a mess!" Haley stood, fluttered around the lunch room till she found a tissue, then came back to Carly, pushing it into her hand. "You poor thing."

"No, no," Carly stated emphatically. "I'm fine. I'm just grateful that you care about me and want to make me have fun. Thank you, Haley."

Haley clamped her mouth shut over a sad smile. "You're gonna get through this, sweetheart. Life ain't the best right now, but it always gets better."

Carly concentrated on pushing back the tears and getting herself under control. They made quick plans for the evening.

RYAN WRAPPED UP HIS workday of shoveling mulch over all the dormant flower beds on campus. A thin film of the stuff covered his skin and his clothes had turned a brown color. He headed for the showers and clocked out on the way.

"You got big plans tonight?" asked one of his co-workers, Ben. They'd never really talked on a deep level, just weekend plans and superficial stuff.

"Yes, I do. I have a date with a special young lady."

Ben chuckled salaciously, a meaningful laugh that Ryan knew was way off.

"My daughter."

"What? Seriously? I didn't know you had a kid."

"Yep. Two years old. She's the most precious little thing I know."

"Well, congratulations."

"Thanks, man." He waved and took his shower in the locker room. Slipping on some fresh clothes, he stuffed his dirty ones in a back pack and was walking through the Maintenance office when his boss, Marlin, walked in. His eyes were wide and the panicked look on his face was replaced with relief when he saw Ryan.

"Oh man, Ryan. So good to see you. You're the last one here."

"Yeah, I'm on my way out."

"I'm in a bind. The department head just called and wants us to deliver some stuff down to the maintenance shop in Horry County. Several of our riding mowers need repair and the forklift needs an oil change."

"Okay ...."

"He pulled some strings and got us an appointment with the maintenance shop, but we've got to get them there before the weekend. I know you're done for the day, but could I ask you to help me? I need an extra hand."

"Uhhh, yeah."

"I'll pay you time and a half. It shouldn't take longer than ninety minutes or so."

"Sure, Marlin, I'd be happy to help out. But I need to make a phone call or two. Is that all right?"

"Absolutely. Go to the equipment garage when you're done, and you can help me load the stuff."

The first person he called was his mom. Things had been tense between them at home, and he avoided her as often as he possibly could. As much as he resented her for what she'd said about Carly, and the result of her hurtful words, he realized with chagrin that he needed her help right now. He'd been working hard with Carly to prove his reliability, so she would find him trustworthy. But Marlin's last-minute request meant he wouldn't be able to pick up Grace on time.

He placed the call and was relieved when his mother picked up on the second ring. "Hi, Mom. Are you doing anything tonight?"

"Well hello to you too, son," she said pointedly.

"Sorry, Mom, I need a favor. I'm getting Grace tonight and Carly's expecting me at six to pick her up, but I have to work overtime. Would you be able to go get her and take her home to wait for me there?"

"Sure," his mother said, her surly mood and tone perking up noticeably. "I'd be happy to."

"Thanks. I should be home by seven or shortly after."

Next, he called Carly and filled her in. He couldn't pick up much from her monotone but imagined that Carly dreaded her first confrontation with his mother since the wedding. Fortunately, Carly agreed to hand Grace over to Ryan's mother, so he could do the overtime shift before he started his weekend with Grace.

His business taken care of, he headed over to the large equipment garage to help Marlin.

THUNDER'S REHAB WAS going well. Shaw spent at least an hour a day with him at Waccamaw Trails, walking him on a lead rope all over the pasture, putting miles on that leg. He was growing strength its back, and the horse barely limped. What Shaw didn't want to do at this point was to increase Thunder's speed to a trot or canter, or to put an adult's weight on his back. Shaw wasn't sure if he would ever be able to do that post-injury. But he'd take it slow and look for small successes.

After a month, Shaw felt Thunder was ready to start providing equine therapy. Good thing too, because he had been working his connections and he had a small handful of potential clients. It would be good for Thunder to feel useful again, and this was a community service that Shaw felt strongly about.

The day for meeting their first client arrived. Shaw came early, visiting Thunder first, feeding him, grooming, and running a calming hand over his muscles. When he was finished he snapped a lead rope onto his halter and led him outside. Using a longer lunge rope, he got Thunder walking in a circle around him, Shaw standing in the middle. He wanted to warm up the horse's muscles for later exercise, but he also wanted to wear him out just a little so when it came time to put a small body on his back he'd be calm and accepting.

Finishing up, Shaw walked to the mansion and tried the doorknob. It was unlocked so he walked right in. It was an agreement he and Nora had come to. She didn't want him to feel like a guest; she wanted him to feel at home. Walking straight in when the door was unlocked was a start.

"Nora?" he called. It was early for a normal visit, but she was expecting him today. They both wanted to experience their first equine therapy patient together.

"In here!" she called from the kitchen. As he approached, the wondrous smell of bacon reached his nostrils.

"Wow, breakfast?" He grinned and wrapped his arms around her from behind as she stood at the stove. She rested her head back into his neck.

"Special occasions only. Don't get spoiled."

Shaw chuckled and let her go. He went to the cabinet, found two plates, two forks in the drawer and placed them on the table. "Can I do anything else to help?"

"Just eat," she said, bringing the frying pan over and loading up both plates with scrambled eggs and several slices of crisp bacon. As they ate, Shaw filled her in on their first client.

"Rusty is eight years old. He's had cerebral palsy his entire life. But he's got the spirit of an athlete and he works hard to stay active and enjoy life. A year ago, his muscles had deteriorated to the point that he needed a walking frame to get around."

"What's that?"

"Three-sided frame on wheels, the opening in the front. The child stands inside it and holds on for support while he walks. There's a seat behind him for when he needs to sit."

Nora's face crumpled. "Poor little guy. He was born with this?"

"Yes, as far as they know. He's got physical disabilities, but he's got the perfect mindset to enjoy getting to know Thunder."

They finished eating and went outside. Soon, a minivan rolled up the drive and parked in front of the barn. Two adults got out and then walked around to the side rolling door. They unbuckled a boy from the seat. Dad picked him up, gave him a hug, then set him on his feet, while Mom pulled the walking frame out, opened it up and placed it around him. Rusty immediately grabbed hold of the handles and started walking, pushing the device along.

Nora stepped forward, reaching her hand out, worry evident on her face. "Can I help you get over this bumpy grass?"

Rusty shook his head with a grin. "No thank you," he said with happy enthusiasm.

Nora looked over to Rusty's mother.

"Bumpy grass wouldn't stop him. He's so excited to be here today, he could barely sleep last night." She gazed at him with fierce fondness.

Shaw made introductions, holding on to Thunder on the lead. "I'm Shaw Flynn, and this is Nora Ramsey. Together, we offer equine therapy services with the help of this amazing animal, Thunder."

Thunder must've known he was being introduced because he lowered his head to Rusty's level and started sniffing his face, ending in a huge exhale. Rusty's red hair blew up and out, and Rusty let out an excited laugh.

"Do you like horses, Rusty?" asked Shaw.

"I love 'em." Rusty held his hand out to Thunder, palm up.

"Atta boy. That's exactly the right way to let a horse smell you, get to know you."

The boy's smile made a rush of warmth flow through Shaw's heart. This is why he was doing this. "Here you go, buddy, here's a way to make friends with Thunder right away." He dug a half-carrot out of his jeans pocket and placed it on Rusty's palm. He put his own hand under Rusty's and together, they made the offering to Thunder. The horse swished his tail and accepted the carrot, his velvety muzzle tickling Rusty's hand. Rusty giggled.

"Rusty, you and Thunder have something in common."

Rusty looked at Shaw. "What is it?"

"Thunder hurt his leg and had to spend over a month in a sling that helps it heal. Now, although his injury has healed, Thunder walks with a little limp sometimes, and he'll probably never be able to do some of the things he used to do, like run and jump."

Rusty turned again toward Thunder, as if seeing him in a new light. "Really? Can I hug him?"

Shaw stepped forward and held Thunder's lead, helping Rusty move his walking frame as he inched closer to Thunder. "Sure."

Rusty leaned into Thunder's chest, his arms wrapped as far around the big animal as he could reach, and rested his cheek against the horse's body. "Don't worry, Thunder. Even though we're a little different, we still have a lot to give the world."

Shaw looked over at Rusty's mother, who was beaming. She glanced at him and winked.

Shaw pulled a brush out of a nearby bucket and handed it to Rusty. "We're going to start with you grooming Thunder. Horses love the feel of a brush going over their hair. Go ahead and start at his chest and brush him all the way to his tail. Avoid his face."

The adults watched as the little guy did as he was told, Thunder appearing to enjoy the attention. At one point he grunted and let his eyelids drift closed. "Look Rusty, you're putting him to sleep, it feels so good to him."

Rusty followed up each brush stroke with his hand, petting Thunder's soft coat. When the grooming was done, Shaw tossed the brush back in the bucket. "Now let's take Thunder back to the barn so we can put his saddle on. Then we can see if you're ready to jump up there and ride him."

Shaw buckled Thunder to the restraints outside the tack room and while he was putting on the horse's saddle and bridle, he said to Rusty's parents, "I assume you read the pre-session material and shared it with Rusty."

"Yes, we did," Rusty's dad said. "We were impressed with the benefits of the therapy. Building muscles, improved confidence and self-esteem, improved coping skills."

Shaw nodded. "Horses are great for all kids, including ones with special physical needs. But more than anything else, especially for a kid Rusty's age, horseback riding is fun. Kids can form a personal relationship with this big powerful animal, and they'll begin to trust each other. We'll also get into goal-setting. Each week we'll try to build our skills, focusing on one thing at a time. Balance, distance, strengthening the core. Once the rider sets a goal, we know what to work on that day to help him achieve it."

Rusty's mom shook her head. "It's a wonderful program and we feel lucky to be asked to participate."

Shaw winked at Nora. "Nora and I felt there was a gap that wasn't being filled. We partnered to fill the need and provide equine therapy with our buddy Thunder." He finished up putting on all of Thunder's gear. He turned to Rusty and knelt, so their faces were even. "Rusty, how do you feel about riding on Thunder's back?"

Rusty's eyes went wide as he displayed an excited smile. "Yesss!"

Shaw glanced at Rusty's mom and she looked nervous but heaved a fortifying breath. "He'll be completely safe, Mom and Dad, trust us. I will lift Rusty up and place him in the saddle, then you see, I installed this seat belt." He tugged on a leather add-on to the saddle. "He can't leave the saddle with this on. In addition to that safety feature, we'll have Nora leading Thunder, walking at his head, and I'll walk along beside Rusty. At first, I'll have my hand on his leg for support. But once his balance is good, I'll let go. He'll ride on his own, and I'll just walk along beside in case a problem arises."

Rusty's mom gave a determined nod, then gripped hands with her husband.

"You two stay on the other side of the fence in the pasture. You'll have a good view from there."

They made their way out of the barn, across the paddock and through the gate into the pasture. Shaw turned to Rusty. "I'm gonna lift you up, buddy, is that okay?"

Rusty nodded enthusiastically. Shaw lifted him and handed his walking frame to his parents. He loaded Rusty onto Thunder's saddle and strapped him in, then he took his place right beside the little boy. "Okay, Rusty. You can hold onto this thing for balance, it's called the horn of the saddle. You can also lean forward and pet Thunder's neck. He'd like that. Nora will take care of steering and we won't let Thunder go very fast today. If for some reason you think you're gonna fall, I'll help you."

Falling off the horse looked like it was the last thing on Rusty's mind. He was a typical little boy Shaw would rather see racing down the field with a football, sprinting around a court with a basketball, or swinging a bat for a homerun. It broke Shaw's heart to see this tough little kid afflicted with cerebral palsy, and he knew his disabilities would probably get worse as he got older. But gazing up at him on this majestic animal, sitting tall and proud and excited about this experience, Shaw said a prayer of thankfulness in his mind that he and Nora were embarking on an endeavor that could help kids like Rusty.

They walked in a big circle in the pasture. Shaw not only kept an eye on Rusty, but he also kept an eye on Thunder's recovering leg, searching for a limp, a flinch or any sign of discomfort. However, both his patients were doing great. Thunder loved the attention, the movement, the outdoors, and Rusty loved the riding.

"Hey Rusty, do you like the beach?"

"Yeah." The response wasn't particularly enthusiastic, and Shaw could imagine why. Walking the beach, maneuvering the dips and mounds of sand, while relying on the walking frame would be awkward and difficult. Why would Rusty enjoy the beach under those restrictions?

"Thunder likes the beach too. Let's head down there."

Rusty grinned and nodded. He was up for it. Shaw turned Thunder in that direction and they continued to walk. He winked at Nora and she smiled back. Shaw caught a quip of conversation on the breeze and he turned to see Rusty leaning forward in the saddle, talking to Thunder. The two were bonding.

They reached the beach and Shaw turned to catch the sight of Rusty's face beaming with excitement. "Wow!" the little boy said. Maybe he'd never been to the beach. Or maybe he'd been exposed briefly. But never, Shaw was sure, on the back of a horse.

"You like it, buddy?"

"Yeah!" Rusty gazed out at the waves, the shoreline and the distant water. He lifted his nose and Shaw knew he was sniffing the distinct scent of salt water. Thunder seemed to enjoy it too, his ears forward, his head up and his tail swishing. "It's amazing!" the little boy shouted.

They took a short break, standing on the soft sand of the beach and Shaw took the opportunity to unwrap Thunder's leg, run his hands down it to check for swelling and rewrap it. The leg was doing well. This was just what the doctor ordered.

They turned and made the slow walk back to the barn. When they arrived, Rusty was looking a little worn out but still happy and positive. When he saw his parents, he waved happily. They waved back, their relief at his return showing in their faces.

Shaw led Thunder into the barn and hooked him at the grooming station outside the tack room. He came around to Rusty's left side. "I'm gonna get you down from there, and then you can help with grooming again. After a good ride, you always help the horse by brushing him. It helps soothe the muscles and remove any perspiration due to the exercise."

Rusty agreed. Shaw reached up and grabbed hold of Rusty firmly. Rusty leaned left and ended up in Shaw's arms. Shaw lowered him to the ground and put him on his own feet, hanging on until he felt Rusty was solid. His parents were right there with the walking frame and put it in place.

"Mom! Dad! It was awesome! We rode all over the pasture and I didn't fall off. Then we went to the beach and rode on the sand. It was the best thing ever!"

"Oh, sweetheart, I'm so glad." Rusty's parents looked at each other, then at Shaw. "Thank you so much. This was such a great experience for him."

Shaw removed Thunder's saddle and hoisted it onto a stand in the tack room. Coming back out, he handed a brush to Rusty who again showed his expertise in horse grooming.

"Does that feel good to him?"

"It sure does. He knows you're taking good care of him. He appreciates that."

Rusty moved to face Thunder straight on, brushing the barrel of his chest while continuing to murmur words to the horse.

"What are you saying to him?" asked Shaw.

"I'm just telling him that he's my best friend. We have a lot in common because we both have problems with our legs. But we can help each other and be friends."

Shaw chuckled. "I'm sure Thunder's happy to hear that."

Rusty turned to his mom and dad. "Can I come back and go riding again?"

They looked at each other and back at their son. "I don't see why not. This experiment was a total success."

Rusty cheered and threw his arms around Thunder's chest, hugging the massive animal. Thunder lowered his head and muzzled the top of Rusty's head.

"We're going to recommend you to Rusty's doctor for other patients to check out. This is a wonderful program for kids like Rusty."

"I appreciate that."

When they were done brushing Thunder, they put him back in his stall, and Shaw showed Rusty how to measure the oats and pour them into the bin for Thunder to eat. Then they were done. They walked back out to the car and as his mom was helping him in, Rusty turned and put his arms around Shaw, hugging him fiercely. "Thank you," he said.

Shaw blinked back an attack of tears. This little boy had so much ahead of him to battle, physically, emotionally and socially. He was glad he could give him a whole afternoon of love, companionship and fun.

"And thank you, Rusty. You were Thunder's first rider after his leg injury. You were exactly what he needed. He can't wait for you to come back and ride him again."

With that, the boy climbed into the van, and they drove away.

Chapter Twelve

Carly stood in the doorway of her small closet, scanning the choices. She sighed. Two things became apparent to her: one, her wardrobe choices were limited. Two, she had no idea what to wear for a girls' night out. Because she honestly couldn't remember the last time she'd been on one.

The doorbell rang, and Grace yelled helpfully, "Mommy!" Carly went to the door, opened it and was relieved to see Haley. "Hey you." She smiled and then noticed Haley's hands were full. "Oh, thank goodness. You brought reinforcements?"

Haley stepped in with a big smile. "Yes, I couldn't resist." Then she kneeled in front of Grace. "Hi pretty little girl, remember me?"

Grace nodded vigorously. "Yes. Haley. Mommy's friend."

"That's right. And I have a little gift for you because you're so smart." She handed her a small white plastic bag with red print boasting the name of the girl's accessory store at the mall. Grace opened it and peered inside. Then she squealed and pulled out hair scrunchies and a few barrettes.

"Mommy, look!" She held out her stash with a beaming smile.

"Well, what do you say to Miss Haley for bringing you a gift?" She twirled back to face Haley. "Thank you."

"You're welcome, sweetie."

Grace raced down the hallway to her room where she could experiment with placing the treasures in her hair.

"You didn't have to do that." Carly patted her on the shoulder.

"Hey, I want the kid to like me and be excited to see me. A quick trip to Claire's Boutique and for five bucks or less, I can guarantee that reaction."

Carly laughed.

"Now, I brought along a few things just in case you need some wardrobe assistance."

"How did you know? Oh my gosh, I have nothing to wear." Carly ran her fingers down several of Haley's offerings before she set eyes on a turquoise form-fitting blouse with a V-neck and layered cowls. A fitted waistband would hug her middle and add shape and form.

"You like that one?" Haley said with a grin. "That'd go nice with a pair of dressy jeans or black pants."

"I'll go try it on. Thank you again." She leaned in, placed a peck on Haley's cheek and ran to her room. Once on, it was a hit. It was the perfect top for a classy evening out between two girlfriends, just as Haley had said.

She made her way back to the front of the apartment and just as Haley was giving her the thumbs up and gushing about how great she looked (how had she ever lived without Haley?) the doorbell rang. Haley gave her an eyebrows-up look of anticipation. She obviously thought it was Ryan behind the door. Carly shook her head quickly. "It's Ryan's mother."

Haley gave an exaggerated frown and pretended to gag. Carly smacked her shoulder on the way by. "Behave!"

She opened the door to Ryan's mother. "Hello, dear," she said blandly. "Had Ryan let you know of the change in plans?"

"Yes, he did," she answered. "Please, come in. I'll get Grace and her stuff for the night." As she headed for the bedroom, she remembered her manners. "This is my friend Haley. Haley, Mrs. Melrose."

She left the two of them to try to make conversation. She didn't feel too sorry for Haley. She could talk to a rock and get it to laugh.

"Sweetie, your grandma is here."

Grace looked up from her mirror. She had successfully placed three randomly scattered ponytails around her head and secured them with scrunchies. Carly held back a laugh at her rag-tag appearance and wondered briefly what her perfectionist grandma would think of it.

"What? Gramma?"

"Yes, honey. You're going to spend the night tonight with Daddy, Grandma and Grandpa. Is that okay?"

Grace rose to her feet and jumped up and down. "Yes!" Carly's heart eased at her daughter's reaction. Regardless of what she thought of Ryan's mother, and what Ryan's mother thought of her, Carly would never want to impact Grace's love for her extended family. Every child deserved the love of as many people as they could get, and grandparents were a child's treasure.

"Okay, I've already packed your bag. I want you to be a good girl for your grandparents. Mind your manners, be a little lady, and do as you're told. All right?"

"Yes!" Grace raced out the door, down the short hall and threw herself into the arms of her grandmother.

"Well, my goodness," the older woman said. "Careful now." Then she eased into a warm grandmotherly hug.

When she stood, Carly handed her Grace's child-sized suitcase full of pajamas and a few changes of clothes, as well as her diaper bag filled with the last of her supplies. The handing over of the child and all her weekend material goods was quick and conversation was short. Carly kneeled and pulled Grace into her arms. Grace rested her head against Carly's chest. It was easier now to relinquish her precious daughter to extended family. But it would never be normal. "I love you, baby," she whispered, more for herself than for Grace. She didn't want Grace to know she was melancholy about her leaving, because she truly did want her to have a good time. Her mother's loneliness without her was not something she wanted Grace burdened with.

She rose and watched Grace scamper over to her grandmother for their Melrose weekend together. Ryan's mother waved and opened the door, disappearing through it without a word.

Carly closed her eyes for a moment, then turned to face Haley. "I can't tell you how glad I am that you're here."

"I can see why. That woman is not exactly a ball of sunshine, now, is she?"

Haley and Carly decided where they were going and since they both planned to have a glass of wine or two, they decided to call Uber for their ride. That way, they wouldn't be at risk of driving under the influence.

An hour into their evening, Carly was grateful for the night out. As she'd promised, Haley had taken her to a higher-class bar, and she felt like she fit right in with her pretty top, her dressy jeans, and not a care in the world since she'd passed her mothering responsibilities over to Ryan's mother for the night. She could see why young professionals came to places like this to unwind after a busy week of office work. For her, it was a first, but for many that she met there, she knew they did this to kick off every weekend.

Haley suggested that they order appetizers to fill their stomachs with a makeshift dinner. They selected potato skins and shrimp cocktail off the appetizer menu and shared the delicacies.

"THANKS AGAIN FOR YOUR help, Ryan. I sure appreciate you being flexible like that," Marlin said as he drove the truck pulling the flatbed trailer into the campus equipment garage.

"Not a problem. Happy to help." Ryan helped Marlin with the garage door, and waved goodbye. Pulling his phone out of his pocket he saw it was 7:20. On his way to his car, he called his mother, however it rang and rang with no answer.

Next, he tried calling Carly. He just wanted to touch base with her to make sure the pick-up had gone off as planned. Carly's phone rang three times and then went to voice mail. "Hi Carly. I'm done with my overtime and I'm heading home now. I just wanted to make sure everything went okay with my mom picking up Grace. Okay, talk to you later."

He drove home and parked on the street out front. Letting himself in the front door, he walked straight to the door that led from the family room into the garage and opened it. He blinked at the two empty stalls. He figured his dad was still working. His job often had him working till seven or later in the evenings. But where was his mom? He fully expected to see her red Lexus sitting on its side of the garage, but it was not there.

A tinge of nerves tiptoed down his esophagus. He expected his mother to be home with Grace, waiting for him. If she'd taken his little girl somewhere else, she should've called him and let him know of her change in plans. Or at the very least, answered her phone when he'd called her.

He placed a call to her again, hoping that she had just missed the first one, and would put an end to his anxiety. But no answer.

He closed the garage door and stood staring at it for a moment. This was what it was like to be a parent. Worried over the slightest thing, if it involved his daughter. Imagining the worst-case scenario.

He turned into the family room, settled into a recliner and worked hard to intentionally put his mind at ease. He was sure there was a logical explanation. He'd just need to be patient.

"ARE YOU UP FOR THAT movie?" Haley asked.

"Oh, I don't know," Carly responded. Truth was, she was having way too much fun to go sit in a dark theater and concentrate on a movie. She was enjoying the rare and unfamiliar night life and didn't particularly want it to end this early.

"Want to stay?"

Carly smiled. Her heart was light, and she figured this night was exactly what she needed. What so many other young people her age were doing at this exact time on this exact night. She never got out and enjoyed herself like this. There was nothing wrong with this.

Nothing.

"Or do you feel like dancing?"

Carly looked around. "I don't see a dance floor."

"No, I'm talking about going somewhere else. Rocky's has a fun DJ and lots of people dancing. Want to go there?"

Why not? Why, for once in her life, would she not go dancing on a Friday night with a girlfriend? "Sure!"

They made their way outside where Haley summoned the Uber driver with her phone app. They only had four minutes to wait. The miracles of modern technology.

"I'll have to download that Uber app too." Carly pulled her phone out to see if she could find the app and noticed that she'd missed a call. "Oh, Ryan called me earlier. Let me see what he wants."

She stepped a few feet away and placed the call to Ryan. He picked up on the first ring. "Hey."

"Hi," she said. "I noticed you called. Sorry I didn't hear my phone ring at the time."

"No problem," he said, but she detected some tension in his voice.

"Ryan, what's wrong?"

He let out a breath. "Probably nothing. Have you talked to my mother?"

"Your mother? Well, no. Not since she picked Grace up earlier tonight."

"Hmmm. So, she picked Grace up on time?"

"Yes."

"Okay." The pause caused a crackle of tension over the phone line. "I'm sure it's nothing. But I've been trying to call my mom since I got home from work and she's not picking up."

Dread gripped Carly's heart, and she purposely downplayed the unwanted emotion. "Is your mom good about keeping her cell phone nearby? My mom throws hers in her purse and doesn't even hear it unless she happens to be carrying it."

He didn't laugh. "We tease my mom about having a third appendage – she's never far from the thing."

"And you're sure she has Grace with her."

"I'm honestly not sure of anything right now."

"What can I do to help?"

He paused. "I don't want to worry you and I don't want to interrupt your free night. I'm sure it's nothing. They're probably at the mall or something and my mom accidently left the phone in the car."

But even as he said it, Carly knew he didn't believe it. He was just saying it to make her, and himself, feel better.

"I'm sorry I bothered you, Carly. Go have a good night and I'll call you when I get in touch with her."

She didn't want to hang up and break the precious tie they had formed over their mutual worry of their daughter. She gripped the phone and didn't speak until the pause had drawn out. There was nothing more to say, really. "Okay. Please call me, no matter what time."

"You bet."

She dropped the phone back into her purse and turned unsteadily to Haley.

"What is it? My gosh, you look drained."

"Ryan's mom has Grace, but he can't get a hold of her."

Haley shrugged. "So, is that bad?"

"No, not necessarily. Just unusual. I guess we're both a little worried. We'll feel better when she answers her phone."

The Uber driver arrived, and Haley and Carly got in. "Rocky's Bar and Grill on 21st Avenue." They settled in for the ride. Carly leaned her head back against the seat and closed her eyes. She couldn't shake the feeling of worry over Grace's well-being. Where was she? Was it just a simple case of Mrs. Melrose not answering her phone? Or was there something wrong?

She slipped into a silent prayer, "*Dear Lord, please keep my little girl safe. I can't be there to watch over her and Ryan and I have this strange feeling that something is wrong. Please keep her safe and watch over her for us.*"

She kept her eyes closed while her thoughts went on a continuous loop to God. She felt Haley's hand on hers and she put a second hand over Haley's and squeezed.

Soon the car came to almost a complete halt, moving forward in spurts and stops. Carly peered out the windshield and saw red brake lights on a long line of cars in front of them. She looked over at Haley and rolled her eyes.

"Friday night beach traffic, gotta love it," Haley said with a chuckle. Carly tried to smile but she couldn't adopt the carefree attitude Haley was projecting. The evening had taken a turn for the worse. Gone were the carefree moments of Happy Hour and chatting with peers, without a care in the world. The truth was, she was a mother. She had responsibilities. And even when someone had given her a break from them, she still cared.

She turned to Haley. "Would you hate me if I changed plans for the evening?"

"Of course not! What do you want to do?"

"I want to find my baby."

"Okay! Where do we want to look?"

"I think my first step is to hook up with Ryan. We can join forces and figure it out together."

"You got it. Where's Ryan?"

"He's at home. Let me ..." She didn't have his parents' home address memorized, but she had made a note of it in her phone. She pulled up the note and tapped the driver on the shoulder. "Excuse me, change of plans. Can you take us here instead?" She read him the home address.

He nodded and tapped the new address into his GPS system. "Sure. There's a two-lane back road up here in about a mile where we can get off this highway. Only thing is, it gets real dark at night because there are no street lights. But it'll cut over and get us there."

"Thank you."

The moments dragged on, torturing Carly. Inside, she was pounding the back of the driver's seat with her fists. She was driving herself crazy. Instead, she repeated a prayer in her head, *"Lord, keep her safe. Let us find her. Let her be fine."*

The sound of the driver putting on his turn signal brought her out of her reverie. He maneuvered the car into a left turn lane. Finally, they were getting somewhere. It still took several moments to complete the turn but soon, they had left the world of stop and go traffic and brake lights and entered a quiet road covered with peaceful darkness. The driver increased his speed. "Okay," he said. "If the road stays like this, we'll be at your destination in fifteen minutes."

A few minutes later, the driver slowed. "Whoa," he said under his breath. Haley, sitting on the passenger side of the car, let out a low whistle. A red sedan had partially left the road, its hood down in the ditch and its rear end still on a portion of the road.

"I'm going to call 9-1-1 and let the police know this car is obstructing the road. This could cause future accidents."

"Yes, please do," Haley said. They came to a stop behind the wrecked vehicle. Haley turned to Carly, "Someone had a bad night."

But Carly was focused on the vehicle – a red Lexus sedan. In the back window was an adhesive bumper sticker that looked familiar. Dreadfully familiar. "I'm gonna get out," she murmured, and opened her door. She approached the back of the car and saw the light blue logo of a N and a C on top of each other. The logo of the University of North Carolina Tarheels.

Ryan's old school.

Her heart jumped into overdrive, pumping furiously as she ran around to the front of the car. She ignored shouts from Haley to be careful and to stay out of the road. The sight that met her was bone-chilling. A deer, embedded in the broken front windshield of the car, its front legs dangling into the car through the shattered glass, its torso and back legs on the outside of the car. Blood covered the shards of the windshield and spattered across the exterior.

"Oh, dear Lord," she said out loud. "Please take the soul of this deer and let me help these people inside this car."

She turned and dashed to the driver's side of the car. The driver was a woman, slumped over the steering wheel, her hair pushed forward and covering her face. And that's when it became clear to Carly. This wasn't just any red Lexus with a Tarheels bumper sticker. This wasn't just any woman driving.

This was Ryan's mother.

She let out a scream, a piercing, painful scream and heard a "What is it?" from Haley before she reached for the backdoor handle and attempted to fling it open. "My baby!" she heard herself wail, and those same words came running out in an endless stream that she couldn't stop.

But she couldn't get to her. She could barely even see her through the dark window, but the door was locked so she couldn't get in there to grab her sweet child and pull her to safety. Was it too late? Would God have brought her here to this spot at this precise time, only to find that her precious daughter had died in a terrible car accident?

She found Haley at her side. She continued to tug at the locked car door and she pointed into the back seat, wailing wordless screams, a stream of nonsense because her brain wasn't working. Instinct had taken over. The maternal need to protect and save the one little life that meant more than any other life in this world.

"We'll get her, we'll get her, we'll get her out," Haley started her own endless stream of words. At least they made sense, and they were exactly what Carly needed to hear. Carly felt like sinking to her knees, no longer having the strength to stand, but she couldn't lose sight of the glimpse of Grace she'd gotten while standing next to the dark window and looking in.

She wasn't moving. She was snapped into her car seat, but there was no movement whatsoever.

"Come on!" Haley's shouted words snapped Carly out of her daze. "Help me!" She looked up and saw that Haley had moved over to the front passenger side and was attempting to move the deer, so she could reach in the broken windshield and unlock the car doors. It was crazy, it was insane, the deer was too heavy for her to move, but she was the only clear-headed one and it was a plan.

Carly raced over to where Haley was, and soon the Uber driver was there too. "They're on their way with a tow truck and an ambulance." He frowned at the frantic actions of the two of them, and Haley yelled an explanation, "That's her daughter in there!"

"Oh, my Lord," said the Uber driver and he hesitated not a moment longer. "Here, let me help." He took hold of the deer's back legs and began pulling, and Carly and Haley grabbed wherever they could and helped move the heavy animal off the car. It took several moments and they all got completely covered with the animal's blood but with a final hoist, the animal dropped to the ground beside the car. Carly jumped onto the hood, reached in through the broken windshield, pushed back the expelled air bags with both arms and unlocked the passenger side door. Sliding off the hood, she opened the door and climbed in, and scrambled into the backseat. "Baby, Grace, it's Mommy, I'm here, how are you sweetheart ...," an endless stream of words, words that helped herself as well as, hopefully, her daughter.

She unfastened Grace from the car seat and saw with elated thanksgiving that the seat had done its job. It had protected Grace and kept her secured inside during the accident.

But the little girl wasn't moving. She hadn't seen that her mommy had come to rescue her. She wasn't seeing or responding to anything. Her eyes were closed, and although there wasn't a drop of blood on her, Carly had no idea if Grace was alive or dead. She lifted her precious daughter from the car seat and cradled her in her lap, rubbing her hair, caressing her cheek, whispering in her ear, "You're going to be okay, you're going to be fine," and just hoped beyond hope that it would be true.

Carly heard sirens, and soon saw flashing red lights through the backseat window. First responders took control of opening the drivers' side door and removing Mrs. Melrose from her seat. Another one helped her and Grace out of the back seat and into the ambulance. Everything was fine now. The professionals were here, and they would take care of everything. The only question in her mind now was Grace. Would she be okay? Or would this be the worst night of her life?

Instead of letting her mind wander, she focused instead on prayer. God would not let her precious daughter lose her life before her third birthday. Not like this – not now. She needed to trust and have faith that everything would be okay.

If only Grace would just open her eyes and say hello.

She clutched the toddler in the back of the ambulance. Haley appeared and looked in. "I'll meet you at the hospital, okay, sweetie?"

Carly's mind was racing but she pinpointed on one thing and yelled, "Get my phone and call Ryan, Haley. Tell him to meet us at the hospital."

Haley gestured an "Okay" with her thumb and forefingers and the ambulance door slammed shut.

Chapter Thirteen

Ryan stared at the television, which was on, but although the volume was up, he wasn't hearing it. His phone sat beside him on the arm of the chair he occupied and when it rang, he answered it immediately, "Carly."

"No, it's Haley. I'm on Carly's phone."

"Oh ..."

"Ryan, there's been a car accident."

"Oh, God."

"Your mother and Grace were taken in an ambulance to Tidelands Hospital. Carly wants you to meet them there."

Ryan wasn't sure if he even said good-bye before he disconnected the call and ran for his car.

ABOUT TWO MINUTES INTO the ambulance ride, Carly's prayers were answered as she stared fixedly at her daughter's face. The sweet angel stirred, then opened her eyes. They flickered around their surroundings before focusing on Carly's face. Then she said, "Mommy."

"Yes, sweetheart! You're okay. You're going to be fine."

An Emergency Medical Technician came over and shone a flashlight into Grace's eyes, took her temperature and blood pressure, and did a quick examination of her joints. "She looks pretty good," he said to Carly, "but the ER doctor will want to have a look at her."

"How's my ..." Carly paused. She was about to say 'mother-in-law' but boy, what a faux pas that would be. Where on earth had that come from?

"The driver?" the EMT asked.

"Yes."

"She's still unconscious. She hit her head pretty hard, whether on the steering wheel or the airbag, not sure which. She's got some abrasions and a laceration on her arm. But don't worry. She should have a full recovery. These two were lucky." He scooted to a bench on the other side of the truck and started writing in his folder.

Carly pulled Grace closer and hugged her gently. Lucky? Could've been luck. But she preferred to believe it was something else that had protected them in their accident. Or, someone else. She said her silent thanks to God.

RYAN PARKED HIS CAR and raced into the Emergency Room. He went straight to the receptionist and asked, "Has Barbara or Grace Melrose come in? They were in an ambulance from a car accident."

The receptionist shook her head. "Not yet, but they're on their way. You can wait right here."

Only a few minutes passed before the ambulance pulled up. As they unloaded its patients, Ryan ran outside and was relieved to see Carly holding Grace tightly in her arms. He pulled them both into an embrace, thankfulness flooding through him. Carly clung to him with the arm that wasn't holding Grace. He pulled back long enough to ask, "How is she?" When Carly responded, "She's just fine. She might have a slight concussion but other than that, she's perfectly fine."

"Oh, thank God," he murmured and pulled his two women back to him. If he'd ever needed a concrete reminder that being in the lives of these two special ladies, every day, day in and day out, was the right thing for his life, this was it. He didn't know what he would do if he didn't have them. His life would have no meaning, no purpose. And to have had them and lost them. He couldn't think of anything worse.

He looked down and noticed something sticky and red on Carly's clothes, and now, due to the hug, it was also on his. "What is this? Are you okay? Is this blood?"

Carly nodded. "Oh, yes, it's blood, but it's not mine."

"My mother's ...?"

"No, she ran into a deer. Or more likely, the deer ran into her. That's what's caused the accident. It was on a dark, thin, windy road, and judging from how the deer had crashed into the windshield, I imagine he jumped out of the woods and onto the road and your mother couldn't do anything about it."

"But, why ...?" he gestured to her clothes covered with it.

"I couldn't get into the car to get to Grace, so Haley and I, and the Uber driver, in fact, pulled the deer off the car."

"Wow. I wish I could've helped."

A stretcher holding his mother rolled by and Ryan left to catch up to it. "Mom?" She didn't answer but he stayed even with the stretcher, reaching for her hand and holding it in his own as they moved. "Will she be all right? How bad are her injuries?"

"We'll find out when we get in there," the EMT said. "And you are?"

"Her son, Ryan Melrose. She had my daughter in the back seat."

"Ahh, the little girl. She was kept snug and safe by her car seat. I'm not too worried about her. Your mom doesn't appear to have severe injuries, but I'll feel a lot better when she's conscious."

He followed the stretcher through the reception area of the ER and into one of the cubicles in the back. He sat with her for a few minutes, and then it dawned on him that his father needed to know.

Everything had happened so quickly. He leaned over his mom's deceptively peaceful-looking face and whispered, "I'll be right back, Mom. I'm gonna call Dad."

He looked at the sign in the cubicle warning against making cell phone calls in the ER and walked back outside. Carly and Grace had moved on, so he assumed they had been taken to an ER cubicle too. He placed the call to his father and gave him the news. "Dad, they think she's going to be fine, but she's unconscious so that's their first order of business."

"Oh, son, I'm so sorry. I'll be right there. How's Grace?"

"Grace is good." He got the three words out before emotion escaped. He ended the call and took a moment to get himself under control. *Thank you, Lord*, he said silently. *Thank you, thank you.*

He went back into the ER and this time, found Grace's cubicle. "Hi, baby," he said when he went in, holding his hands out to grab hers.

"Hi Daddy," she said, her sweet voice clear.

"I'm so sorry you were in a car accident," he said. "You are going to be fine. How do you feel?"

"Good."

Carly said, "The EMT gave her a physical exam when she was in the ambulance and he feels good about her, but they want the ER doc to look at her too."

"Where's Grandma?"

"She's got her own cubicle and she's waiting for the doctor too."

"Grandma screamed."

Ryan looked at Carly. Grace harbored memories of the accident. He hoped they wouldn't traumatize her or cause issues down the road. "Grandma screamed because she saw the deer coming?"

Grace's forehead creased with thought and she nodded hesitantly.

"Did you see the deer, sweetie?" Ryan asked her.

Grace shook her head.

"That's why Grandma wrecked the car. A deer came from the side of the road and jumped into the window."

Grace's eyebrows furrowed as she tried to picture this unimaginable scene.

"Isn't that crazy?" Ryan said.

"That crazy deer."

"Yes. Grandma wasn't expecting it and she ran off the road. But guess what. The most important thing is that you are safe and sound."

"And Grandma will be safe and sound."

"Yes." As he said it, he hoped and prayed it was true.

Twenty minutes later, Grace was officially released from the hospital with no restrictions. The doctor recommended baby aspirin in case she complained of a headache, but he was convinced she had no concussion symptoms.

"Let's go find your mom," said Carly.

They went to her cubicle and Ryan was glad he had his two ladies with him for support. Carly held back. "It's crowded in there. Grace and I will wait out here."

Ryan nodded, pushed back the fabric divider and went in. His dad was there sitting beside Mom, who lay with her eyes closed. Ryan went to his father's side and gave him a hug. "She's gonna be fine, Dad. Have faith. Just you wait and see."

"You're right, Ryan. I am fine." His mother's voice had him pulling away from his father in shock.

"Mom!"

"She came out of her coma about ten minutes ago. Docs want to admit her for observation overnight, but they don't see any serious injuries."

Ryan rose and walked to her bed. "Thank God."

"How's Grace?" Her voice was hoarse, and tears formed in her eyes. He immediately answered to ease her worries.

"She's fine, Mom. Perfectly fine."

"I'm so sorry ...," she said and then sobbed.

"No, Mom, you have nothing to be sorry about. It was an accident. A deer jumped out of the woods and landed on your car. No one could've avoided that, especially in the dark."

His mom took a deep breath and pushed it out of her lungs. "Carly must be furious with me. I wouldn't blame her if she never let me drive Grace again."

"Nothing could be further from the truth." They all turned toward the cubicle door flap at the sound of Carly's voice. She had a beautiful, translucent smile as she walked into the small room, holding Grace. "It was an accident, and it could've happened to anyone. I just thank God that you and Grace are all right."

His mom held out her hand, and both Carly and Grace grabbed it. "You're so kind and generous to say that, Carly." And then his mom stopped speaking because her voice broke.

HALEY AND THE UBER driver sat in the lobby of the ER, coming to their feet in unison when Ryan, Carly and Grace walked in. In a flurry of questions and answers, they learned how everyone was doing.

Ryan shook hands with the Uber driver. "I can't thank you enough, man."

He shook his head. "I didn't do anything."

Ryan gestured to his blood-stained shirt. "Yes, you did. You pulled a deer out of a car, so my little girl could get out of there. And," he checked his watch, "you've lost out on an hour's worth of fares, just so you could sit with Haley and find out how everything turned out. In fact," he said and pulled some bills out of his pocket, "take this. This was the OT I made tonight. That's the whole reason my mom was on that dark road at that hour in the first place, because I agreed to work OT. Next time, I won't be quite so anxious for the money. Take it, please. It'll help."

The driver hesitated.

"Heck, you might need that much to dry clean your shirt," Haley joked.

He laughed and went ahead and accepted the small stack of bills. "Thank you."

"What's your name, by the way?" Ryan asked him.

"Blake," Haley answered for him. They all turned their heads toward her and stared. She blushed, a faint pink covering her cheeks. "What? His name is Blake."

They all laughed, and Blake said, "Well, all's well that ends well. Glad it all worked out. I better get going. Can I drive you home, Haley?"

They all said their good-byes, and Ryan turned to Carly. "So, you don't have a car here, huh? How about I take you and Grace home?"

Carly was grinning, but not at him. She was looking over toward the door and he followed her gaze. Haley and Blake leaned close in conversation. He smiled, and she did too. He slipped a hand into hers and they headed together through the exit door.

"What on earth ...?" Ryan puzzled.

Carly put a gentle elbow in his ribs. "Looks like those two bonded over near tragedy."

"Oh."

They loaded into Ryan's car, Carly spending extra time and attention hooking Grace into her car seat. Thankfully, his little girl did not demonstrate any concern or fear getting back into a car after the scare she'd experienced.

"So," he said when they'd taken off, "fill in some gaps for me here. How did you know where to find my mom and Grace?"

"I had no idea. But we were stuck in bumper-to-bumper traffic on Ocean Highway and I knew we'd be sitting there for a while. I was feeling more and more nervous and I wanted to do what I could to locate them. So, I told the driver ... well, Blake now ... to go to your parents' house. I figured the two of us could put our heads together and find her better than being apart."

Ryan's heart rushed with emotion. Better together than apart. Yes, he thought so too. And he hoped she didn't just feel that way about finding their misplaced daughter, but about their relationship as well.

But he didn't interrupt her with his thoughts. She went on, "So Blake's GPS took us down some dark beach road that wasn't well lit. We came upon the accident. But I guess since I had told him to go to your parents' house, that's the shortcut your mom had taken too. Probably to avoid the same beach traffic."

He pulled into Carly's apartment parking lot and a desire overwhelmed his senses. He turned to Carly. "Would you pray with me?"

She watched his face for a moment, smiled gently and said, "Sure."

He reached for her hands and they held hands as he prayed. "Dear Lord, thank you for keeping Grace and my mother safe. Thank you for family. Thank you for being able to lean on each other when there are times of concern and worry. Thank you for Carly, for the great mother she is. And thank you for our daughter Grace, who we love very much. Amen."

He kept his eyes closed and held on to her hands for just a few more seconds while he added a silent addendum, "And please find a way for the three of us to live together as a family."

They walked up to Carly's apartment. Ryan and Carly watched Grace closely for signs of worry, but after an hour of playing with her toys on the living room floor, she started yawning. Carly took her to change into pajamas and brush her teeth, and then returned.

"Ready for a good night kiss and hug?" he asked her, his heart so full it might explode. He wouldn't have to miss this. So close.

"No, she has something else in mind," Carly said.

"Daddy, read me a story?" Grace said and of course, there was no way he could refuse. Both Grace's parents sat on the bed, one on each side, while she selected a book and then crawled into her sheets between the two of them. They'd never actually done this before— bedtime stories all together—and Ryan was determined to treasure each second. He read something silly about farmyard animals and he managed to come up with a different accent and voice tone for each of the characters, which delighted Grace to no end.

When he was done, Grace rolled onto her stomach and he rubbed her back while he sang a lullaby his mother used to sing to him, that he pulled out of the far reaches of his memory bank. Soon, her heavy, even breathing suggested that she was out.

He winked at Carly and they tiptoed out, Carly closing the door quietly behind them.

He knew he should leave Carly to the rest of her evening and get home, but he didn't want to. He had the strong sensation that he was right where he was supposed to be and leaving would be a mistake. On the other hand, Carly had broken up with him in no uncertain terms, and his presence in her living room after Grace had gone to bed, was not what she wanted.

He looked up from his thoughts when she approached him. She held a DVD in her hand. "Care to watch a movie together?"

"Sure." He hoped he didn't sound too anxious. On the other hand, he really didn't care if he did.

They watched a five-year-old comedy that they'd both probably seen ten times before. But Ryan didn't care. He was sitting with the woman he loved, and his precious daughter was sleeping just feet away, healthy and fine. It really didn't matter what they did. He was just thankful to be here.

Carly paused it once to make popcorn and Ryan took the moment to take a peek at Grace. Her breathing was even, her eyes were peacefully closed, and he breathed a word of thanks for the happy outcome.

"How is she?" Carly asked when he returned.

"Perfect."

They watched the rest of the movie and it was late when it was over. Carly stood to take the popcorn bowls to the kitchen and then lingered. "Well, thanks for everything, Ryan."

He shook his head and got to his feet. "You don't have anything to thank me for, Carly."

"You were here for me and helped me get through this."

"You were the Superwoman. Figuring out where they were, dragging a dead deer off the car! Golly!" They laughed together. How he yearned to lean in and kiss her, pull her into an embrace and enjoy every bit of her. But of course, he couldn't. He wouldn't put whatever future they had in jeopardy by doing that. "The doc suggested we check her out after four hours of sleeping to make sure we could arouse her. That would convince them she had no concussion symptoms."

"Oh, that's right. I'll have to set my alarm for four am."

An idea gripped him, and he didn't want to let it go. "No, how about this? You sleep. I'll stay here on the couch and get up at four to check on her."

He watched an expression flicker over her face. First, she looked like she liked the idea, before she clamped it down. "I couldn't ask you to do that."

He shrugged. "You're not asking. I'm offering. I want you to get a good night's sleep. And I want to help Grace if she has any trouble through the night. So what better solution than for me to stay here and help you?"

She hesitated, but the fact that she was staring at his face seemed to indicate she was considering his offer. "You wouldn't be comfortable on that couch. It's not even as long as you are."

He laughed. In his mind he squelched the question he wanted to ask, "I'd be more comfortable in bed with you." Instead, he said, "I've often spent the night on a couch and slept just fine. What do you say Carly? Can I stay?"

She relented, and he gave a fist pump like he'd just made the winning three-pointer at the buzzer. She laughed and headed down the hall, returning with sheets, a blanket and a pillow.

Chapter Fourteen

Carly awoke, a quiet peace covering her as she opened her eyes. Blurry-minded for a moment, she turned her head and saw that the digital clock was displaying, almost like a shout, 8:45!

Eight forty-five? She hadn't slept this late in years! What was wrong with her?

She struggled to get her legs out of the sheets and got to her feet, stumbling to the bedroom door. First, she ran to Grace's room, and seeing it was empty, she realized she heard voices. One sweet little girl voice. One deep man's voice.

Of course. Ryan had spent the night and had taken care of Grace's needs, throughout the night and in the morning. And she ... was able to sleep like she hadn't a care in the world.

She felt like kissing him. If only she hadn't ended their relationship.

She made her way to the living room and he immediately lifted his head at her approach. His eyes went wide at the sight of her, rested on her for a moment, then he dipped his head. "Good morning," he said with a forced joviality. Realization dawned within her. She must look horrid to have invoked that reaction. She could only imagine. Bedhead hair, streaked face, wrinkled pajamas. Not to mention her morning breath. She'd never had to worry about these things before. She'd never lived with anyone but Grace, and Grace certainly didn't care.

Speaking of Grace, she got to her feet and ran over, throwing her little arms around Carly. "Hi sweetheart, how are you feeling this morning?"

"Good!" She went back to whatever she and Ryan were doing. On closer look, it appeared to be a big jigsaw puzzle laid out on the coffee table.

Ryan spoke to her while he concentrated on the puzzle. "I got up at four, but she had no issues at all. Then she wanted to get up at six. I hope we didn't disturb you. Did you get a good night's sleep?" He looked up at her again and smiled into her eyes. She noticed he pointedly ignored looking anywhere but her eyes.

"Yes, I did. In fact, I can't believe I slept this late. I haven't slept this long since before Grace was born."

"Ahhh, good. I'm happy to help."

"Well, the least I can do is make breakfast for the two of you." She started for the kitchen, wondering what she had in stock as far as breakfast food items went.

"We ate," Ryan said abruptly, and his head went back to the puzzle.

"Oh, right." She sighed and ran a hand through her messy hair. "Well, how about if I take a shower. You all right here?"

"Yes. Yes, good."

HE SENSED, RATHER THAN saw her walk out of the room, but as soon as she did Ryan breathed a deep sigh. Carly, in her normal state of dress and makeup and hair styling, was a beautiful, desirable girl. One that Ryan had always been extremely attracted to. But Carly, first thing in the morning, with her hair tousled from bed, and her complexion pink and creamy from the warmth and ... God forgive him ... her body accentuated by those skimpy pajamas she had on? Her mere presence in the apartment, looking how she had, made it impossible to control his feelings for her. The woman was gorgeous. No doubt about it.

The woman also was not his. But one thing was certain. They weren't done. Not by a long shot. Not if he had anything to say about it.

And he wasn't going to give up without another try.

CARLY GOT OUT OF THE shower and listened briefly. No cries, no shouts. Everything seemed to be under control. She took her time to powder, lotion, and take care of her hair and makeup. She got dressed and returned to the living room where Ryan and Grace now sat on the couch, her on his lap, watching cartoons.

The minute she arrived, he glanced up and she thought she detected a look of relief. At least he wasn't acting strangely like he had earlier. He was her normal Ryan, calm, happy, friendly.

She caught herself. Not *her* Ryan. Not anymore.

But it sure was nice having him around. Maybe if they tried, they could work out an arrangement where he could be around for her and Grace, while not committing to a personal relationship.

Was that even possible? And if so, was it fair to the two of them?

"Well," Ryan said now, "I better get going. I'm going to check in with my dad and see how my mom's doing, and what their plans are for releasing her."

"Oh, right. Keep me posted. And Ryan, thank you for all your help last night and this morning."

He walked by her on his way to the door, but paused, put his hand on her jaw and leaned in to inhale. Then, he let go and kept moving, almost to the point where she wondered if it had happened at all.

RYAN DROVE STRAIGHT to the mall, and once inside, strode to the jewelry store. His plan wasn't even fully concocted in his head, but he knew a ring would be a part of it. He could figure out the rest later.

He looked through the glass cabinets at the rows of petite gold bands and diamond solitaires. He couldn't see the price tags, and that was okay. He'd rather concentrate on picking the perfect ring for Carly's finger, and then figure out how to pay for it later. The saleswoman let him do his own review, and when he'd narrowed it down to just two rings, she came over, smiling at him. "Good morning."

"Good morning."

"Looks like you have a special occasion coming up."

He stared at the rings until his eyes swam. "I sure hope so."

The lady laughed. "Can I pull anything out of the case for you?"

"Yes." He pointed out his two favorites and she took them out for him. Even though they were tiny, the diamonds were beautiful, at least they appeared so to his untrained eye. "Tell me about these diamonds."

The lady talked for a while about cut and clarity and caret and color. She assured him that they were good quality rings. He couldn't go wrong picking either one. He made his selection and cleared his throat. When she told him the price, he let the sting of the number make its way through his bloodstream and then he said, "I'll need some payment options."

She understood and pulled out a flyer, giving him some assurance that he wasn't the only one who was poorly prepared to buy a diamond ring. "We'll set up a payment plan with the monthly amount that you're comfortable with, and when you have paid 50% of the purchase price, you can take the ring along with you."

He calculated in his mind what he could afford from his lawncare job, and she did the math. He wouldn't have the ring in his hand for another four months. Well, it would have to do.

RYAN DROVE HOME AND was happy to see that his mom had returned. She had a stack full of prescription meds to take, and a schedule of rest she needed to adhere to, but for the most part, she was healthy. That didn't stop Ryan and his dad from taking turns sitting with her, running to the kitchen whenever she wanted a drink or a meal, and helping her however she needed.

During the quiet moments when she was either resting or watching TV, Ryan pondered on his dilemma. The accident had driven home a lesson that he believed in fully. Life was too short not to live it to its fullest. If you wanted something in your life, you needed to grab it by the horns and do everything you could to make it happen.

He loved Carly. She was the woman for him, there was no doubt in his mind. He wanted to propose to her and he wanted them to be committed as a family.

He needed that engagement ring to let her know how sure he was. But he couldn't wait four months. He needed it now. How would he get the money he needed?

NORA SWIPED A LAST brush of powder over her cheeks and checked herself in the mirror. The fall sunshine had colored her complexion and she was tanner than she'd ever been this time of year in Philadelphia. Being outside in the pasture or on the beach, instead of stuck in a law office had had a healthy effect on her.

She went to her closet and slipped into a casual dress, a red sleeveless sheath that skimmed above her knee and fit her form snugly but comfortably. She slipped her feet into leather sandals. She ran a brush through her hair, its waves falling to her shoulders.

Shaw was taking her out tonight to celebrate their launch as an equine therapy center. She knew he'd plan something fun. He always did. And she absolutely loved that he took the responsibility of planning their evenings out without expecting her to come up with ideas. He'd lived here his whole life and wanted her to experience his favorite things. It made her feel warm and loved.

She paused to close her eyes and let her mind drift toward gratitude. It eventually resulted in a silent prayer to God: *Thank you for leading Shaw back into my life. Thank you for forgiveness and second chances. Thank you for love. Please watch over the two of us and guide us along our way. Amen.*

Downstairs, she heard the door open. Shaw was here. She wrapped up and went down the stairs. As she descended, he came to the bottom of the steps, his head lifted to watch her. He wore an expression of appreciation, his eyes unwavering. He reached out a hand as she approached, and she took it. "Don't you look gorgeous," he said and pulled her close and kissed her. As they joined lips she realized that God was answering her prayer. This was love, undoubtedly. This was her chance, and she was not going to give it up.

"So do you," she managed when he let her go. She took a moment to admire him in his khaki pants, cowboy boots and golf shirt. "You look great."

They made their way out to Shaw's truck. On the way there, he said, "I've heard a lot about this place and I'd been wanting to give it a try. Do you like theater, by the way?"

She glanced over at him with a grin. "I do. Do you?"

He laughed. "Well, I have to say it's not usually in my Top Five favorite things to do, but this place combines food and theater. And anyplace that feeds me well gets a thumbs-up in my book."

They drove south on Route 17 to Pawleys Island, crossed over the causeway to the island itself, and drove along on the quaint beach road till they reached a sandy parking lot. They parked, he helped her out, then they walked across the street to a big wooden house. Nora saw the sign, "Seaside Inn."

"It's an inn that offers three meals a day to its guests. It's been written up in cuisine magazines for having delicious food. On weekends they also offer a theater experience."

"Dinner theater?"

"Yep. Their first production was *Music Man* and they featured actors from New York City. They've moved on to other shows since then. Tonight is *Mamma Mia*."

"I love that show! And the music!" A bubble of excitement filled her chest.

They climbed the front steps and entered. The door opened into a homey great room filled with couches, bookshelves and beachy décor over a hardy wooden floor. To the left was a line of people forming. Shaw led them there. After a brief wait, they reached the doorway to the dining room. It was a good size, filled with tables and people, with a stage set against one wall.

"Welcome!" said a friendly looking woman. "Tickets please?"

Shaw pulled out his wallet and handed her two tickets.

"Thank you," said the woman. "Oh, you have great seats. The table is center to the stage, so you'll have a good view. I've placed two other couples at your table. Our dinner tonight is prime rib, baked potato and roasted vegetables, and our dessert is cheesecake with strawberries. Every bite is homemade in our kitchen. My name's Marianne Muller, by the way. I own this place with my husband, Tom."

Nora liked her instantly. The woman bubbled over with cheerfulness and positivity. A true picture of a person who loved her life and was exactly where she was meant to be.

"Oh, here he is now. Tom! Come here."

A solid man walked over and ran his hand behind her, pulling her close.

"Tom, I want you to meet our guests, the, uh, Flynns." She glanced down at the reservation name in her book. "This is my husband Tom."

Nora looked over at Shaw, eyes challenging. He just laughed and shook Tom's hand. "We're looking forward to a great night. In fact, we're celebrating."

"Oh?" Tom said. "What's the occasion? Thanks for picking our place to celebrate, by the way."

"Nora here," he gestured with his hand, but she noticed he didn't correct them and say she wasn't his wife, "owns the Waccamaw Trails facility for horses in Murrells Inlet. Recently we partnered on offering equine therapy services."

"Really!" Marianne said.

"Yes. We're thrilled to offer this to our community. All kinds of people can benefit from riding horses. Kids with physical disabilities, veterans with Post Traumatic Stress Disorder, lots of others. I'm Shaw Flynn, by the way. I'm a veterinarian."

"What a perfect fit. Do you have a card for the equine therapy? I'd be happy to offer them to our guests."

Nora was about to tell her they'd only just started, and before this week, had no idea if they even had a horse strong enough to offer the service, but Shaw pulled a short stack of business cards from his breast pocket and presented them to her. "I'd much appreciate that."

"Hey, we always help our neighbors. So glad to know you, Nora and Shaw."

Nora looked behind her and noticed the line of dinner theater guests getting longer. "Well, we don't want to hold you up."

"No problem. Our daughter Stella will see you to your seat." She raised a hand and an adorable little girl, maybe nine years old appeared. Marianne handed Stella their tickets and the little girl gave them a polite smile. "This way, please."

They followed her to their table and when they'd sat down she gave them a little bow and said, "Your waitress will be right over with your water."

"Thank you, Stella."

The evening was an absolute delight. Their table partners were a newly engaged couple, along with her mom and dad. They conversed a short time and then their meals came, the aroma of the beef circling and tickling Nora's nose. They had just finished dinner when the lights dimmed, and the music started, and soon they were swept away in the story of a young bride in a quaint Greek island inn, trying to solve a mystery of her paternity before her wedding.

At intermission, their cheesecake came, along with coffee, and then the lights dimmed again for the final act. Nora knew the songs so well she fought her inclination to sing along, but at the very end, the actors encouraged everyone to stand up and sing a few of the well-known songs with them. It was a raucous ending to the evening.

They tumbled out of the inn, thanking Marianne and Tom, who stood at the door, for the fun evening, and promising they'd come back again.

The drive home was quiet, and Nora glanced over at Shaw, his brow firm like he had something on his mind. "Did you enjoy the play?"

"Yes, I sure did."

"And the dinner was out of this world."

"Yes. I agree with all the reviews. That chef is fantastic."

They continued to drive and where he should've turned to take the causeway back to the mainland, he stayed straight. She glanced over at him, but he was concentrating on the thin dark road. Finally, he drove to the very end of the island, to a parking lot of a public access beach. He parked and turned to her. "Could I interest you in a walk on the beach?"

"Of course."

They got out and left their shoes in the truck. Shaw rolled up the legs of his pants to his knees. They joined hands and made their way down a wooden walkway to the beach. The sand was cool, and the waves were more heard than seen in the darkness. They walked along slowly.

"Something on your mind?" Nora asked.

Shaw stopped, took both her hands in his, and faced her. "Yes, there is. It's you."

"Me?"

"Yes, you are on my mind. Always, Nora. Even when I'm doing something else, you're always there, on the fringes."

Nora's heart started to beat faster. She moved closer to him, trying to see his eyes in the moonlight.

"Nora, I love being with you. I look forward to partnering on more projects together. I want to build a life together. I can't imagine life without you. But I have to know. What are you thinking? About me?"

A smile burst onto her face. His words made her happy, of course they did. They were exactly what she wanted to hear. But his question reminded her that she'd never really told him. In her cautiousness at approaching their "re-do," she thought it was going well, but she'd never told him. He had a right to know.

"I love you, Shaw."

His eyes went wide, his mouth dropped open and he went motionless for a moment. He was absorbing her simple words and processing them. So, she helped him out by saying them again.

"I love you. I think God has led us together and I don't want to mess this up. I want to be with you, I want to work with you, I want to have fun with you. I want to love you."

He freed her hands and cupped her cheeks, leading her mouth to his. His lips were warm on hers, and the kiss became deeper and deeper still, causing a heat to spread down her core and fill her entire body. When he pulled back, she was shaking.

"I love you too."

She laughed because in true Shaw fashion, he didn't want to leave her hanging; he wanted to assure her he felt the same way, but his actions had already told her that. He was a good man, a loving man, a man of God, and he'd been led to her by God himself.

How did she ever get so lucky?

"I'm the luckiest man in the world," he went on. "I've finally found the love of my life."

She grinned. It had been a long haul for them both to get to this moment. She had long ago given up on having love in her life. And she was sure he had too. But good things were worth waiting for.

"What comes next?"

"Well ... I imagine ... a ring? A proposal? A wedding?" He was grinning so wide she could see his white teeth in the darkness. And she couldn't mistake the delight in his voice.

"Yes. That all sounds great." In time, she almost cautioned. There was no rush. They had all the time in the world.

Then, no. She wouldn't overthink this. She wouldn't analyze and plan and overdo. She'd simply let this happen the way it was supposed to.

She leaned in close to him and found his mouth again. She kissed him, letting her hands stroke his hair, his short locks tumbling through her fingers. She loved this man, and it was all going to happen, in good time.

She shivered, and he noticed. "You're chilly. Let's go back to the truck."

They walked, their feet buried in sand with each step. She climbed into the truck and he helped her with the seatbelt, then kissed her again before he closed the door firmly.

The rest of her life was just ahead of her, and she couldn't help thinking, what a great second act.

Chapter Fifteen

Monday started a new workweek and Carly delivered Grace to pre-school as usual. She alerted Grace's teacher to the events over the weekend, so she could watch out for unusual signs or symptoms.

Carly waved at Haley on her way past the front desk but a breeze-by was not going to be enough for her friend. She gestured Carly over with a loud hiss.

"So, what happened with you and the gorgeous one?"

Carly laughed. Haley had all kinds of nicknames for Ryan and never hesitated to let Carly know how much she approved of him and wanted the two of them to end up together. Carly grinned, thinking of a way she could truly start Haley's work week out with a bang. She gave her friend a sly grin. "He spent the night."

As expected, Haley gave a hoot, causing several of their co-workers to stare. Carly shushed her, and Haley said, "I knew it! I knew it! He's crazy about you, girl. I knew you would get back together."

Carly chuckled. "Don't get crazy. I said he spent the night. I didn't say we spent the night together. He slept on the couch and let me sleep while he got up every few hours to observe Grace."

"Oh." Poor Haley sounded disappointed but she recovered. "Now, if that doesn't show you how devoted he is to you and your daughter, what does?"

Carly nodded. "I know. He's so sweet. And he really does seem devoted to Grace."

"And to you."

Thoughts of Ryan filled her mind. "I have to admit, I do think he wants to be with me. Not just because I'm Grace's mother. But because he has feelings for me."

"Yahoo! So what are you waiting for? That man is fine, he loves you, and you love him. Go get this thing kickstarted."

"But his mom ...," Carly began.

"Nope, huh uh. You can't use his mom as an excuse. She's not a reason to keep the two of you apart. Ryan's a grown man and he can make his own decisions. It's almost a cliché that a woman doesn't approve of her son's choice because she's never good enough for her baby. Put that out of your mind."

Carly nodded thoughtfully. Maybe Haley was right. Maybe after all they'd been through together, Ryan and she and Grace could be a family, together, in love. She'd definitely need to think about it some more.

Changing the subject, she said, "So, you and Blake, huh?"

Haley blushed and ducked her head with a smile. "Me and Blake. He's a cutie, isn't he?"

"What happened after you left the hospital?"

"He took me home and I invited him in for hot tea."

"Hot tea." Carly smirked and waited to see if Haley would come clean with more details.

"Yeah, it was soothing after all the craziness of that night."

Carly patted her arm. "Are you going to see him again?"

She beamed. "Friday night. He plays in a band and he invited me to come and watch."

"I'm so happy for you." Carly gave a wave and went to her desk.

MID-WEEK, RYAN NOTICED his mom was up and about more than usual, and probably more than the doctor wanted her to be. But she was always like that. She never was down for long.

"What do you want for dinner?" she asked when he'd returned from his day of school and work.

"Something easy, Mom. A sandwich?" he said over his shoulder as he walked down the hallway to his room.

"How about spaghetti and meatballs?" His mother's voice came from the kitchen.

"Don't go to any trouble."

He heard muttering. Although he couldn't make out words, he was sure his mother was making it clear that she was done sitting around like an invalid, and she needed to do something productive. He supposed boiling some noodles and warming up a jar of spaghetti sauce was productive without being exhausting.

He washed his hands and face and went back out to the kitchen. "Is there a Delta Tau Delta chapter at Myrtle Beach College?" his mother asked.

He paused before answering. He didn't want to stumble into the ever-present landmine of his mother's disapproval of his college choice, not tonight. Not when she was doing so well with her recovery, and their quiet days of rehab had provided them with more friendly conversations than he'd ever had with her. "Nope. No fraternities at MBC."

She lifted her eyebrows, then shrugged. "Letter for you on the table."

He found it and saw that indeed, it was from his old fraternity at Chapel Hill. He opened it, unfolded the paper, and a smaller piece of paper slipped out and landed on the table. His gaze followed the escaped paper and he picked it up. He blinked.

It was a check.

His stunned gaze focused on the amount, while his brain tried to process. It was a large check. Enough to pick up Carly's ring.

He looked over at the letter that accompanied it. It was a refund from the fraternity for fees paid. Since he'd dropped out of Chapel

Hill this semester, he was finished with the fraternity, and he no longer owed the fees.

This money was rightfully his. The answer to his prayer.

He went from motionless to running in seconds. He grabbed the check and raced for the door. "Mom! I have to go do something. Don't count on me for dinner!" He left before he could hear her protests.

He drove through the lane at the bank and cashed the check, then drove straight to the jewelry store. He dashed inside and scanned the faces of the employees until he saw the one who had helped him pick out Carly's ring. He covered the distance and stood in front of her. "Excuse me."

She looked up. "Yes?"

"I'd like to pick up the ring I picked out. I have the money."

She chuckled, took his name, and went to the back. She returned, carrying a black velvet box. She opened it so he could admire it. "I polished it for you. She's going to love it."

He hoped so. But he wouldn't know until he presented it to her and discovered if he could convince her that he loved her, he loved their family and he wanted to spend the rest of his days with her.

"We never spoke about the size. Do you know her ring size?"

"No idea."

"It's okay. If it doesn't fit, just bring her in and we'll size it."

He handed over the envelope of cash he'd just received from the bank. She finished the transaction and handed him the ring box and the receipt. "Congratulations."

He thanked her. He headed for the door, and then changed his mind. He turned. "Could you help me with one other thing?"

CARLY HAD FINALLY COME to a decision. Breaking up with Ryan had been wrong. They deserved to be a couple, to see if they had what it took to be together. She needed to see if he was still even interested in being with her after how she'd torn them apart. Would he forgive her for her bad judgment? Or had he moved on?

Gathering up her courage, she picked up her phone and called him. "Hi Ryan. I was wondering if you were busy. Could you come over here?"

He hesitated a moment. "Yes."

"Great. I wanted to talk to you."

He chuckled, but she had no idea why. "Okay, see you when you get here," she said. She put the phone down. She could use the time to figure out what she was going to say. She didn't want to blow it. This may be her only chance to get Ryan back. What she wasn't expecting was a knock at the door less than a minute later. She opened it. It was Ryan.

"What are you doing here?"

His happy smile brightened the entire room. "You invited me over, didn't you?"

"Well yes, but ...."

He laughed and let her off the hook. "I was on my way. Great minds think alike, I guess."

She brushed it off and stood aside so he could come in. It was go time; now or never. Although she hadn't had time to prepare, he was here, and the time was now. "Ryan, I had something I wanted to tell you."

He went motionless and looked at her. Then he held up his hands. "No, stop. Before you do, I have something I want to tell you, too."

No, no, no. He may have been dropping by to tell her they were done, thinking that she still wanted that. But she couldn't let him make that decision without knowing about her change of heart. If she had the chance to tell him, and he still wanted to end it, then it was her own fault and she'd have to deal with her missed chance at love.

Grace must've heard him from her room because she came roaring out like a racecar, yelling, "Daddy!" She launched herself into his arms and he lifted her up into a loving hug. The sight tugged at Carly's heart and she had to control the rise of tears in her eyes. How could she have thought to give this up? How could she have decided it wasn't what she wanted? Of course, this was what she wanted. It had always been what she wanted.

Ryan settled into the couch with Grace and the little girl climbed into his lap and hugged him. Carly sat beside them and said, "Grace, calm down. Stop climbing all over Daddy. Here, sit on his lap quietly."

Ryan gave her a grateful glance. "It's okay. She's just excited."

"Yes, she sure is. She loves you so much, she is absolutely ecstatic every time she gets to see you."

Ryan's face went soft. "And I feel the same way about her."

Carly took a fortifying breath. "I know you do. But what I want to talk about now is the way you feel about me, and the way I feel about you."

His eyes widened but he nodded. "Okay."

"Ryan, you're the only man I've ever been completely in love with. Well, I should say, boy. Because when I fell in love with you, you were a boy and I was a girl. Now we're adults, and I learned how painful it was to be abandoned by the boy I loved with all my heart."

Pain crossed his countenace and he took her hand and examined her face. "I'm so sorry ..."

"No," Carly said emphatically. "That's not what this is about. We both know how you hurt me, but you've apologized for that, and you've made changes in your life to remedy it. You told me that you wanted to be Grace's dad, and you and she are getting along great. And that makes me happy." She paused to take a tissue from the end table and brush her eyes. "I want that. I want Grace to have you in her life. But until recently I wasn't sure how I felt about having you in *my* life."

"Carly, please, before you go any further, could I say something?"

She looked at him and he looked so sincere and so loving, but she had to get this out. She had to let him know. "I need to go on." He nodded. "I wanted the whole shebang. If you were back in my life, I wanted the love story. I wanted the happy ending. I didn't just want to be friends with my baby's daddy."

"You want the fairy tale," he said softly.

"Exactly," she whispered.

"Do you love me, Carly?" he asked, cutting to the chase.

There was so much more she wanted to tell him, needed to tell him. But he'd gotten right to the heart of it. He must've wanted the same thing. "Yes, Ryan. I love you." Her heart felt like it was exploding.

His smile was the answer she needed. This was good news. She hadn't waited too long. He'd waited for her and he still felt the same way.

He lifted Grace and placed her on Carly's lap. He slid off the couch, onto the floor, resting on one knee. "Carly and Grace. You two have made me see what being a man of integrity is all about." Carly gasped. His stance was making her nervous, making her excited, making her hopeful. But she needed to concentrate and listen to his words. "I've made my share of mistakes but you two are the absolute best things in my life. You both make me want to reach my potential as a father and as a husband."

"A husband?" Carly blurted.

"Yes. Carly, I loved you when I was seventeen, and I think I've loved you every day since. What I definitely know is that I'm madly in love with you now. The woman that you are: hardworking, ambitious, loving, caring. The mother you are, nurturing, loving and attentive. I don't want to spend another day without knowing that we are together."

She drew in a deep breath. "Oh, Ryan."

He pulled something out of his pocket and held it out to her on the palm of his hand. It was a velvet ring box. Of course. This man, who she loved with all her heart, who she'd lost faith in, who'd earned her love and trust back, who told her he loved her, and proved that he was ready. Of course, he would come to her with a velvet ring box on the very same day that she decided she loved him and wanted to give herself over to him fully.

He popped it open and she gazed upon a beautiful petite, simple diamond solitaire on a gold band. "Carly, will you marry me, and make me the happiest man in the world, and let me make you happy every day of your life? Will you join me in raising our beautiful daughter together, as a family? Just the three of us?"

The beautiful thing about this was that she'd already decided on the answer before he'd even asked her. "Yes!" He pulled the ring out of the box and slipped it on her finger.

"It fits," he marveled. But he wasn't done. He focused now on Grace. "Grace, my beautiful, sweet, precious daughter. I know it's been you and Mommy together for your whole life. I know she's been the best mommy in the world and is perfectly capable of taking care of you by herself. But I love you both, and I want to be your daddy, and Mommy's husband. Would you like me to marry your mommy and live with you both here, all three of us together?"

Carly laughed out of pure, heart-exploding happiness. It was a word-filled speech and Grace probably didn't follow all of it, but she certainly got the gist. She yelled, "Yes, Daddy!" Ryan's smile beamed as he pulled out another velvet box, this one oblong. He opened it and pulled out a tiny toddler's gold chain with a 3-diamond pendant. "This is for you, sweetheart. It demonstrates my commitment to our family. You see these shiny stones?" He pointed to each of them. "This one is me, this one is Mommy and this one is you. See? There's no way to separate the three stones. They will be together always."

He unclasped the chain and reached for her neck. Carly lifted Grace's hair and Ryan secured the necklace. Grace jumped to the floor and started to run to her room. Carly knew she wanted to look at her new necklace in her vanity mirror. But she stopped midway down the hall and came back with a question. "Can we add shiny stones to this necklace?"

Ryan's expression was confused. "Why would we add stones, sweetheart?"

"When I get a brother or sister," she explained, then raced out of the room. Carly and Ryan looked at each other in surprise, then burst out laughing.

"I guess she's okay with this," Ryan chuckled. Then he quieted and searched Carly's face, using a knuckle to caress her cheek. "I love you so much, Carly. You can't imagine how happy you've made me."

"I love you, too. That's what I wanted to tell you tonight. I was wrong to end it with you. I was scared. I didn't want to cause trouble between you and your parents."

He shook his head. "I love my parents, Carly. But my future is with you. If they can't accept that, then I'm okay with making my way in this world without them."

"You and me," she whispered.

He nodded. "You and me." He ran his fingers into her hair and came closer. "And now, I have been waiting for this moment for so long, I can't tell you." He placed his lips on hers and they shared the finest kiss she had ever experienced in her whole life.

Chapter Sixteen

Life with Carly as his fiancé was better than he could imagine. He didn't have to hide his feelings for her. He didn't have to continually feel guilty about his past mistakes. By accepting his proposal, she had wiped all that clean. The only thing left was their future. And it was looking pretty bright.

The weekend following their engagement, they were in Carly's kitchen, working together to make dinner. Carly was warming tortillas to wrap the taco mixture in, when she tossed them on the counter and said, "I want to go tell your parents."

He looked at her and wondered if she was crazy. Or maybe she was just the more mature one of the two. He'd wanted to break the news to his parents, but he figured the best way to do it was when he was alone with them. He didn't want their reaction to hurt Carly's feelings. He just hadn't worked up the nerve yet.

"Tonight?"

"Yes. I mean, we're engaged. They have a right to know."

He nodded. "Are you going to be okay with their reaction, whatever it might be?"

She grimaced. "Let's face it, we know what their reaction will be."

He shrugged. "Probably. But you never know, they may just surprise us."

They sat at the table for dinner, and when they were finished, and the kitchen was cleaned up, Carly said to Grace, "Sweetie, we're going to go visit Grandma and Grandpa Melrose."

Thirty minutes later, they arrived at the Melrose house, parked in the driveway and made a plan to keep it simple. Direct. Ryan would do the talking.

They entered the house where Ryan's parents sat in the family room, watching the TV news. When the three of them came into the room, his mom looked startled. His dad just looked confused. Ryan realized he'd never brought Carly and Grace over there together. "Mom, Dad, we have something to tell you."

They stood in the middle of the room and he slipped his hand into Carly's, as much for her fortification as his. "Carly and I love each other. We already have a beautiful daughter and we want to be a family and raise her together. We realize you probably don't approve, but we're moving forward with our plans anyway, and we ask that you support us." He glanced over at Carly and she gave him a nervous nod.

His father sat in a stunned silence. But not his mother. She stood and came over to them. She cupped her hands and placed them, one on Ryan's cheek and the other on Carly's. "I'm happy for you both."

"What?" Ryan blurted.

"When I had that car accident, I had a lot of time to ponder. One conclusion I reached was that there was an error in my thinking about you two." She gestured to the nearby table and they all sat together, facing each other. Even his dad sensed the importance and came over, too. "Carly, you have done a wonderful job raising Grace. I mean, look at what a great little girl she is. So well behaved. Respectful. Smart. Inquisitive. That doesn't just happen. You made her like that because you're such a good mother."

Carly blushed but didn't argue.

"When I was in that terrible accident with that precious angel in the backseat, I knew what a horrible tragedy it could've been if Grace had been severely injured. All our lives could've been devastated. But the way you handled the situation, Carly, cemented for me what a quality human being you are. Obviously, you love Grace more than anything, but you didn't blame me for the accident. You didn't say one mean word to me about putting your daughter in harm's way. I wish I could say I would've done the same, but I'm afraid I wouldn't have."

Ryan put a hand over Carly's hand and beamed at her.

"I hope you can forgive me for pushing Ryan away from you when it was time for him to go to college. I had some crazy thought that he would meet an appropriate woman at Chapel Hill and marry her and live the successful life we had planned for him. The life I expected him to lead. But what I finally realized this week is, sometimes things don't go according to a mother's perfect plan. Although it wasn't what I had in mind for him, he'd already met the one true love of his life. It was you. And you are a fine choice for my son."

Ryan's eyes went wide, and he looked at Carly. He'd been praying for his mom to see how special Carly was, and now that prayer was answered.

"Do you really mean that?" Carly asked breathlessly.

"Yes, yes, I really do. My son loves you, my granddaughter loves you, and I want the two of us to love each other too. Will you forgive me, Carly?"

Carly stared. "I do. I do forgive you. And I guess now would be a good time to show you this." She held up her left hand to show off her ring.

His mom gasped and recovered. "I can't say that I'm surprised. I'm happy for you, I really am. Congratulations." She stood and hugged first Carly, then Ryan. His dad got up and followed suit.

"When are you planning the wedding for?" his mom asked.

Ryan looked over at Carly. "We haven't discussed it. But I can't imagine we'd wait very long."

Carly beamed at him. "Not long at all. Can you get the afternoon off tomorrow?"

Ryan stared, hoping he didn't dream it up. "Tomorrow?"

She nodded with a grin. "The courthouse is open tomorrow afternoon and we could get married before the weekend."

"Are you serious?" he asked, his heart in his throat.

She wasn't sure how to take his response. "Unless you want to wait ..."

"Heck no!" he yelled. "Tomorrow it is. I've got to get my suit together, make sure my shirt is clean, oh, and get a blood test."

His mother piped up. "And when you're done, bring Grace by. We'll keep her for the weekend, and as our wedding gift to you, we'll send you on a weekend trip for your honeymoon. That is, if you trust us with her, Carly."

"Of course, I do. You're her grandparents and you love her."

His mom squeezed her hand. "Thank you," she murmured.

CARLY PULLED GRACE'S dress out of her closet and laid it on her bed. The same dress she'd worn to Charlie and Jessica's wedding. It was time for another wedding.

Grace walked in, excited about putting on her fancy dress again. Carly wanted to at least try to explain what was happening today. "Sweetheart, remember when you went to Daddy's cousin's wedding, wearing this dress?"

"Yes," she enthused. "Flowers and music and pretty dresses."

Carly chuckled. "That's what some weddings are all about, true. But some weddings don't have all that."

"Why not?" Grace said, in a tone of disbelief.

"When you come right down to it, a wedding is about two people who love each other, who have decided that God has put them together and they want to live the rest of their lives together."

Grace nodded.

Carly went on, "Today, your daddy and I are getting married."

Grace gasped and jumped up and down.

"But we won't have a fancy wedding like Charlie and Jessica's. We'll have a simple wedding. But the meaning is the same. It's our chance to say we love each other and want to be together forever."

Grace's expression evolved into a happy beam. "Forever?"

"Yes, and you'll be there too. Because we'll be a family forever, the three of us."

"Will Daddy live here?" Grace looked around.

They hadn't discussed it, but she had to assume that was the most logical solution. "Yes, he will."

Grace let out a "Yaaaaay!" and started jumping around her room. Carly calmed her down, got her dressed and then worked on her own face and hair.

Later, they drove to the courthouse. The Justice of the Peace was on the second floor. They climbed the stairwell and when she opened the door, Ryan was standing there. He looked resplendent in his dark suit, his hair all in place. She couldn't imagine he was there for her. But he was.

Grace beat her to his side, taking off and flying to him. "Hi baby girl," he said, kneeling and swooping her into his arms. She giggled.

"Happy Wedding Day," she said.

"Thank you. Today's the happiest day of my life."

"Why?"

"What do you mean why? Because I get to marry the most beautiful woman in the world, that's why." Carly approached, and he pulled her into a kiss that if it'd had words, would've told her exactly how happy he was they had gotten to this point. "I love you," he whispered in her ear, and a shiver started at the top of her spine and traveled all the way down.

"I love you, too. I love you so much." It was true. She'd always loved him, she'd just learned to protect her heart. Never in a million years did she think she'd get her happily ever after. But here he was.

He lowered Grace to her feet, turned to Carly and took both her hands. "Look, I know it's just a courthouse wedding, but someday I want to give you the wedding you deserve. With all your friends and relatives there, and the big white dress and the church. But this counts too. And for me, it's the beginning of the rest of our lives."

Carly shook her head. "I don't need all that. I don't want all that. All I want is you, Ryan. I want you and Grace and our family together. It's all I've ever wanted and I'm getting it today."

He swept her off her feet with another mind-blowing kiss, and then she heard their names called, "Melrose and Milner." She shook the cobwebs out of her head and walked toward her future.

THE END
Laurie's Letter

Dear Readers,

I hope you enjoyed reading about Carly and Ryan, and of course, continuing the love story between Shaw and Nora. I was really pleased with how this book turned out and I find myself in love with my feature couple!

The writing of this book was somewhat difficult. Although I've been balancing my demanding day job with my writing career for 18 years now, I had settled into a good pace of producing two books a year, throughout my Pawleys Island Paradise series. That enabled me to continually present you with the next installment of the story at a pretty reasonable pace. However, life interrupted the writing of this book. So many life events made me put the writing on the back burner. My younger son graduated from college and we moved him 800 miles away from home. My parents sold their house in Illinois and I helped them locate a new place at the beach. My project at work was hitting a high point and implemented in the fall (very successfully, I'm happy to say).

And then my company announced their plans to transform, which started with eliminating 25% of their experienced leaders. This led me to ponder whether I wanted to stay and try to compete for a new job in the new organization or accept their very generous offer to retire early.

It truly didn't take me long to decide. I took the offer! And I'm absolutely thrilled to be retiring (or *graduating*, as I often think of it) at an age young enough that I still have lots of energy and good health (fingers crossed!). I'm looking forward to spending more time and focus on my writing business. I'm looking forward to moving permanently to the beach! But of course, after close to 34 years of working for one company, the thought of leaving, however exciting and pleasant, takes a lot of getting used to!

For all these reasons, it took me longer than usual to write this book. But here it is, and I'm pleased that it came together as a cohesive, smooth story despite all the behind the scenes challenges. When I was doing my final read-through I was reminded of why I loved this story and these characters so much.

So now, enjoy. And thank you for being along on this ride with me! If you haven't already, please subscribe to my monthly newsletter mailing list to get the latest news, contests, offers and release information. Just click here to sign up.[1]

Oh, and one more big favor. You wouldn't believe how helpful it is to authors when readers post reviews of their books. It does way more than you realize! So could you please take a moment and post a quick review on the retailer where you bought the book? Here's the book page[2] where you can click to your retailer. THANK YOU!

Blessings,
Laurie

---

1. https://www.authorlaurielarsen.com/reader-group
2. https://www.authorlaurielarsen.com/restoration

Excerpt to Book 3 of Murrells Inlet Miracles

Haley Witherspoon drove her Acura into the parking lot of Winners Lounge. She parked underneath a street light and hoped that it would still be lit at two in the morning. She cut the engine and peered around. Not exactly her kind of place. She'd never frequented Winners Lounge before. She'd never been in this part of Myrtle Beach before. And she'd certainly never walked into a bar alone before.

But, when Blake asked her out on their first date, listening to his band perform, she'd said yes. And, when she'd asked all her girlfriends to join her, so she wasn't sitting there all by herself all night, they all had reasons to say no. She thought they were legit. Or, at least she hoped so.

She'd be fine. Blake wouldn't have invited her here if she would be in danger. Would he? Honestly, she didn't know him well enough to know. She'd only met him once.

She took a deep breath, checked her lipstick in the rearview mirror and opened the car door. She walked purposefully to the front door, and once inside, she scanned the room for a table with a good view of the band. Finding one, she walked straight there and sat down. She checked her watch. Nine pm. The band should be starting any minute.

A waitress stopped by and she ordered a light beer and left her tab open. Once it came, she took a long, fortifying sip. She definitely didn't want to get drunk tonight, but she needed something to occupy her attention while sitting here all by herself. She picked up her phone. Maybe she could web surf until the band came on. She checked the time again. Nine ten. Where were they?

Two girls about her age approached her. "Haley, right?"

"Why, yes."

"Blake told us to watch for you." They joined her at her table by climbing up into the high bar stools. "I'm Lindsay. Jake the drummer is my boyfriend. And this is Helen. She's with the bass player, Robbie."

"Oh, hi!" Relief flooded through her body and most likely, out through her voice. "So nice to meet you. I'm Haley."

They chuckled. "Yeah, we know."

Haley rolled her eyes good-naturedly. This, she could do. She'd always made friends easily. Her laid-back, friendly personality made her approachable and accepting. She suddenly felt a sense of community. Three gals watching and cheering on their men. "We're with the band," she imagined them telling onlookers. A sort of sorority. Instant membership because of Blake.

Finally, the band took the small stage in the corner. Haley clapped and cheered, then realized she was the only one at the table doing so. She looked at the girls.

"Look, Helen," Lindsay intoned. "A band groupie virgin."

The comment flustered Haley and she frowned and swiped at her hair. "What do you ...?"

They both laughed. "We're not criticizing. We both went through it too. Everything's so new and fresh and fun when you first start coming to these gigs. You're excited, you clap and cheer. But after a couple hundred of these you start to tarnish."

Haley gave them a grim smile. A couple hundred? They must've been with their boyfriends for years.

The band was all set up now, and Blake took the microphone, his guitar strapped over his shoulder. "Good evening, ladies and gentlemen, and welcome to Winners Lounge. We're Ace in the Hole. Let's let it roll." The music took off, a cover of a Luke Bryan hit, and Haley immediately settled into the tune. The song wrapped her in a blanket of familiarity and the band sounded great together. Guitars, a keyboard, drums. "Oh my gosh, they sound great!" she yelled to her tablemates over the noise. They nodded.

Then Blake started singing. She didn't know if he was trying to imitate country superstar Luke Bryan, but he sounded just like him. His voice had a clear, deep tone, with just a little bit of raspy on the corners. She couldn't take her eyes or ears off him. He closed his eyes as he cradled the mic in his hand, swaying his hips along with the melody. He dipped his head back to hit the higher notes, and then when he opened his eyes, he zoomed in on Haley. A rush of adrenaline went down her esophagus and settled deep in her core. She went breathless.

They finished the first song and Haley didn't care what the more seasoned girlfriends thought. She jumped off her barstool and clapped and yipped for Ace in the Hole. They were fantastic. The rest of the bar clapped quietly. Blake smiled and winked at her, then started in on the second song.

Haley got absorbed in the first set, listening to every lyric, every note, every stanza. The band's talent overwhelmed her, especially Blake's singing. This man had talent.

The set ended and while the band was putting their instruments down, she turned to the girls. "My gosh, they are good! Why are they still playing in little tiny dives like this? Have they tried to get a recording contract? They deserve a shot!"

They stared at her, each of them raising one eyebrow, as if in unison. "Gee, Helen, why didn't we ever think of that? You mean they could be playing nicer bars? Stadiums? Recording music? Hmmm. Maybe we need to look into that."

The way she phrased it, and the deadpan monotone of her voice clued Haley in that she was being played. "Oh. So, they have tried? And what, hit roadblocks?"

Just then, the men of the band approached the table, each putting an arm around their woman. Blake stepped in front of Haley and leaned in for a hug. She pulled him in close, squeezed him, and then placed her lips on his neck. She had no idea when she'd met him that he was this talented a musician. After all, he was an Uber driver who'd picked her up one night. One very traumatic night.

Blake released her as the waitress came over with beers for the band. He took a long gulp.

"Oh my gosh, you are so good!" Haley said.

"Aww thanks." He looked over at the other girlfriends. "Ladies, I guess you met my date, Haley Witherspoon. I want you to take good care of her tonight while we're up there."

Haley beamed her appreciation at him. From beside her, Lindsay's voice hit her ear, "Witherspoon? Did he say your name was Witherspoon?"

Haley's heart skipped a beat and she took a deep breath in. The joys and curses of a well-known family name.

Blake said, "Yeah, why?"

Lindsay maneuvered so she could look straight into Haley's eyes. "Of the Witherspoon dynasty? The jewelry? The wineries? The clothing lines?"

Blake frowned and scoffed. "Just because she has a famous name doesn't mean she is a descendant of the Witherspoon dynasty. Right, Haley?"

She stared at him and her eyes widened. This certainly wasn't how she wanted to tell him. She wouldn't lie to him. But she also didn't want to spill the beans of her family's wealth and prosperity while sitting at the Winners Lounge with a bunch of near strangers.

Instead, she tried to make a joke of it. "Oh yeah, you know, me and Grandpa Emerson, taking over the world."

Blake chuckled but Lindsay wouldn't let it go. "Emerson Witherspoon is your grandpa? Seriously?"

She hesitated, and Blake jumped in. "Can't you tell she's joking Lindsay?" The conversation moved on to other topics and soon the men finished their beers and headed back toward the stage. Blake leaned over her and placed his lips on hers, a quick kiss for good luck.

Leaving her with the stares of Lindsay and Helen. "Okay," Lindsay said, "if you are a multi-millionaire with the Witherspoon dynasty behind you, I can understand why you wouldn't want to fess up. However, if Blake knows, and just isn't spilling the beans to us, then that sort of explains why you're here."

Haley let the words spill over her. She was usually pretty good at ignoring jabs, especially involving her family's wealth and prestige. After all, she was the black sheep of the family, uneducated and unambitious. She had no desire to take part in the family business, preferring instead to work her own little job, live in her own little place and enjoy her life without pressure. But the truth was, Lindsay was insulting her, intentionally, and she couldn't let this one slide.

"What are you talking about Lindsay?"

"No offense, but Blake is sort of a lone wolf. He never brings girls to the gigs. Too distracting for him. He wants to hit the country music big time, and he'll do everything he has to, to get there. You won't find a harder working musician than Blake."

Haley shrugged. "What does that have to do with me?" She stared at Lindsay, willing her to say it.

"Knowing your name, maybe he sees you as a fast track. You've got the money to help make it happen. You said yourself they've got the talent to be mainstream. Maybe he thinks you'll payroll them to get there."

Haley's mouth dropped open and then she clenched it shut. When would she ever learn? Her family's wealth was a hindrance, much more than a help, in any situation.

"Blake doesn't know anything about my family. And what's more, he doesn't care."

"Yeah, right." Lindsay drew out the last word, then leaned in to Helen, both laughing like it was the biggest inside joke in the world.

"Hey, look. This is my first date with Blake. We met when he gave me an Uber ride. We pulled a dead deer out of a windshield together and bonded in the waiting room of the ER. We talked for hours and my family didn't come up at all. So, I don't like what you're insinuating that he only asked me here because he's interested in my bank account." Her chest heaving with the unaccustomed effort of the forceful words, she locked eyes with enemy Lindsay and wouldn't let go.

Lindsay sat motionless, staring back.

"Thanks for sticking around. We're Ace in the Hole." Blake's magnified voice filled the room, then a few guitar strums.

Lindsay held her hands up. "Okay, okay, I'm sorry. I had no right to say that."

Haley looked away, then her gaze flickered back at Lindsay and she nodded. She'd let it go, but she'd never be friends with Lindsay. Never.

She enjoyed the next two sets of flawless country music from Blake's band and managed to say only a minimal number of words to Lindsay and Helen. She didn't want to believe what they said about Blake, but God knows, they knew him better than she did. She'd have to proceed this "relationship" with a cautious heart.

Be a Part of Laurie's Reader Group

One of my ongoing goals is to continually connect with readers who love Christian fiction, and engage with them throughout the year. I have lots of great ideas about how to do that—to give readers what they want without killing your email Inbox and being a pest. <u>Sign up now</u>[1] and you'll get TWO free books, a monthly newsletter with all the latest news and a free giveaway! Contests that will excite and amaze you! Exclusive previews to upcoming books and special features only available to you, my reader group. C'mon, it'll be fun!!

Laurie

---

1. https://www.authorlaurielarsen.com/reader-group

Christian Fiction novels
by Laurie Larsen
The Pawleys Island Paradise series:

BOOK 1: Roadtrip to Redemption[1]. *It started as a trip to lose old memories. It became a journey to find her heart.* A woman facing the most desolate summer of her life, follows God's direction and instead has the most rewarding and life-changing summer of all.

---

1. https://www.authorlaurielarsen.com/roadtrip-to-redemption

BOOK 2: Tide to Atonement[2]. *Life knocked him down. Faith raised him up.* A man has paid his debt to society and is released from prison. Determined to create a life to be proud of, he realizes his past isn't quite as willing to be done as he wants it to be.

BOOK 3: Journey to Fulfillment[3]. *A traumatic family event. Distinctly opposite ways of dealing with it between husband and wife. Let no man put asunder.* A married couple deals with a family tragedy in different ways and works through the resulting collapse of their marriage to reconcile their love for each other.

---

2. https://www.authorlaurielarsen.com/tide-to-atonement
3. https://www.authorlaurielarsen.com/journey-to-fulfillment

BOOK 4: Bridge to Fruition[4]. *The old is gone. The new is come.* A young woman from an affluent family finds love with a man who grew up in the foster system. Can they let go of the trappings of their past and find love together in their present?

BOOK 5: Path to Discovery[5]. A brokenhearted New York actress welcomes the escape from the hustle and bustle of the big city to take the lead in a beach-town dinner theater show. It's the solace and sanctuary that she's needed ever since her world came crumbling down. But then he walks in... back into her life and her memories of her worst nightmare.

---

4. https://www.authorlaurielarsen.com/bridge-to-fruition

5. https://www.authorlaurielarsen.com/path-to-discovery

BOOK 6: Return to Devotion[6]. *Can men and women be "just friends?"* A military wife deals with unbearable loneliness on her husband's third overseas deployment, leading to an indiscretion with her new male friend. Will the truth destroy everything she and her husband have built as man and wife?

BOOK 7: Pawleys Island Paradise: A Companion[7]. Discover the stories and inspiration that led to the Pawleys Island Paradise series! A short, fully-illustrated non-fiction companion to the beloved Pawleys Island Paradise series of inspirational romance by award-winning author Laurie Larsen.

---

6. https://www.authorlaurielarsen.com/path-to-discovery

7. https://www.authorlaurielarsen.com/a-companion-nonfiction

PAWLEYS ISLAND PARADISE boxset[8]: First three books in one easy download!

PREACHER MAN[9]. Laurie's 2010 EPIC Award winner for Best Spiritual Romance of 2010: A beautiful, heartwarming Christian love story that will leave you feeling good.

---

8. https://www.authorlaurielarsen.com/boxset-books-1-3

9. https://www.authorlaurielarsen.com/preacher-man

The Murrells Inlet Miracles series:

BOOK 1: Sanctuary[1]. An ambitious Philadelphia lawyer is offered a generous inheritance when a beloved aunt dies: a ramshackle mansion, a state-of-the-art horse barn, and miles of beachfront property in Murrells Inlet, SC. She partners with a handsome veterinarian, and her decision is almost made, until she discovers the secrets he's hiding could destroy their future forever.

---

1. https://www.authorlaurielarsen.com/sanctuary

BOOK 2: Restoration[2]. He broke her heart once. Can she take a chance on him again? Carly Milner is doing all she can to make ends meet. Left pregnant and alone by her high school sweetheart, Carly has struggled to provide for her daughter while getting her career off the ground. Just when she is getting her life back on track, Ryan Melrose walks back into her life.

---

2. https://www.authorlaurielarsen.com/restoration

Don't miss out!

Click the button below and you can sign up to receive emails whenever Laurie Larsen publishes a new book. There's no charge and no obligation.

https://books2read.com/r/B-A-WTLE-ZDMR

BOOKS 2 READ

Connecting independent readers to independent writers.

About the Author

Award-winning author Laurie Larsen leads a double life. During the day she's a respected Project Manager in the fast-paced world of Information Technology. After dinner and a glass of wine, she becomes a multi-published author of Christian fiction grounded in today's modern world.

Laurie's been published for 17 years, but feels she finally found her writing "niche" in 2009 when her first inspirational romance, *Preacher Man* was published. It won fans, accolades, and the prestigious EPIC Award for the Best Spiritual Romance of 2010. From then on, her path was clear. She was put on this earth (in part) to tell love stories combined with a strong message of faith. Her Pawleys Island Paradise series is a much beloved, at times best-selling series of six books following Leslie and Hank, and the Harrison clan, as they face the daily challenges of life while trying to include prayer and praise. Reviewers say the books are heartwarming, life-changing and an example to follow for including God in your life.

Laurie loves the beach (obvious to anyone who's read the Pawleys Island Paradise series) and she's fondly looking forward to a day (not too far away) where she can retire from the demanding day job, and spend her days living at the beach and writing novels. Until then, she travels back and forth between Illinois and South Carolina just as often as possible.

Read more at https://www.authorlaurielarsen.com.

Made in the USA
Columbia, SC
18 June 2019